Twelve O'Clock Sharp

Michael Eisele

Other books by Michael Eisele:
Without Tears And Other Tales

Contents

The Huntress

ark Russel was glad to get back again. After
spending years in the never-ending flatness of
Manitoba, he yearned for the pristine mountains of
his home town Radium. At the sight of the Rocky Mountains
an elation gripped his large frame, which turned to euphoria
when he crossed the Great Divide. Ahead, deep down in the
valley, lay Radium, a little town with a big reputation, where
the bighorns walk unmolested on Main Street.

First he would knock on Justin's door, his friend since early
youth. Since their surveying days long ago they felt a brotherly
affinity for each other. More than once they risked life and
limb in rescue operations above the turbulent Toby Creek, a
misnomer if ever there existed one. Creek indeed! torrent
would be more fitting.

Russel's joy was short-lived; Benta was not home,
moreover, his small house up on the hill seemed forsaken.
Soon unpleasant news came to his ears. Pierre, the Frenchman,
gave it to him undiluted.

"Didn't you know, Mark, Justin is in jail?" he was told.

"You are jesting, old chap," Russel retorted with a tinge of
rebuke.

The man from Montreal was known as a wag and practical
joker, but some of his witticisms annoyed more than they
amused.

"I wish I were, my friend, Justin is imprisoned down in
Cranbrook."

"Impossible! what happened?"

"That German woman at the Hot Springs finagled it, that's what we all think," Pierre informed a flabbergasted Russel.

The short of it was this: Justin Benta, the manager of the facilities, his intimate friend, was found guilty of theft and breach of trust. He received a six months sentence, which he started serving three months ago. The woman, Lena Bauer, a major prosecution witness, now held Russel's position.

"There is a schemer for you, a veritable Mary Magdalene with all her devils intact. Justin hired her about two years ago as a counter girl, then shortly after promoted her to assistant manager, thereby paving a road to his own downfall."

"You mean she aspired to his position?"

"Exactly. You know Justin better than I, he forever seems to bet on the wrong horse," Pierre summed up.

More he neither knew, nor wanted to know. Happy go lucky as always, he went his way.

Why Russel did not rush to his friend's side, seemed a riddle even to himself. A whispering oracle admonished him to wait till more information had been garnered. Obtaining additional news proved easy in that small place with a far-reaching reputation.

The town lay on many people's tongues; not only on account of its fabulous hot springs, but also because of an incomparable scenery, and unpolluted air in abundance. Everyone he talked to made unpleasant remarks about Lena Bauer.

"That woman is a sly one, she soon will have snared the administrator's job," one and the next said.

Some added with a significant wink:

"She and no one else stole and planted those jewels in Justin's safe."

Others however, with a more developed sense of justice, pointed at the difficulty of such doings.

"Only Justin knew the combination, surely he would not have left the safe open or unguarded. After all, the day's cash receipts were deposited there."

Soon Russel learned details which reinforced his conviction that his friend was innocent; Lena Bauer had framed him, nothing less. Justin would never commit such a perfidious deed. Manslaughter, yes, murder perhaps, but tiptoeing around lockers and filching someone's belongings? Not in a hundred years! Not Justin Benta, whom he remembered as a daredevil, with a heart as large as all outdoors.

The core of the matter was this: The Hot Spring facility contained a number of lockers to store clothes and other belongings, while patrons soaked in the pool. Since they looked sturdy enough, plus were lockable, some people left more in there than they should have. Despite reminders to leave valuables with the staff for safekeeping, they chose the lockers.

Complaints about missing items, though rare, were nevertheless voiced. The staff just shrugged them off. Outwardly they commiserated with the alleged victims, but inwardly they had little sympathy with them. First, they lent no credence to these reports; second, their attitude had hardened over the years towards these fanciful accusations.

"They are doing it out of boredom," it was suggested.

"Perhaps even out of spite," some declared.

"Just to be ornery," others said.

Even after a slew of such complaints did the management pay much attention. Pointing to a sign above the counter, the complainants were reminded that they should have left their valuables right here for safekeeping.

Then a very precious ring went missing, belonging to the park commissioner's wife. Now, that woman knew how to make a fuss, she had years of experience in it. At first her hue and cry produced scant results. But as mentioned she was no novice in the area of scolding and intimidation. No amount of appeasement and indulgent explanation dampened her zeal. She demanded an immediate investigation; moreover, that none should be allowed to leave the premises prior to submitting to a search.

Then she contacted her husband. Within the hour the police arrived, who immediately interviewed everybody involved. After talking to Lena Bauer, the assistant manager, a request was made to open the company's safe under Benta's control. There was the purloined ring, glittering between bundles of cash, which was quickly identified by the jubilant victim as hers. Benta vigorously denied all knowledge about it; he apparently flew in a rage and roundly accused his assistant to have engineered all.

After a short investigation he was charged with theft and breach of trust. He was found guilty after a hasty trial. The most incriminating prosecution witness was Lena Bauer, though Russel was told that Benta did not help himself either. His testimony showed itself to be tenuous, contradictory, and occasionally false. Bauer never wavered while giving evidence. Although the defence unmasked her as a covetous schemer, the judge obviously believed her.

How Benta, a man, could gain access to the women's compartments without creating a stir, was quickly explained. One had to know the layout to understand it. According to Bauer, who several times observed her boss, he entered late at night when few bathers remained in the pool, after ascertaining of course whether the locker room was empty. Entering from the opposite side imposed no difficulties for an authorised person with a master key, as little as shutting out anyone while inside.

The night of the theft remained vividly in Bauer's memory. She proved unshakeable in her testimony. Benta stayed in the locker room, all by himself, at least ten minutes. When he came out he hurried to his office, opened the safe, deposited a small object from his pocket, and quickly closed it again. Being unduly absorbed, he took no notice of her as she followed almost on his heels. That was the essence of the information obtained by Russel.

He still felt disinclined to visit his friend at the jail. That same oracular voice kept on repeating not to. First he intended to take a closer look at Lena Bauer. The Hot Springs, as well as every long-term employee were no strangers to him. The locals, as he had learned, were not enamoured with the German woman whose rampant ambition rubbed them the wrong way. Moreover, her disquieting penchant for hunting, deemed unwomanly, stuck deep in their craw. Her moniker, the huntress, could not have been uttered with greater disdain. Strange enough, Lena Bauer seemed oblivious to such condescension. Even being called 'Lena Popgun', or 'Miss

Shootmenot' elicited rather smiles than scowls from her broad, somewhat doltish face.

For some time she had been pestering every guide and outfitter in the region to take her hunting. Bagging her first grizzly, she announced, stood high on the agenda. None of the professionals deigned to consider such eccentric requests. Accosting individuals, all male chauvinists, earned her nothing but derision and abuse.

"Taking a dame hunting, what next!" some snorted.

"My name would be mud from thereon," others gave her to understand.

Discouraging Lena Bauer however, would have been more of a chore than performing one of the labours of Hercules. She possessed a strong obstinacy seldom found in anyone but the insensate and tuft hunters. Her roving eyes did not tire in the search for a suitable candidate. To the wild mountains she would go, despite the tongue wagging viragoes and the prejudice of their henpecked men.

When Russel turned up, her alert mind started to shift into high gear. Obtaining information about him proved easy; his name lay on many people's tongues. While he studied her from afar, incognito he hoped, she approached him.

"Mr Russel, I hear you are a big game hunter, a licensed guide even," she chirped.

Russel felt an urge to scamper off. Dumbfounded he looked around for someone to bridge his embarrassment. Her chipper, direct approach took the wind out of his sails. Feigning amnesia he hemmed several times prior to responding:

"Yes. I – I used to be an outfitter," he admitted haltingly.

"Used to, Mr Russel?" she echoed, raising her eyelashes suggestively.

Then giving way to a sudden, inexplicable inspiration, he conceded:

"Come to think of it, my license might still be valid."

Pretending to be puzzled he asked:

"Why do you want to know?"

"Because I would like to go hunting, bagging my first grizzly, to be exact."

He was uncertain whether to laugh or curse. He was out to harm the woman, not fulfil her dearest wish. Taken aback by her brazen approach, repelled by the notion to help a woman stalk the king of the mountains, he nevertheless signalled interest. For in a flash he sensed an opportunity to pay her back. High up in the Purcell wilderness, amid savage nature, who knows what could happen.

"There might be a possibility," he granted, thereby casting the first bait.

For a moment he felt an impulse to duck behind the counter, out of fear that she was going to fall around his neck. Recalling that the hunting season was about to start, he inquired:

"When would you like to go?"

"Whenever you are ready."

With the words, "I will let you know in a few days," he went his way.

Avoiding friends and acquaintances he tried to work out a scheme worthy of a friend's service. Conjuring up favourable circumstances, repudiating them as unworkable, finding new ones, he spent several days wandering around in solitude.

Finally he had mapped out a mode of action. He would take her hunting alright, way up in the shadows of Saffron Peak, on the banks of Dutch Creek. Tony Hicks owned a cabin there, rustic, but comfortable enough.

Tony, a half-breed, lived in Wilmer, a small town on the west side of the Columbia River. He was a character as much as a gay Lothario. Under a shock of coal-black hair radiated a laughing face that could lift clouds from the gloomiest heart. Hicks played the fiddle quite well, but the gamut of love even better. Russel paid him a visit.

"Tony, I need a favour," he announced after customary salutations.

"What is it?"

"Your cabin at Saffron, could I use it a few days?"

"That can be arranged. Let me know when and for how long."

"From the start of the hunting season, say, two to four days thereafter."

"Two weeks from now? done!" Hicks declared.

Russel lingered a while, during which time he cast glances at the river and the gardens behind, but evaded Hicks' questioning glimpses. They were fairly close at one time, but over the years had drifted apart. After early manhood their characters developed diversely. Hicks' penchant for levity, crowned by a propensity for amorous adventures, began to grate on Russel's sensibility. In earlier years they had walked on a riotous path, and hoisted more than one at the pub. Maturity affected them differently. Hicks' laughing fiddler's heart wandered close to his sleeve, in contrast to Russel's, which burrowed deeper into layers of reticence.

He had left the Kootenais to seek his fortune out east. The far end of the Great Lakes was his destination, which he never reached. As so often, life's vagaries played light with him. Barely had he travelled half the intended distance, when they inveigled him to stay. Take a rest, catch your breath, the ever tempting voice of irresolution intoned. It ended up to be more than a breather; four years to be exact. What made him endure the teeth-chattering cold, the hairlifting wind, and bone-bleaching sun in summer, he lacked words to explain. But now he was back, charged with a duty no decent man could circumvent. Lena Bauer had to be dealt with.

Their halting conversation gained new impetus when Hicks suggested:

"Mark, I sense you have something else on your mind."

"Indeed, I have, Tony."

"Well?"

"You have to come with us."

"Who is us, and where to?"

"Us is a woman and I; the place of course is Saffron Peak."

Hicks stared at his erstwhile friend as if he had seen a ghost.

"The answer is no. Just the same, who is the woman? Not that amazon at the Hot Springs?"

"Yes, it is."

"Then my reply is twofold no. I have heard all about her. Lucky for me she hasn't ferreted me out yet. I might have a predilection for ladies, but none for mannish dames."

"Tony, I need your assistance as never before. First, you are a seasoned tracker who knows that area like the inside of every pub between Cranbrook and Golden; second, you are stronger than Atlas in his youth."

"I don't know who that fellow is, but nothing doing, Mark, find someone else. How about the Frenchman?"

"He is a regular gadabout, besides, being weaker than flies in November."

Then followed a discourse highlighted by insistent demands and emphatic denials. Russel, weaker physically, but mentally more astute, ground away at his pal's resistance till it crumbled.

"Remember how I stood up for you when the mayor tried to put the mark of the beast on you, following your dalliance with his wife?"

"Hm – no."

"Have you forgotten Russel Chadwick, the wild boar? Tell me, who saved you from his terrible paws when he found out about his wife's escapade with you?"

Seeing Hicks' countenance soften, Russel began to load his second barrel, when he was cut short:

"You are doing it for the money?"

"Nothing else, I'm broke, my pockets are empty to the seams."

"Anything left for me if I come along?"

"Half."

An understanding was reached with the proviso that not a syllable about it should roll over anyone's tongue.

The next day Russel informed Lena Bauer about the arrangement. He cautioned.

"I have no wish to dampen your enthusiasm, but be aware that this is no picnic."

"Don't worry about me, I am no trembling mimosa leaf, nor am I made of sugar," she replied.

"Part of the trip will be on horseback," he added, knowing full well that all the wrath of the gods could not deter her.

"I can ride," she assured him.

"I take it that the quarry is of no further interest to you," Russel inquired.

"None, beyond being photographed with it. The rest I leave to you."

About two weeks later they were on their way. Hicks, the tracker, joined them at the end of a dirt road, past Whitetail Lake. No force on earth could have persuaded him to be seen on the trail with a petticoat, he avowed. On the near side of the creek Oom Johanson maintained a stable with horses and gear year round. He also offered a service to transport and dress the quarries.

As they rode along the narrow trail, Hicks in the back repeatedly shook his head. Russel's demeanour puzzled him. How a man could play up to a woman, pushy beyond endurance, mouthier than ten oracles, and plain to boot, his ingenuous temperament was unable to fathom.

"Miss Bauer here, my dear, there," it went on and on.

Hicks could not fend off the impression that his pal tried to convey an image of amity that he did not feel. On the whole, this entire undertaking grew more distasteful by the minute to him. More often than once he felt an urge to turn around. Only the lure of compensation induced him to persevere.

It will not take long, he promised himself, for he knew how to proceed. The bears' behaviour contained no secrets for a man of his experience. Besides, as Russel justly said, the entire area he considered to be his back yard. Those ever hungry Silvertips must be prowling at their usual place. He could almost see them, positioned at the outflow of a small lake, a pond really, catching fish by the ton. Chasing one of them into that amazon's line of fire, should not prove difficult.

Hicks could not suppress an appreciative chortle, as he called into mind her singular request, which inspired a certain amount of respect in a man who was no stranger to daring. That trouser clad, domineering woman showed pluck seldom found with her sex. She insisted on nothing less than to face her intended quarry alone, and let him have it at close quarters.

Peculiar enough when he, Hicks, balked at such a wayward demand, Russel came to her aid. So be it, he told himself, he is the leader, furthermore the client's wishes are sacrosanct. Just the same he voiced some concerns, which Bauer pooh-poohed with gusto.

"Don't be a chicken," she snorted, "I have been shooting big game for years, just never grizzlies," she advised reprovingly a grimacing Hicks, who murmured more to his horse than anyone else: "That woman sours my days."

Upon arrival Russel announced:

"First we will set up camp, then look at the lay of the land."

After tending and tethering their horses they went on foot to the spot intended. Soon Hicks, blessed with the vision of a bird of prey, detected some grizzlies far down at the creek. Remaining windward, they cautiously approached. Keeping their voices down, a plan of procedure was worked out. Russel explained:

"Tony will position himself on the other side of the creek, waiting for one of the bears separating himself from the others. He is well adept to direct him onto the right path, namely, through the clearing right into your line of fire, Miss Bauer."

After further discussions, Russel asked:

"Everybody in the clear?"

Both nodded, thus indicating a readiness to return to camp.

Autumn in the Kootenais makes one forget paradise. The sun over the snow-capped mountains becomes playful. The weather turns into pure delight, inviting men to laugh more and fret less. Having lost its parching fierceness, the calm warmth conjures smiles to lips, and gives the heart ease. Not a cloud darkens the blue sky, seldom does a wind stir the leaves, now ablaze with bright colours.

Eastward, across the Continental Divide, the spectacle of an alpenglow can be seen. Who could forget the phenomenon capable of transforming barren, forbidding masses of rocks into resplendent incandescence, that provides an incentive to rise before dawn, and fills the mind with soothing happiness in the evening before retiring.

After supper they gathered around a crackling fire, talking, or rather listening to Lena Bauer's narrations, during which they were unable to hide a deeply felt discomfort. It affected them adversely that a woman should brag to have penetrated a

man's domain, especially in the last bastion of masculinity.
They felt shamed and dishonoured while listening to her
various hunting adventures.

The chase, so commendable to a man, in their opinion had
lost its sheen. Their indignation, however, was mitigated by
Bauer's foreign accent, which lent an air of unreality to these
boasts. Besides, imbibing freely also helped to lessen their
discomfort.

The huntress quickly got into full swing. Anxious to
ingratiate herself, she overstepped propriety. As happens so
often, someone's endeavour to emulate obtains results opposite
of those aimed for. The ones imitated, pleased no doubt, at the
same time feel the spurs of contempt.

The men were casting clandestine glances at each other,
carrying a message more explicit than words: namely, to
escape Bauer's nonstop revelations. When she stopped to catch
her breath, Russel announced:

"Time for bed, I guess."

"Yes, tomorrow will be an eventful day," Hicks, already on
his feet, agreed.

Next morning they set out at dawn. Tarrying not for a
moment to admire the splendorous scenery, they hurried on.
Russel advised Miss Bauer:

"I have inspected your rifle as the rules demand, all is in
order."

"Don't wait too long, shoot at the first opportunity," Hicks
recommended."

"And keep shooting till the bear drops," Russel added.

Soon they had taken their respective positions, where they
waited for a propitious opportunity to start the hunt. It arrived
when a lone grizzly ambled onto the clearing. Bauer, the
impatient huntress, immediately stepped from her hiding place
and took aim, waiting for the bear to come nearer. Startled, the
Silvertip stopped, then rose up and started to sniff and sway.

From thereon everything happened so fast that neither
Russel, close by, nor Hicks across the creek had a chance to
act. The bear, growing angrier by the second, growling and
chopping his jaws, acquired a frightful posture, meant to scare
away the figure at the end of the clearing. But the huntress

stood her ground. Heartened by the fully loaded rifle levelled at the bawling beast, she waited for the right condition to pull the trigger.

Suddenly the bear charged with lightning speed. Like a ball of fury, snarling and squalling, he hurled himself towards the huntress. Shots rang out, yet the bear kept coming at a clip unimaginable to anyone who had not seen it. Noticing that her shots took no effect, Bauer ran, or rather attempted to. She stood not the ghost of a chance. Before she turned, the terror of the woods, by now a bundle of wrath, was upon her. By the time Russel's bullets found their aim, Bauer breathed no more, the huntress lay dead on the ground.

Hicks, who meanwhile had arrived at the scene, could not hide his disbelief. Shaking his head he muttered:

"I can't understand it. Some of her shots must have lodged, yet the beast neither stopped, nor seemed to be fazed."

"She probably missed," suggested Russel.

"Mark, four shots were fired, at least one at close range, no more than ten steps away," Hicks protested, then added:

"One sure thing, she is a plucky woman."

"Was, Tony, was."

Shortly after Hicks galloped back to Invermere to make a report. He was in a snit. Accusations and recriminations were hurled across the roan's crest.

"What a predicament I got myself in. I should never have come for all the money of Croesus."

Money? that word made him bolt upright. He repeated it through clenched teeth.

"Money? What money? I won't see a red cent now."

He realised in a flash that besides wasting time, furthermore opening the gates to the house of troubles, he ended up poorer than before.

"What a pickle, what a fix," he wailed into the horse's ears.

So it went till he reached the fork at the dirt road. He knew, that blasted woman with two piercing eyes was bad news, who should have been avoided like the bubonic plague, but a friend in need can not be ignored.

Russel, who had stayed behind, found his mind occupied by more than one thought. He recognised there would be a coroner's inquest. Not a pleasant experience for someone on the carpet. He could expect reprimands, if not charges.

Surveying the area in silence, forming theories, repudiating them again, he finally reached a conclusion: He regrettably would have to disclose Bauer's foolhardy action prior to the attack. She goaded the grizzly, perhaps in a burst of bravado, or out of nervousness, but she stepped right into his path stomping and waving her arms. That more than tugged at the strings of patience of an already annoyed bear. Hicks might disavow such aversions, but it will carry little weight, considering the distance, plus obstructed view he had to content with.

No doubt, some reproof could deservedly be voiced for not staying closer to Bauer, which too might readily be explained. Surely Hicks would endorse his contention that she intended to face her quarry alone. It meant much to her, like a baptism of fire, both were told. Such requests raised no eyebrows, many of his clients insisted on it.

Only the question why he did not shoot earlier required a measure of substantiation. It is easy to judge after the fact, within secure, calm surroundings, he would remind the jury. Out in the wilderness, confronted by a ferocious grizzly, changes all aspects. Decisions had to be made in a flash: whether to shoot after Miss Bauer's first bullet failed to fell her quarry, perhaps after the second. Was it safe to fire? All looks easy on hindsight, especially after one is beyond harm's reach.

At the coroner's investigation all would have gone well, except for that ornery Gardner, who raked Russel as well as Hicks over the coals. Other jurors, though knitting brows and making wry faces, hardly pierced the surface of their testimony. Not so the retired trapper and guide.

Jack Gardner, crusty as ever, fearless and articulate, reprimanded them without mercy. Many stories, wild and in part true, circulated about him. He never related his hair-raising experiences, not even in younger years, when he camped among growling bears and howling coyotes. He was one of the very few men that had faced down a charging grizzly and lived to tell about it. A dying breed he could be called, of a wild land losing spirit fast.

Fiercely independent, even at advancing age, he remained a true type, to which North America can raise its head in pride. One thing the old-timer knew: running from a grizzly was tantamount to committing suicide. His scathing rebuke stung Russel more than Hicks, for understandable reasons.

"I don't understand you fellows, whom I had known since you outgrew diapers. What in the dickens were you thinking by taking that woman grizzly hunting!"

He knew the area well.

"You could blindfold me at the end of the dirt road, and I would find the exact spot where you committed your tomfoolery."

Then he went on:

"Alone the thought to take a woman, any woman, hunting in that inhospitable region, and be it only rabbits, should be indictable."

Hearing these words the coroner, along with the other jurors, winced. It needed a brave man to utter such sentiments in a society were timid men are cowed by strident women. But Gardner, undaunted, sprinkled with the smell of Canada's past, had never learned to be wishy-washy. Teaching him otherwise would have meant more trouble than learning a lion to roar different.

The judicial inquiry's verdict followed as expected:

Death by misadventure, accompanied by one or two trite recommendations. Although neither Russel nor Hicks were imputed with wrongdoing, they did not escape some criticism; not harsh, but nevertheless vexatious. Just the same, Russel heaved a sigh of relief, he had anticipated something more severe after his erstwhile teacher's censure.

Luckily the old fogy took the sting out of his reprimands, when he announced that the chase is meant for men only. He thanked his guardian angel for once more shielding him from harm. Hicks just grumbled about never hunting with Russel again, and no woman need apply, period.

Three weeks later Benta was paroled. Stepping out from a warm prison cell into a cold, wind-blown November morning, he was surprised to see his friend Russel.

"Mark, old horse, where did you spring from?" he cried.

"I thought you had left us for good."

"I came back, and just in the nick of time it seems."

They had much to tell each other, since writing letters was neither one's strong point. Benta almost at once broached the subject which haunted him since awhile.

"Did you hear about the accident up in our old stamping ground?"

"I have, sure."

"I guess you did not know the victim?"

"Not too well," came an evasive answer.

"Poor Lena, what a way to end," Benta commiserated to Russel's astonishment.

Looking sideways at his friend, he remarked:

"I know it sounds absurd, Mark, but the prison grapevine mentioned your name in connection with Lena's demise."

"It is true."

"But it can not be, you were not even here," Benta protested a bit miffed at the notion of being made sport of.

"I came back two months ago."

Benta's surprise, as much as disappointment was written all over his face.

"Two months ago?" he echoed in disbelief.

Russel interjected:

"I know, I know, why did I not come to visit you. I had good reasons not to show up."

"Man alive, tell me about it," Benta urged.

"Not here, Justin, let's make ourselves comfortable at my place first. I saved a few bottles of old brandy, just for such an occasion."

Soon they sat in a small log cabin up on a hill, where the view alone made life worthwhile. It was a clear cold day, made inhospitable by a raw northern, which blew down from the icecaps of the towering Rockies. The strong breeze, a sure indication of winter's arrival made people huddle, and the wilted foliage dance across the valley. Deep layers of snow covered the upper regions of the Purcell Mountains. Day by day the white carpet moved lower, soon it would spread over the entire valley.

After a substantial sip of eau de vie, Benta was unable to contain his impatience any longer.

"All right old man, out with it," he entreated his pal.

Aglow with satisfaction, imbued by an anticipation of forthcoming praise, Russel quipped:

"Easy does it, what you are going to hear is worth waiting for."

Benta looked at his friend expectantly.

"Impatience is beginning to strain my nerves. Poor Lena, how unfortunate, what a pity," he murmured.

"Never mind that, she is dead and buried, and good riddance many of us say," Russel remarked.

"Come now, Mark, she was not bad. Overly ambitious perhaps, but having myself felt the talons of that demon, I will neither condemn nor judge," Benta remonstrated.

"Really, Justin, I fail to understand you. Turning the other cheek was never your strong point. After what she has done to you, she deserved twice over what she received," Russel reminded.

Benta called out astonished:

"What are you driving at?"

"It is this: When I returned from Saskatchewan, my first steps led to your house, which was locked up and forsaken."

"Small wonder," Benta interjected.

"Soon your misfortune, caused by that perfidious woman, unfolded before my eyes. Pierre, the Frenchman, apprised me of the ugly facts."

When Benta attempted to interrupt, Russel signalled him to remain silent.

"Wait, Justin, hear me out. I failed to show up at the jail because an inner voice, coming from heaven knows where, bid me to stay away. Soon a more insistent one urged me to settle with that woman."

Noticing Justin's uneasy movements, Russel commanded:

"Don't say anything, let me finish. I hatched a plan which quickly grew to fruition."

"To take Lena grizzly hunting?" Benta interjected.

Russel looked at him obliquely, as if he deserved to be pitied.

"Yes. But my designs extended beyond that, for which reason I asked Tony to come along."

"That must have taken some arm-twisting, considering his aversion for women hunters."

Russel chuckled.

"It did, but the lure of money swayed him at the end."

"Lena paid you money?"

"An idle promise, that is how it ended up."

"How did the accident happen?"

"It was not an accident."

Benta started.

"What do you mean?" he called out.

"I wangled it," Russel said nonchalantly.

His friend grew utterly confused.

"Mark, you lost me. How can anyone, even an experienced hunter, engineer an accident involving a grizzly, known to be one of the most intractable and unpredictable creature on earth?"

"Yet I did. Maybe luck stood by my side, but this is how I managed it. Sit still, I'm coming to the end. Before we set out that morning I removed all live bullets from her rifle's chamber, and replaced them with blanks."

Benta jumped to his feet, aghast he cried out:

"Mark, you are not serious!"

"I am. I took every bullet out as I said."

The revelation proved too much for him, he staggered back to his chair where he slumped down. Burying his head in both hands, he moaned:

"Why, Mark, why?"

"To pay her back what she had meted out to you. Don't you remember our slogan? Nobody injures us with impunity."

Benta raised his head slowly, his face took on a mask of pale horror. His whole frame shook in disbelief and loathing. Gaping at his friend harder than ever before, he gasped:

"What have you done!"

"Nothing that a friend would not do."

Deliberately, emphasising every word and stressing each syllable, Benta groaned:

"You have committed a murder, senseless and unjust. Mark, you should have visited me."

"What good would that have done?"

"It would have spared an innocent life, plus me a lot of grief," he said visibly shaken.

Thunderstruck Russel jumped up.

"Justin, what is going on? Have you gone soft, did prison life grind you down? How can you feel sorry for that treacherous woman who almost ruined your life?"

Still staring ahead, suppressing a mournful smile, Benta snapped:

"Who says Lena harmed me?"

"Pierre, the Frenchman, told me everything, he apprised me of the facts. She testified against you, lying through her teeth, accusing you of a felony which she had committed. All in order to push you aside, to feed that insatiable demon ambition."

Moving his head reproachfully from side to side, Benta remarked:

"There is something you are not aware of, Mark. Pierre, a vengeful fellow by any measure, duped you. He has been going around for a while imputing Lena with all sorts of evil deeds. He maligned her character at every possibility. The saying, there is no wrath like a woman scorned, fits him like a glove. You see, she jilted him, thereby calling to life an implacable enemy."

"You mean she did not plant that ring?"

"No."

"How do you know?"

"Because it was I who placed it there."

"For safekeeping?"

A wry grin appeared all over Benta's face.

"You might say that if you like. I was going to take it home after work," Russel was informed.

He seemed utterly befuddled.

"I don't understand," he admitted.

Then by degrees something dawned on him. Frowning he asked:

"Are you saying that Bauer did not testify against you?"

"More than that, she lied to help me."

"Then why were you found guilty?"

"Because I was, I am. Not only did I steal that ring, but other jewellery too."

This unthinkable admission, shamelessly made, took a while to sink in. Offhand it proved too prickly to digest. But the unassailable truth, rising before his eyes like the pillars of heaven, could no longer be denied. He suddenly saw leagues beyond the boundaries of mere vision.

As he was about to ask his friend why he had stooped so low, he took a closer look. He unfailingly knew the reason: The man in the room with him, middle aged like himself, had changed. Gone was the lithe frame; the firm, ever active muscles had turned flabby prematurely; his face, often the only compensation for advancing years, showed signs of resignation. Russel needed not to be told anything beyond his perception.

The once confident man who touched every female's heart with his laughing eyes and lilting tongue, now had to bestow trinkets to obtain what once was so freely given. As he looked again, he could have sworn to see the sap of life drying up in his friend.

"Tomorrow morning I shall cross the Continental Divide again," he decided.

Flight

*M*arriage is known to tame the wildest spirit. It can stifle imagination over the years and render the mind tepid. The young man, or woman for that matter, just spreading his wings to soar with eagles, soon finds it wiser to stay on the ground with serpents. Add to this spiritual choke encroaching old age, and there we have Rudi Faron.

He was an intrepid youngster once, brimming with initiative, adventurous in spirit, and daring as few before him. He virtually hungered for the brilliant rays of intellectual achievements, which he had sworn to bend around himself.

It turned out to be a chimera, a dream that he occasionally attempted to revive. Lately, however, just raising his eyes towards the sun of glory blinded and tired him. Conjugal duties, enshrined in society's expectations, had sapped his strength, he avowed. For this premature loss of vigour, and his failure to reach the corona of excellence, he blamed Lora, his wife of thirty years. She rejected such notions with more than a hee-haw.

"It's pure bunkum, Rudi, not worth wasting one's breath over," she countered every time he alluded to it.

Privately, however, there were moments of doubts, accompanied by pangs of guilt. For she too, like Montaigne, felt the need to own up to the truth with advancing age. She had to admit that her predilection for worldly possessions over intellectual pursuits provided no stimulus for her husband's mental endeavours. A dollar in her pocket meant more than well turned phrases or grandiloquent poetry. Was their union unhappy? Not really, just stagnant.

"You are going out again I see," Lora remarked in a listless tone, neither vexed nor sympathetic.

"Yes, I want to catch some fresh air," he answered without turning.

"Be careful, I hear that some peculiar characters are starting to frequent the park lately, especially after nightfall," she admonished.

These words, said in jest, somewhat sarcastically spoken for no other reason than to be heard, set the stage for a drama worthy of a Greek master's mettle. As mentioned, although kisses and laughter had left the Faron house some time ago, deep resentment had not yet entered. There still existed a bond between them, tenuous to be sure, slowly disintegrating, but it prevented a complete separation. Vexation could have been called the needle, bickering the thread that stitched the ever widening gap again and again together. Faron at times revived his latent ideas of grandeur, which to him was within reach, but unattainable because his wife blocked the way.

Night was setting in rapidly. As he reached the park, darkness began to swallow the shadows of trees and shrubs. Following the narrow footpath, at times well maintained, other times merely tamped down by sturdy feet, he hardly met a soul. This seemed odd, or perhaps he just paid no attention to it before, since he usually walked amid a cloud of bitterness, which veiled his mind and blurred his sight.

Not tonight, however. This evening he perceived his surrounding with an awareness that simultaneously roused and soothed his whole being. There, under the rising moon, walked a different man who after untold years of shilly-shally tried to steel himself for action. For the first time in memory he noticed the rising moon, smiling, tending to give courage, and heard the rustling in the trees, whispering to be bold.

A few weeks ago he had turned sixty-five, not an advanced age by any reckoning, but devastating to a man whose lofty aims remained not only unfulfilled, but who never undertook the first step. This situation had to change. Commencing

tonight he would forge ahead without intermission to reach his
goal before the age of seventy. It was not too late; only
yesterday he paged through an encyclopedia where he found
names of men who had accomplished great deeds beyond that
age.

First he must find an objective however, then he would
show the world and his doubting wife his true colours.

"My wife," he muttered aggrieved. He would make her
swallow every sneering word she had uttered. Let her suffocate
on her own vapour of apathy, so stifling to the spirit and
paralysing to the intellect. He had resolved to escape from this
ring of smothering haze; quite soon that is.

As he walked on, engrossed in reflections and reveries, he
could not quite banish the impression that something was
amiss. It was a lovely summer evening, warm without being
oppressive. A light wind drifted up from the Fraser River,
stirring the leaves and tickling one's face. The moon shed
sufficient light to make the path clearly visible, thus render
shapes recognisable and friendly.

Nevertheless, he felt ill at ease. As mentioned few people
were abroad, a fact which disconcerted Faron for reasons he
could not, rather would not acknowledge. For his mind was
occupied by weightier matters. He recalled his youth, when
inspired by a steadfast purpose he wished that fate should make
time leap ahead faster. To be older was his desire, so that his
stirring ambition could be given free rein.

At twenty he talked of achievements which would
flabbergast the world. When he reached his thirtieth year he
allowed himself another ten years to reach the apex of success.
Then came marriage, bringing untold bliss in its wake.

"In ten years, Lora, we shall be clothed in silk," he
announced to his wide-eyed wife.

Some years later he declared, still enthusiastic:

"Lora, guess what I see. A mansion, my dear, surrounded by
cultivated grounds, and you the mistress waited on by a host of
maids."

His wife smiled, infected by his eagerness, yet somewhat
sobered by reality. Then the children arrived, three in a row,

spaced less than two years apart. That of course erected hurdles on his path to success.

"But don't worry," he consoled Lora, "the setback will only be temporary. Just wait, darling, in five years we shall rub elbows with all the nabobs up on the hill," he announced more often than once.

Lora smiled, she understood. The expected arrival of their first child meant more to her than fame and riches. Besides, there was still time to map out and carry his ambitious plans to fruition, she indicated.

That was thirty years ago, not much had happened in the meantime. Just thinking about their lacklustre life, for which he increasingly blamed his wife, forced his steps to slow down. It allowed some people behind to overtake him.

"Good evening," he greeted, relieved that he was not alone in the park.

"Good evening," they answered with surprising reluctance.

Then quick as lightning the realisation hit him: they are dissembling their voices. Surprised, he ventured to take a closer look, but did not succeed. Before he managed to open his eyes wider, they had gone by. Just the same, what he saw made him uneasy. They looked familiar, yet he could not place them, since the next moment only their backs were visible.

Beyond a doubt, however, it were two young men, judging by the way they walked and moved their limbs. Youthful and sturdy they could be called, as much as suspect. Both wore light clothes resembling joggers on the surface, who strove to cast an aura of casualness.

"No, no," Faron argued with himself, "these fellows are not innocent strollers, they are up to no good."

Even the dim light of the moon revealed that fact. Sinister they looked despite averted faces. Hardly had he given vent to these extravagant notions, when he chortled in derision:

"Now, Rudi, what next!"

Just the same he stopped, pretending to be fascinated by a cluster of bushes. What did Lora say?

"Be careful, there are some weird creatures out there lately, I hear."

Did she know something, or was that just another of her
fatuous remarks? The words in themselves bore little
significance, much less than the way they were uttered. A
message was intended, no doubt a warning mixed with hope
that harm might befall him. He had good reasons to make such
assumptions.

Their lives together, for years not a bed of roses, had lately
taken a nasty turn. Both were pensioners beset by ailments,
which society termed signs of advancing age, and Faron termed
symptoms of progressive ignobility. But no worry, he would
escape from that vicious circle, before the end of the month to
boot.

A weak heart beat in his narrow chest, more than one doctor
told him. Let them diagnose till resurrection, as of today he
would hurl their prognoses into the Fraser River below.

"A bit of wisdom and circumspection, Mr Faron, and your
heart will last another twenty years," one of the quacksalvers
told him a few days ago.

"Remember, no exertions, and listen well, no fast running,
and above all take your medicine."

Twenty years? what of it? It would suit him fine, allowing
ten years to complete his work, leaving the other ten to receive
the deserved acclaim.

"No running, indeed, I bet I could outrun those two
youngsters ahead of me," he told himself.

His thoughts returned to Lora, the stumbling block in his
path to fulfilment. The cornerstone towards his freedom had
been laid. Tonight, after his return the project would be
completed. Telling all, mincing no words stood on his mind. A
total separation was necessary, nothing else would do.

A week ago they had a powwow, as he called it, the most
incisive for decades. He had tried to be casual about it, jovial
really, in order not to alarm her.

"Come, Lora, out with a bottle of the best, let's get in the
mood," he announced with forced gayness.

It made his wife wince visibly. Despite her ever present
arthritis she bolted upright.

"In the mood for what?" she demanded to know with more
than a tinge of alarm in her voice.

He understood; a smile stole around his lips.

"Now, now, don't worry, I harbour no untoward designs upon the virtue of a – an honourable maiden," he chortled.

Nettled just the same by her priggish demeanour, he resolved to be more forthright than intended. For decades they had spoken seldom with each other seriously, heart to heart that is. Hardly ever did their conversation extend beyond hackneyed remarks or general gossip. Whenever he made an attempt to speak about weightier subjects, like their lives for instance, she appeared to be busy. At the first hint at it she had developed a habit of scurrying away. Not tonight she would, he swore to himself.

Setting bottle and glasses on the table he practically ordered his wife to sit down. Gazing at him surprised, she obeyed his bidding. Some ring in his voice, a peremptory undertone, moved her to comply. Altogether he seemed to have changed into a man she had not encountered for decades. Of course she did not know that Rudi, almost a teetotaller, had fortified himself prior to requesting this discussion. More than one snifter filled with Seagrams' best had been poured down his throat.

"As you know, Lora, I'm working on a book," he said.

"For three decades, I might add," she retorted, still peeved because she had failed to elude him this time.

"Well, I intend to finish it quickly, and then write a few more."

"Am I stopping you?" she snorted.

Hearing no immediate response, she took another glimpse. The man, her husband of many years, sitting across the table suddenly acquired a stranger's appearance. Odd, she thought, how can someone, invariably frail and timid, transform into a veritable pillar of fortitude within a few short weeks. For untold years he was known to be pusillanimous, turning fogyish, yet always conciliatory. Behold him now! she thought, he has developed into a dissenter of the first magnitude, causing strife far and wide, besides making me uneasy.

"No, you are not," he conceded reluctantly.

Sensing his hesitation, she added angrily:

"I don't understand you at all. We are alone in a house of five rooms. Surely you can find peace and quiet in one of them. I certainly will not bother you."

Faron wished he had hoisted a few more, the fire in the liquid might have encouraged him to tell the truth, something like this:

"Lora, how can I write knowing there is an anguished soul in the house praying for failure, hoping fervently that my efforts be cut to shreds by the Sword of Zoilos. Knowing that, plus having to breathe in air contaminated by ill will, how indeed can I work?"

He did not say it, but while thinking it he managed to smile. For he knew what must and will be done. In a way he regretted having to leave her. Not that she would miss him, for she cultivated a never-ending string of acquaintances and friends. In addition she had her ailments, ostensibly hated, yet in reality nursed and enjoyed.

They had met almost forty years ago, in the wilds of the West, which then was not yet encumbered by conventions. People, surrounded by ice fields, who encountered bears and coyotes almost at their door steps, did not kowtow readily. It was a wonderful time, marred only by his restless yearning to excel. Their conversation had ended as many previous ones: acrimonious and fruitless. So be it.

He intended to finish his stroll and right after let her know the inevitable. He was just directing his steps towards the narrow path leading to a cluster of houses, when he caught sight of someone standing there. Faron instinctively stopped. He could not explain it, but his heart missed a beat or two. In no time the recognition surged through him: these were the same men who passed him a little while ago.

There they stood, two dark silhouettes steeped in suspicion, whispering to each other, sending significant glances his way. Unwittingly he retreated behind a dense bush. Had they seen him? Were they waiting for someone, him perhaps, or was his imagination running out of control? Lora's wry smile came to mind again, along with her cryptic words, which now took on a less obscure meaning.

"Watch out, they are going to get you," she had muttered as he closed the door.

These words, in retrospect sounding like a message full of significance, now absorbed his attention. Were they spoken in jest, intended to warn him, or a slip of the tongue? He vividly recalled an odd vibration in her voice, sounding intense, and jubilant at the same time, indicating fulfilment of hope. That was it! Lora secretly wished him harm. Could that be possible? No! was his spontaneous reaction, which he repudiated the next instant. Did she not cast lurking glances at him at the first sign of nightfall?

Ever since their recent powwow, ending in a quarrel really, her whole demeanour had changed, especially at the approach of evening, when signs of an astounding impishness flitted across her pinched face. Even more striking he found symptoms of restlessness stirring her limbs. Tonight these indications were exceptionally expressive, a fact he now realised fully. A palpable, all consuming tension surrounded her whole being, a crackling suspense he had never sensed before in her presence made him feel on edge. She was nervous alright, no doubt about it; besides, being anxious to see him going out. Did she say twice, three times, or more often?

"Rudi, what a beautiful evening to go for a long walk. How glad I should be to accompany you, but my arthritis is acting up more than ever. Take your time, dear, enjoy yourself."

These were welcome words, encouraging and supportive, but marred by that final, fateful utterance:

"Watch out! they are going to get you!"

To be sure, she perceived him beyond hearing distance, yet he heard all, and now understood. Something was in the wind; ominous vibrations disturbed the night air, sending tidings of impending perils, of hazards aimed at him; but why? He was a peaceable man just trying to escape from spiritual atrophy.

Lora! No one else had an interest to do it, she possessed more than one reason. No doubt she divined his intention to fly the coup, as it were. Preventing it could well be uppermost in her mind.

"Lora, Lora, no matter what you hope for, or have hatched, come Sunday I am gone," he murmured.

A glance at his watch told him it was getting late, quite past his usual hour of return. It was high time to go back. Not along the customary route however, since he harboured no desire to brush past the two men farther ahead, although they were no longer visible.

As he stepped from behind the bushes voices were audible, among others a woman's. Hearing it he felt reassured, his agitated nerves calmed down somewhat, till he realised it was Lora making loud requests which sounded more like an order to him, especially after hearing his name mentioned several times. It could only mean they were about to set their plan into motion. What it entailed he could neither explain, nor wanted to. The truth was, reason had kicked the traces, given rampant imagination the reins.

Getting away from here, to some safer well lit place was all he could think about, before the moon disappeared behind the mountains.

"Good luck, Lora, whatever you have concocted will fail, be assured of it," he said loud enough to lend encouragement to his quivering heart.

Turning on his heels he rushed back to the main path. He would fool them good, since he was intimately acquainted with every trail, clearing and crossing of these extensive grounds. Walking faster, soon falling into a trot, he felt the crackle of danger, and heard the voice of prophecies louder than before. Lora's sibilant words rang in his ears again and again:

"Leaving me, are you? To write in solitude, are you, Rudi? Try it! Go on, try it! You know what? I bet you will never write, never write!"

The sound of footsteps crunching on gravel made him lurch forward. He remembered that about two hundred metres ahead branched off a winding lane leading to the main road, towards which he ran with ebbing strength and gasping for air. His heart was pounding, but reassured by the fact that his prescribed pills would sustain him, he pressed ahead. Urged on by thumping steps behind, he hurried up the hill.

Then the first shooting pain raced through his chest, followed by a numbing sensation which paralysed every muscle in his body. His last thought, a silent wail really, belonged to his lifelong ambition, which would remain but idle hope. In this peaceful park, surrounded on three sides by dwellings, he was about to meet his Waterloo. Clapping a hand on his throbbing heart, moaning pityingly, staggering violently, he collapsed. Three hours later he was dead.

"Cardiac arrest," Dr Meunier diagnosed.

Shaking his head he looked at Mrs Faron.

"Why would a man in such precarious condition, at an age where prudence should prevail, plunge headlong through a neighbourhood park," he mused.

"Doctor, I have no idea," she answered.

"Hm, hm, an autopsy might reveal the reason," he suggested not too resolutely.

Mrs Faron almost burst out:

"Surely, there is no need for that, excessive exertion caused his heart to fail, nothing further."

Considering her closer, Dr Meunier remarked:

"I was only kidding, I guess."

Two weeks later Lora Faron had a visitor. It was Enzio Furgetti, Rudi's best and only friend. They of course knew each other; furthermore, they had a common bond: namely, a reciprocal dislike for one another.

She opened the door reluctantly, and was even more disinclined to invite him in. Such minor omissions, however, were scant deterrents to the man from the heel of Italy. He was cut from a different cloth than his tame friend. Burnt by the sun of Catania, his veins afire with the spirit of Garibaldi, he was not easily daunted. Before she could protest he stood inside.

A strange expression darkened his already swarthy face, it was ominously set. Around the ever laughing eyes hovered a grim aspect; she had never seen him so determined. Ignoring her inimical attitude he said:

"I just returned from a trip abroad. The news I have received is devastating. How did it happen?"

This was more of an accusation than question. Annoyed she advised:

"As the death certificate says, Rudi's heart gave out after undue exertions. It took place right down in the park."

"Exertions, you say? Was he not just strolling like always?"

"No, he ran, rather sprinted. Foolish man, I can't think what induced him to do it," she explained haltingly.

"Rudi running? it sounds incredible."

These words were drowning in a stream of scorn and disbelief. He knew his friend's habits well. Running was never one of them, but indulging his heart was.

Putting his hands in one of his pockets, he fished out a vial which he shook gently. The tinkling obviously rattled Lora, she sprang back as if bitten.

"Guess what I have here?"

"I have no idea," she snapped.

"Your pills, Lora, your pills."

"I don't understand."

Her attempt at defiance appeared feeble even to herself.

"I think you do. Let me explain. Two days before Rudi's mishap, manslaughter we might call it, he came to visit me. Since I was all set to go on a business trip the next day, I was more than happy to see him. He was no whiner as we all know, but without a preamble he commenced to complain about intermittent chest pains."

'My heart is acting up in a queer way, Enzio,' he confided.

'Don't your prescription pills help?' I demanded to know in a voice showing signs of alarm. To tell the truth he looked like a harbinger of distress. His next words confirmed my impression.

'They make it worse,' he told me.

'Since when?'

'Since about a week ago,' he admitted meekly.

'In what way?'

'Right after I take them my whole inside changes. I don't know what I fear more: the disorientation or the stabs right through my heart. In short, Enzio, I get panicky.'

As Furgetti talked, his eyes never left Lora. He studied her with sidewise glances which soon changed to stares of scrutiny. Oddly enough she neither protested nor stirred during these portentous revelations. Her eyes however, riveted to the vial, were like an open book to him. Raising the little bottle occasionally, Furgetti rattled it suggestively in front of her face. He said more:

"I berated him mercilessly."

'First you give me those pills, every one of them,' I barked.

'Then straight from here you go and see Dr Meunier, tell him to write out a better prescription.'

"Before Rudi left I obtained the name and location of his pharmacist."

Lora was unable to restrain herself any longer.

"Why are you telling me all this?" she asked.

"You will soon find out. After my return I made some astounding discoveries. As you noticed I did not approach you immediately. For two reasons: First, I never trusted you since the day you ruined Rudi's manuscript."

"That was an accident," she interjected.

"Was it now? A mishap similar to Rudi's demise, I guess. I have stated the first reason, let me tell you the second one. At his last visit my anguished friend made me privy to some disquieting news, to the extent that I almost cancelled my trip; in retrospect I wish I had.

"Anyway, when upon my return I heard about Rudi's death, the sluice gates of suspicion opened wide. As luck would have it the pills, I sort of confiscated, were still in the house. Pocketing them instantly, I practically raced to the pharmacist. Now, that fellow, much younger than I, almost manhandled me when I suggested that Rudi's prescription was wrongly filled. He coughed and roared till I pulled out what I had. Three hours later when I returned, the ambience in the whole store had changed."

Facing Lora squarely he remarked:

"You are a graduate nurse, are you not? Never mind, don't answer."

He then chortled:

"How well I recall Rudi's tiresome eulogies about your pharmaceutic skills, of which he now became a victim."

"What are you saying?" she protested.

"Just this: You substituted Rudi's pills, meant to soothe the nerves and strengthen the heart, with psychedelic drugs, which looked similar on the surface, but contained substances producing opposite effects. Instead of calming nerves and slowing down an excited heart, the pharmacist stated, they conjure up hallucinations and accelerate pulsation. You knew exactly what you were doing."

"And you are talking nonsense. There might not have been much love left between us, but hate? I think your brain has shrunk in that southern sun."

Ignoring her snide remark, Furgetti continued:

"Who would suspect a solicitous wife beseeching neighbours to bring back her errand husband, ailing and disoriented, probably lost in the park. It had the anticipated result. Mistaking the approaching men as evil-minded pursuers, he fled, thereby overtaxing his already vulnerable heart, which soon after stopped beating."

Raising both hands to prevent her from interjecting, he went on:

"What now, that you have rid yourself of a man always kindly disposed towards you? Only being guilty of aspirations loathsome to you. But this is not the end."

Alarmed she asked:

"You are going to the police?"

"No."

Visibly relieved, growing bolder, she mocked:

"I know, you are going to hurl the Sicilian curse at me."

"No."

Reassured by now, Lora sneered:

"Horror upon horror, a contract will be put on my life."

"Not that either. Yours will be the ultimate punishment."

"What might that be?"

"To your grave you shall nourish the scorpions of a guilty conscience. A rivederci."

On The Way

*T*oday Nemaska, a Cree settlement, about a thousand kilometres north of Montreal, can easily be reached. Contrary to the time when three government surveyors were on the way towards it. To reach Matagami took little effort, but the final two hundred kilometres required more than good intentions to get through.

A settlement was planned at the shores of Lac Nemiscau, a wild isolated area a hundred kilometres from the closest town. It was slated as a future home for the Crees, now settled in the Sekami region at the banks of the mighty La Grande River, below the fifty-fourth parallel. A compulsory resettlement stood in the offing within the coming three years, ahead of inundation, which would take away their traditional hunting grounds. For the present only roads and services were under consideration; the village would come later.

Lac Nemiscau can be termed small compared to other lakes around. Resembling an inverted St. Anthony's cross, it measures over forty kilometres one way, and somewhat less the other. It is not wide, hardly three kilometres average.

Peter Dudinka, the chief of the trio was considerably older than his two co-workers. Sure-footed, of sturdy built and weather-beaten, he did not fear the most arduous march nor heavy labour despite advancing years. Imbued with a sunny nature, his confidence was not diminished by setbacks or misfortunes, no matter how harsh or unjust they were.

Insurmountable obstacles he accepted with ready smiles, while circumventing them with a shrug of the shoulders. Uttering a few phrases of wisdom, of which he possessed a veritable storehouse, and on he went in a different direction. Quibbling he left to others, it held no appeal for him.

After several delays they reached the Rupert River bridge, where gear and provisions had to be loaded in canoes. Then upriver it went towards their destination. Arriving next day in clear June weather, not a moment was lost to start erecting a cabin, to serve as work and sleeping area in the coming months. In less than four days it stood ready for occupation at the northwest shores of the lake. It proved a small effort for skilled hands, guided by plucky dispositions, aided by Dudinka's experience, who had performed similar tasks dozen times.

Lack of light was no concern. Although the walls were built mainly of logs, their upper part, as much as the roof were covered with transparent tarpaulins. They anticipated rain with joy, which is understandable by someone who ever slept under such a roof.

Choosing assistants lay exclusively in Dudinka's province. It had to be so, considering their close living conditions in remote areas, which could render life pleasant, or sheer hell. He had learned the hard way to be careful, after that dismal episode at the lower Orinoco, a region inhabited by warlike Yanomamoes. By a hair's-breadth he would never have seen the sandy shores of Lac Nemiscau. The steaming, oppressive jungle almost became his grave.

He barely avoided a disaster, partly on account of his assistant, but no less because of his naivety, bordering on mindlessness. He was no match for that equivocator's glibness, nor could he parry the selfish weakling's homage. Albeit reluctant, he had taken him along on that hazardous journey, which consequently almost cost his life. Coincidence, looking in retrospect more like fate, saved his neck from a tightening noose.

Since then circumspection governed his choice of assistants. Only acquaintances of many years, colleagues or well-recommended candidates stood a chance to be taken along.

First requirement was equanimity, the second geniality. Inner peace, as much as unshakable self-confidence were desirable attributes on prolonged sojourns in close quarters, where the only distractions are howling wolves and screaming eagles.

Fickle characters, forever jumpy, quickly become an abhorrence to themselves and others in such surroundings. They even affect the animal world like running sores. An abbot of unrest may well have advantages in high society, but in wide open regions where every word resounds a hundredfold, inner turmoil becomes a liability.

Henri Musil and Roland Kreisel did not disappoint Dudinka till now. Both turned out to be admirably suited for this work. They were modest, independent, and despite relative young years imperturbable. True, Musil possessed a propensity for practical jokes, not at all favourable received by Kreisel.

Apart from that, harmony prevailed so far; words intended to malign were never uttered. Their inclination towards sobriety especially pleased Dudinka, for in that respect he had suffered some painful experiences.

It had happened now and then that, after a candidate swore up and down never to allow anything stronger than spring water to flow across his tongue, he turned out to be an unrestrained drunkard. Dudinka, himself a Bacchus admirer, simply could not get over what seemed to move these people. One sip unleashes all twelve major devils, it appeared, who scuffle for the unfortunate's soul.

Gone then is his composure, he must obey an unopposable power to reach an imaginary imp hiding at the shimmering bottom of the bottle. An irresistible urge grips him to come face to face with that spirit. Once arrived at the bottom, something astounding happens: the imp flees. Where to? To the bottom of the next full bottle. Thinking about it might make one smile, having to experience it, however, changes such smiles quickly into scowls.

The work progressed well, the weather proved benign for weeks, hardly a drop of rain fell. Strong winds, the surveyor's adversary, were absent till now. Not a breeze stirred the crowns of the tall, skimpy firs. The mood in the small camp remained upbeat. Pleasant days, rendered agreeable by successful work, were followed by restful nights.

Despite the clement weather Dudinka never neglected to scan the horizon every morning. Sudden squalls in that vast level land amid forests, lakes and swamps were no rarity. He was acquainted with them through first hand experience.

Across Hudson Bay, twice the size of Germany, winds gather at times which push downward and acquire storm-like forces. Howling fiercely, they assail the mainland with only one thing in mind: to cause havoc. Soon the lakes would be covered with whitecaps, and trees start to bend till they creak and crack.

One morning, when he stepped outside as usual, one glance told him all. The air smelled different, the sky above the rising sun had changed. Ominous signs all around spoke louder than the barometer on the wall. Instinctively he started to test fastenings and braces. Conscientiously, without hesitation, he tied ropes, added more, and knocked stakes into the ground. The noise of course awoke his assistants.

"What is going on out there?" Kreisel asked, more curious than indignant.

"Storm, boys, is going on, come out and help, something is brewing," called out a busy Dudinka.

The sky, meanwhile blackening, left no doubt that stormy weather was on its way. A strong wind at this time of the year usually brought heavy, prolonged rain in its wake. Impending storms deserved immediate, undivided attention in the middle of nowhere in an improvised camp. Nothing ought to be left to chance; that is to say tying, propping, and restaking becomes a necessity, for once the roof sails over the lake's whitecaps, no amount of hope will bring it back. It would be a calamity, unthinkable if not fateful.

Six skilful hands were bustling; three pairs of eager eyes skimmed over every nook and corner of their temporary home. Discovered defects were remedied wordlessly; no one gave instructions, none were expected. Three figures acted like one body with six arms, for on the lake the first waves began to rise. Soon they would perform a merry dance above the water, driven by high winds which flap almost playfully the loose canvass to and fro.

Then the increasing wind tugged at the ropes, perhaps to find out how taut they were. Shortly after gusts upon gusts assailed the little hut. Rain did not stay away long; in no time heavy drops jumped around on the roof, carrying out a veritable dance of the dervishes.

It blew and poured for three days already. Outside work was out of the question, even short outings around the hut proved disagreeable. But such occasional trips were necessary, for the stays could come loose, snap even, judging by their precarious whirr.

Gradually a reality manifested itself, gropingly at first, almost shyly, but finally with undeniable force. Time rolled on with increasing effort, in particular did it hang heavy on Musil's and Kreisel's hands. Continual activity was lacking; they missed the discussions after quitting time about completed work and tasks lying ahead. They also longed for the pleasurable lassitude after a day's work, enriched by feelings of achievement.

Musil and Kreisel, being visibly perplexed, succumbed to moping. They were unable to supplant their imposed idleness with either mental or physical activities. That seemed mighty peculiar to Dudinka, who marvelled how two gregarious men, known to rather talk than listen, should now sit around with lips buttoned up. Lack of topics could hardly have been wanting, for one as the other considered himself well-travelled; both prided themselves of an active life. Their profession had led them to unchartered, often dangerous regions, where adventures were encountered sooner than not. Alone their sojourns among Canada's First Nations could be termed exceptional events.

Dudinka knew about Musil's activities at the northern railway tracks between Sept Isles and Schefferville. Kreisel, according to his accounts, had tracked from the Atlantic to the

Pacific Ocean. The Rockies were his home for a stint, moreover, he served on an oilrig near the coast of Newfoundland. Yet having heard and seen a lot, they had little to say. Be it on account of their relative youth, an inexplicable quirk in their characters, or mere coincidence, Dudinka could not guess. As mentioned, splitting hairs he left to others.

The wind abated gradually, but not the rain. Although the clouds almost brushed the treetops, darkness set in late. Twilight made its appearance much earlier, along with an eerie silence inside the hut.

This took a turn on the fifth evening when Kreisel and Musil entered into a lively discussion. Before Dudinka recovered from his surprise about this sudden change, a regular altercation had ensued. It bewildered him to the extent that he could only listen in shocked silence.

"I tell you for the last time that language is the most powerful trait in human beings. It forms and guides us, it is the breath of life. Speech, idiom coming from the heart, elevates and spurs us on," Musil announced as if inspired.

"Pshaw, Henri, a lot of ladida, nothing else. Language is meant for communication, it has no further value beyond that. Contrary assertions are pure self-deceptions. Coming from the heart? you make me laugh. Why not from the brain?" Kreisel retorted.

Musil faltered not a moment, some profound force moved him, a power stronger than the brain. Zealously he defended his opinion:

"Language is our soul, dilute it and you grow depraved. What do you think kept Quebec alert and strong? We Québecoises would have foundered long ago, neither hay nor grass would we be by now, grovelling at the feet of newcomers, who aspired to assimilate us into the tenets of North America.

"How, you tell me, could a small group of people, mostly peasants, have withstood that destructive wave of concentrated will to crush our culture? We not only survived this onslaught, but left our mark. Language, my son, was the glue that held us together, it fanned our pride and formed our character. It helped us to achieve the unthinkable."

Kreisel, taken aback by this sermonic discourse, lacked the
words for a rebuttal; he gazed pleadingly at Dudinka. This
silent appeal made him sigh heavily, signifying indecision with
whom to side. Since both looked at him expectantly, he felt
called upon to say something. Nodding two, three times,
clearing his throat audibly, he said:

"It seems you want my opinion. By relating an experience I
had many years ago my views are most forcefully expressed. It
is a long story, sounding fantastic, yet it is entirely true."

Since both pulled up their chairs eagerly in expectation, he
continued:

"Are you familiar with the Orinoco River in South
America?"

Musil and Kreisel nodded affirmatively.

"At the border between Venezuela and Brazil, where the
river Mavaka empties into the Orinoco, a misadventure befell
me, so remarkable, if not aberrant, that even today it gives me
nightmares. The fact is, in that steaming, tropical forest, my life
was spared by the skin of my teeth. Only through a miracle did
I return whole and hale."

Turning fully towards Musil, he remarked:

"It might sound incredulous, but the miracle was language."

Seeing Musil's eyes light up, Dudinka smiled, but Kreisel's
glowering stare quickly suppressed it. He took up his narrative
again:

"One cold winter morning a telegram reached me in
Montreal. A former colleague, active in Venezuela, invited me
for a visit to Esmeralda, a small city at the lower Orinoco. A
job is waiting there for me, he advised, of a short duration, but
ample remuneration. The tasks, resembling an adventure he
assured, is just your cup of tea. Adventure in the tropics? One
glance through the iced-up window at the swirling snow
outside convinced me. Reading the conditions further on, I
started to pack immediately. In no time did a return cable whirr
through the wires expressing acceptance.

"Everything worked like a charm. True, the unaccustomed
oven-like heat plagued me considerably, especially the first
week or so. Bathed in perspiration I rose in the mornings; with
a feeling like being wrapped in wet blankets, I went to bed in

the evenings. Despite the burning sun, plus the stinging insects which almost devoured me, I felt exceptionally well.

"An inexplicable elation had seized me, bordering on recklessness. The hard cobblestones under my feet felt like cushions of air; the heat I perceived as a stimulus to act. Did the people, curiously free and unconcerned, awake my animal spirits? The luxurious growth all around, or perhaps the strident, yet soothing sounds of an unfettered nature? Who knows, my exultant frame of mind could equally have stemmed from the sight of omnipresent faces, radiant with joy, and ever laughing eyes, or maybe the sounds of lively music at every street corner.

"I must admit, rarely did I feel so thrilled, elevated and in the mood for bold escapades. My whole being appeared to undergo a metamorphosis at the sight of this ubiquitous bloom, and the hearing of beguiling sounds. The work as explained deemed me not onerous; despite assurances that it entailed certain dangers, I looked forward to it.

"A road, rather a pathway had been intended, either on the north or the south side of the Orinoco. Right to the Brazilian border that roadway was slated to lead, a stretch of about two hundred kilometres eastward. My duty consisted in providing layouts, relevant photographs plus extensive descriptions. As my colleague said, the work was exactly up my alley. As much as I could gather, the planned roadway was going to traverse the territory of the Yanomamoes, also known as the 'Fierce People'. Rarely had a stranger set foot in that area, I was told. Concerning this tribe, estimated at about ten thousand strong, scant knowledge existed.

"An assistant was offered me whom I found unpleasant from the word go. He hailed from New York, had lived ten years farther north in Trinidad before he wandered down to Esmeralda on the north bank of the Orinoco. My colleague, supported by others, recommended him unreservedly. He came from the best of families, they assured me, and possessed abilities, although not in surveying, yet highly opportune for such work. 'The last word rests with you of course,' they advised.

"The man, Ron Rawlins, was on the way to us, he should arrive soon, I heard. 'Look at him closer, question him a bit before you decide,' they said, then added: 'Helpers can be found by the dozen, whether they are suitable is a moot point. Most Europeans, more precisely white men in this area, are exhausted characters, prematurely weakened in body, and crushed in soul; besides, being enslaved by the demon alcohol.'

'Rawlins does not drink excessively?' I inquired.

'Not a drop,' came a convincing reply.

"Ha, ha, and ha again, dear colleagues, not a drop indeed! I soon found out quite the contrary. I consented to take Rawlins along, mainly because I had not learned yet to say no. I was too young to be outspoken."

"You did not like the looks of him, you mentioned," Musil interrupted.

"Not in the least, I must admit. After a seaworthy boat with accessories had been found, we commenced our journey. The first stretch, over a hundred kilometres, we covered at a good clip. Serious work began after reaching Jasubibeteri, well inside the Yanomamoe territory, the so-called ferocious area. I must mention that we were repeatedly cautioned about them. Not that they were a menace, we were told, surely not to strangers, but admittedly unpredictable.

'Don't be deterred by their exterior, they pretend to be more ferocious than they really are,' advised the American consul.

"A martial propensity was apparently only displayed among themselves. To be sure, one must refrain from offering any form of physical threats, which they counter promptly with veritable bloodthirstiness, the experienced consul exhorted.

'Therefore in relation with them keep your cool,' he gave us to understand, along with a reminder to demonstrate a friendly, yet firm deportment.

"Our journey to the unknown had begun, a perilous undertaking lasting at least two months."

"I wish I could have been there," interrupted Musil.

Dudinka cast an amused glance in his assistant's direction.

"I fear at that time you had hardly grown out of your rompers," he chuckled.

"Something about that fellow Rawlins is going to surface, I believe, please keep going," Kreisel remarked.

"Rawlins I recognised as a hindrance on the third day already. Expecting assistance from that quarter would have been fanciful. Something depressed the man, he grew more restive by the hour. Indeed, he became so fidgety that I felt the need to seriously request a bit more composure. My inquiries whether something weighed him down, he repulsed morosely:

'No, there is nothing wrong with me,' he announced vexed.

"But nevertheless his eyes scanned the shores steadily, surely not for professional reasons, I thought. He deemed me harassed, seized by an alarming expectation which I could not fathom. A stretch of over one hundred kilometres lay still ahead of us, the source of the Orinoco that is, somewhat beyond our work area.

"Our task began ahead of Bisai-Teri, near the confluence of the Mavaka and Orinoco rivers. To Punto, another thirty kilometres up river, led our destination. Perhaps farther, should time and weather allow, meaning we would push forth till the onset of incessant rain, which practically drenches that area.

"For some time now, still far from our destination, Rawlins refused to go on land. Would you believe that was all? Far from it! he even balked when I disembarked, moreover, soon repulsed every attempt to approach the banks. I had never seen anything like that: the way the man wrangled and raised a hue and cry whenever I steered towards either shore. After the third attempt to interfere with the boat's steering, I lost my composure.

'Fellow, take your hands away! Say, are you completely out of your mind?' I roared.

"This outbreak seemed to calm him down somewhat, albeit not sufficiently to listen to reason. Next morning, as I steered towards a promising mooring spot, intending fully to set up an interim camp, something beyond expectation occurred, rather manifested itself. Rawlins started to act as if all three furies were in pursuit."

"Was he scared of the Indians?" Kreisel asked.

"Scared? that would be putting it mildly, the fellow trembled from head to toe."

"What happened then?" Musil wanted to know.

"As mentioned, Rawlins had behaved quite odd for a while, but not as bizarre as now. As if voices from another world were screaming in his ears, announcing his doom. Disturbed, I examined him closer, thereby noticing his haggard face, flustered, puffed up peculiarly, and above all his bleary eyes. No, I mused, fear alone could not cause such devastation, the man suffers from physical ailments.

"As always he sat at the bow, opposite from me, shivering to an extent that no sensible word crossed his lips. Malaria! it raced through my head. That was it, nothing else could explain his eccentric behaviour. Therefore only one solution offered itself: to turn around without delay.

"At once I manoeuvred the boat till its bow pointed westward, back towards La Esmeralda. Rawlins required medical attention, nothing less would do. When I apprised him of my intention, he protested vociferously. Stuttering, his quivering hand pointed towards the northern shore. I barely understood a word, except 'Indians, Yanomamoes, savages.'

"They stood there alright as expected, with spears, bows and arrows, or sturdy cudgels. But what of it? I said to myself, we knew beforehand of their presence, and that despite their ferocious deportment they are quite harmless if left in peace. So why this groundless behaviour? Oh well, I consoled myself, fear has gotten to him.

"But reason reared its head, it murmured into both my ears: Fever? Does it not relax a person rather than render him stung to the soul? Does it not make one more indifferent, to the point of frivolity?

"Truly, without the assurances from many quarters that he assiduously avoided alcohol, I would have thought him drunk; blind drunk that is. Then he started to curse, raising simultaneously the lid of a crate, which always stood by his side. I had wondered more than once what was in there. When he shouldered it for loading, I quipped: 'What is in there? Gold to bribe the natives?' 'No, just books,' Rawlins replied.

"Instinctively my eyebrows must have lifted. Taking books to the wilderness deemed me highly peculiar for a self-professed philistine, who considered literature bunkum. In the next instant the veils lifted. Rawlins removed not a book from the well-guarded crate, but a bottle filled with a white liquid. Tequila! it shot through my head. Shall I be hit by a thunderbolt if I exaggerate; the presumed sick man unscrewed the cap and poured half of the bottle's contents gurglingly down his throat. Remember, it was still early morning, the sun had barely risen above the palm trees.

"The realisation hit me squarely: the man was a drunkard. He had emptied on the sly one bottle after the other in that crate. Thus his peculiar behaviour explained itself. He suffered not from malaria, but signs of delirium tremens. After several attempts to raise himself, he ultimately succeeded. Stumbling, swinging the half emptied bottle above his head, he came towards me.

"This could not continue; the situation had reached untenable proportions. With one movement I steered the boat towards the shore, all the while talking soothingly to the fuming, staggering Rawlins. Hardly had we moored when he turned from me and clambered on land, at the same time hurling vicious imprecations at the meanwhile gathered Yanomamoes. Then he plunged into them."

Dudinka paused to catch his breath. Looking first significantly at Musil and then at Kreisel, he continued:

"You should have heard the noise, a tumult broke out like in old bedlam. At first the Yanomamoes were puzzled; they stared wide-eyed at this whooping, gesticulating attacker, obviously a maniac. Taken unawares they fell back, but they soon came up to expectation. Don't forget, they were known as the Fierce People. Before Rawlins managed to crash the raised bottle over one of the black tousled heads, at least ten spears had pierced his body.

"Then the roused Indians turned to me. In no time I was encircled by at least thirty naked, growling warriors, who raised their spears menacingly. These grotesque figures alone could have instilled fear in the most intrepid heart. Add to it the murderous clamour, plus yapping curs fighting over my heels, and you get an idea what terror is. Making signs of friendship by folding my arms across my chest, and repeating the word friend, I tried to calm them down. Whether it had an effect I could not even guess, for surely none understood what I meant. They brandished their weapons menacingly around me, and one after the other sent ghastly shrieks towards the sky."

"Could you not have fled?" Kreisel asked.

"Impossible! To begin with I was completely surrounded, moreover, whenever I made the slightest move, up came about fifty spears."

"I'm on tenterhooks to hear what happened next," Musil interjected.

"It got more fanciful by the minute. How I managed to extricate myself borders on the supernatural. But back to the jungle where I shivered for dear life. Topping my misery was the fact that women and children entered the fray. Naked like their menfolk, with even shriller voices, they appeared to incite the excited warriors. Not understanding a single word, I nevertheless sensed that more than just my health was at stake.

"Suddenly the circle opened. Two garishly painted men, wailing and stomping, entered through the opening. At the sight of these daubed, contorted shapes, all turned topsy-turvy around me. Something so abysmal ugly I had never seen before, even less such aberrant demeanour. The two men positioned themselves towards the middle of the circle in a fashion of freestyle fighters about to attack each other. Weapons they had none, only clenched fists were raised. One fist shot forward, the other twitched backward.

"Suddenly they pounced at each other like infuriated fighting cocks. Neither one staggered or gave way, as they pounded each other's chest with all their might. They hammered away with powerful blows till the air resounded. Then both fell back. Taking another run they repeated their onslaught. Oddly enough, an eerie silence had set in, even the dogs stopped yapping. In spite of my predicament I was intrigued by the hollow sounds produced by this chest hammering, whose purpose I did not understand till later.

"They went at it till one of the combatant dropped groaningly to the ground. The victor, expelling a bloodcurdling cry, grabbed a proffered spear with which he belaboured the ground around him. Chest beating, I learned later, was one of their ceremonial customs, conducted by shamans under the influence of the drug ebeni.

"By now my entire attention was directed at the stamping, howling Yanomamoe, who worked himself into a frenzy. Frighteningly gnashing his teeth, he repeatedly pointed towards me. His intention left not much to the imagination after several mock attacks. I stood there transfixed, as if rooted to the ground by the basilisk's stare, surrounded by hissing, groaning, highly excited Yanomamoes. At any moment I expected the death thrust."

"And you could not have fled?" Musil asked.

"I must admit that thought never entered my mind. In any case it would have been senseless because, as I said already, at every move I made more than thirty spears were aimed at me threateningly."

"How did it all end? The whole affair sounds like a bad dream," Kreisel remarked.

"To be more exact like a nightmare," Musil added.

"Anyway, you obviously somehow managed to escape," they remarked almost in unison.

Their argument over the impact of language was forgotten. Their eyes and ears hung on Dudinka's lips, anxious to hear every word, intent not to miss a single syllable. They were not disappointed.

"What happened next I consider to this day a phenomenon from the beyond, at whose threshold I stood. Escape was impossible, that much I knew. One glance at the naked, screaming savages robbed me of the last glimmer of hope. Possible assistance could not even be dreamed of, I was completely at the mercy of these raving barbarians, daubed with war paint.

"Yet somehow, I suddenly forgot my inevitable fate, as my thoughts began to wander far back over the blue Atlantic Ocean. They kept pushing on, climbing, crossing the Ural Mountains to the broad water of the Emisey River in Siberia. It might surprise you to learn that on its sandy banks stood my cradle. My last journey, a flight from reality, led to the place of my birth."

"We figured that you are of Russian descent; but Siberia? that is some distance from here," Musil interrupted Dudinka's narrative.

"Yes, I was born there, and spent the first five years of my life in that region. My parents became victims of an untimely death, of a fatal accident actually, for which reason I was sent to relatives in Canada. Only English was spoken around me, thus my Russian completely fell into oblivion. Also the memory of my parents had paled gradually, including all traces of my early years, till ultimately every vestige of it had disappeared.

"Yet, for some miraculous reason I suddenly heard my father's voice, which I not only distinctly recognised, but clearly understood what he was saying."

"In English?" Kreisel wondered.

Dudinka gazed at him for a moment, than said:

"In Russian."

Ignoring his assistants' surprised glances, he continued:

"In his deep rolling bass he urged me to resist. Something I must mention here: my father, that much I recall, possessed a quiet, equable nature, but woe to someone who aggravated him. Then his composed, well-meaning tone transformed itself into thunder and lightning. He sure could storm and inveigh, which in Russian apparently is much easier than in English. My ears now resounded with encouraging cries:

'Peter Dudinka, son of Igor, resist, fight back! You have nothing to lose but fear! Onward! Go at it! Attack, attack!' That was what I heard."

Dudinka fell silent, during which time he cast tentative glances at his colleagues, like a man disbelieving himself what he is about to say.

Outside the wind tugged and tore at the roof's tarpaulins. Like sails hauled too close to the wind it sounded. But none paid attention to it, for their ears were glued at Dudinka's lips who continued his narrative.

"Voices from my early childhood rose above that infernal din. Men, women and children urged me to attack, in Russian mind you. Amazing as it may sound, I understood every word. More happened. Before my inner eye appeared the brave, high-spirited Cossacks, these legendary wild riders, who too spurred me on to charge right into them. Something stirred in me that I could not explain in a hundred years.

"In one swoop every trace of fear dissipated from me; the trembling lamb turned into a snorting buffalo ready to hurl one after the other through mid-air, and when they came down trample them into the ground. What followed remains inexplicable to my grave.

"I started to roar like a wounded lion, then bellowed, not in the language I had been using for the past thirty years, but in Russian. Rumbling like thunder, inveighing like my father once, I hurled one challenge after another at the jumping, squalling Indians. Increasingly louder, more vehement grew my voice, till it drowned out the shouts of those hopping savages."

Dudinka paused, then sighed audibly, paying no heed to the impatient motions of his listeners. After a while he moaned, louder than the wind over the tossed up water, his colleagues thought. Again those inquiring glances were cast from one to the other. They contained a mixture of doubt, hesitation, and a conviction that nobody would, nor could take him serious. Just the same, he decided to tell the rest.

"A miracle happened. Taken aback, the Indians fell silent and stared at me flabbergasted. Nothing could have restraint me anymore. Raging like a berserker, I plunged towards the shaman, who at first seemed rooted to the spot, then crying out in astonishment thrust his spear into the ground and raised both hands defensively.

"To say that their unexpected change in behaviour surprised me, would be similar to muzzling the truth. No, I tell you, it thoroughly perplexed me. We all know the feeling when an expected certainty not only fails to come about, but quite the opposite happens.

"I froze in my tracks. Startled as never before in my life, I looked around. The widespread silence I found uncanny, almost more a dread than their martial display a moment ago. Children as much as women uttered not a sound anymore, only the men began murmuring, albeit not menacingly as before, but rather conciliatory.

"Just the same, their singsong which they started to intone, grated awfully on my nerves. It sounded ghastly, unbelievable discordant, that I felt tempted to plug up my ears. What now? I thought, for after all I neither understood a word, nor was I acquainted with their customs, except through hearsay.

"Nevertheless, I instinctively sensed that the situation had changed favourably. Despite the stifling heat a chill had entered my bones, thawing quickly now under the rays of hope. Saved! a voice within me whispered, then shouted louder and louder. An elation gripped me, why, only heaven knew, because the whole atmosphere still reeked of danger. True, my chances of survival appeared to have increased, though calling the Yanomamoes friendly would have been foolhardy. Their grotesquely painted bodies and diabolic faces smeared black, still made me apprehensive. Add to it the eerie contrast of white teeth and shining eyes, and you can imagine my dilemma. Their movements, however, did express a peaceable attitude.

"Hesitating no more, my ambition led only towards one destination: namely, down river to La Esmeralda, without Rawlins that is. Gingerly I started stepping backwards in the direction of the boat, never averting my eyes from the chattering Indians while doing so. They followed me, albeit at an appropriate distance, but no doubt intending to be free of my presence.

"Endeavouring to avoid abrupt movements that could be adversely interpreted, I turned around slowly, then proceeded unhindered towards the boat."

"So you made it after all," interrupted Kreisel.

"Hale and sound, as we can see," Musil added, sounding almost disappointed over the harmless ending.

"Yes, no further difficulties stood in my way. To be sure, I had to leave Rawlins behind, since at every attempt to get near him, more than thirty snarling Yanomamoes started to rattle their spears menacingly."

"So, what happened finally?" Musil asked.

"Not much anymore. I arrived in Jasubibeteri, a larger town down river, after darkness. There I encountered language barriers, since I neither spoke Spanish nor Portuguese. English, as much as French was unknown even by the officials. But ultimately everything fell into place, after I was brought in contact with the American consul in La Esmeralda. He promised to dispatch all further matter. Having had more than my share, my only desire was to return to Montreal, cold or not. The tropics had lost their allure for me."

Outside in the meantime it had grown pitch dark. The wind began to abate, but not the rain. It became more intense judging by the patter on the roof, which at times sounded ominous, as if endeavouring to pound a thousand holes into the canvas.

Inside not a word was said, the men listened absorbed to the commotion around them, thankful for the diversion. For a while no one spoke. Dudinka's eyelids, raised expectantly, dropped again when anticipated questions remained unasked. He did not mind really, for how could such queer occurrences be treated with any measure of credulity.

Kreisel strenuously tried to collect his thoughts, which had been thrown out of kilter by this fascinating narrative. With the best of intentions he could not explain his chief's astounding experience, which neither supported nor repudiated his contention about language. Contrary to Musil, whose countenance had lit up in victorious exultation. Turning to his pal he said:

"There you can see how powerful language is. Distress propels one back to the childhood years; when misery knocks, a person instinctively reverts to his mother tongue. No further rebuttals my friend, your speculations are invalid."

Dudinka could not suppress a smile at Musil's self-confidence, whereas Kreisel shook his head in annoyance.

"Henri is partially right," concurred Dudinka before Kreisel could object, but managed to interject.

"How to explain it?"

Dudinka went on:

"Remember, I said partially right, but let me finish. Did a supernatural power guide me, had chance played one of its tricks, or did the hands of fate protect me? I can not profess to know. Till this day I am unable to understand my outlandish conduct, least of all the sudden pugnacity, so foreign to my nature. It was a miracle, I say, nothing less.

"How did it come about that a soft spoken man became vociferous without warning, moreover, in a language he neither had command of before nor after. And what power induced me to roar away in my father's manner whom I hardly remembered, nor rightly knew?"

"Oh well, I still insist that the subconscious, when in distress, hurls a person back to his childhood. Coincidence? I don't believe it," Musil repeated.

Dudinka observed him in silence for a moment, before he said:

"Go easy with these inferences, there is more to it, strange enough to strain one's wits. After I had returned to Montreal, thankful, and still in one piece, two questions plagued me: First, how I managed to use a language long forgotten; second, why these fierce intrepid Indians reversed their stance so abruptly."

When Musil made an attempt to interrupt, Dudinka waved him off:

"Just a moment, hear the rest. As mentioned I found no peace, I felt compelled to search, unconsciously at first, then with downright obstinacy for information about the mysterious Yanomamoes. Rummaging here and there for a while, I finally found a little book about them. A treatise really, I should say, quite informative and possibly containing the solution to the riddle.

"An explorer by the name of Narimanov had written this short scientific work. He had lived among the Yanomamoes for two years. He left the area about a year prior to my arrival. To say I read that little book with interest would be an understatement. I devoured its contents on my feet right outside the store.

"A remarkable book it is, written by a man profound and conscientious. Nothing was lacking: pictures, tabulations, including drawings painstakingly prepared, rendered the booklet extraordinarily informative. Meticulous care had been applied describing their singular language, eccentric deportment, and exaggerated ferocity. My eyes were glued to every line till they hurt. All at once they almost fell out."

"Why was that?" inquired Musil.

Dudinka did not respond immediately. Glancing around significantly he stood up, then walked two, three times to and fro. An inscrutable expression hovered across his face as he continued deliberately:

"From day one Narimanov complained about the Yanomamoes' rudeness, bordering on provocation. Their thievish propensities, however, he bemoaned the most, besides their habit to utter threats. He constantly felt harassed and beset. Although he approached them in a friendly manner, learned their language diligently and proficiently, they treated him like an enemy, with condescension that deeply rankled. He wrote:

'One cloud-veiled morning, oppressive as never before, I lost my composure. Many of my possessions had disappeared over night, the dogs snarled at me bolder than ever, even women and children goaded me incessantly. My patience snapped when one of the warriors stepped from the jeering crowd and shook his spear before my face.

'Suddenly I saw red. From the depth of my being arose a towering rage that shot like a column of fire through my veins. Without warning I began to counter the blasphemers' threats. Louder, ever more insistent my voice grew, till I bellowed at them like a bull ready to charge. At first I did not realise that I was raging and inveighing in Russian. Confounded upon noticing it, I was about to switch to their language in a milder tone, when I became aware of a startling fact; you could have knocked me over with a feather, so thunderstruck was I. Instead of an expected attack, a conciliatory attitude followed. Their martial bearing changed with a jolt, they grew docile like lambs.

'Oho, I thought, Dame Fortuna smiles at me today, she shows me the path to a better future. For some time I stood at the crossroads. Should I continue? The thought had occupied me more and more. To complete my work another full year was required, albeit under much more favourable conditions. No one, not even a miracle worker could have carried out painstaking tasks among a recalcitrant, thievish populace, that hurled one hurdle after another in front of my feet.

'But the situation might change from hereon, I opined. For had I not discovered the means to keep them in check? Fired up by this notion, I lit into them with unrelenting fervour. What followed remains unforgettable to me. One after the other came tripping along with my stolen property under their arms, which they deposited contritely at my feet.

'From thereon the situation improved. I was treated with hesitant respect. Enthusiastic co-operation it could not have been called, for their innate recalcitrance trickled through again. Relief, however, could be obtained by reviling them in Russian occasionally."

That was the end of Dudinka's rendering of the explorer's narrative. Kreisel was the first to comment:

"What you are saying, your life was spared not on account of the mysterious power of language, but because of a whimsical coincidence."

"Of both, I would say."

The Island

Richard Sattler was the born guardian. Already in his childhood his eyes wandered searchingly around. Nothing escaped him. Before he outgrew his youth, a distinct flair to detect developed within him.

"The boy must become a policeman," averred his mother.

But this did not appeal to the father, because policemen were not to his liking. The reason? Oh well, when many years ago he helped taming the mighty Opinaca up north, where he lend a hand to construct dams for the biggest power station of all times, such a paragon of virtue interfered in his affairs. It is well known that, if a man righteous to no end is given four stripes and two brass buttons, he claims the whole world. Father Sattler's offence? Pshaw, a mere trifle. After all, he intended to offer his growing family a bit more than just a roof over their heads, plus simple fare.

He therefore decided to partake in the lucrative smuggling trade with aqua vitae, also known as water of life. After all, it was not his concern that alcohol was forbidden in the camp. Understanding and following rules he left to smarter heads. This memory stuck to this day in father Sattler's throat like a choking morsel. At last they opted for the warden's profession.

Richard Sattler was now occupied for ten years at the state prison in St. Jerome. In no time did he make himself deserved.

His pedagogical propensities, coupled with the gift of being at the right place at the right time, served him well; he rose rapidly. A few short years ago he got sore feet from running errands; but lo! today he sat in the well cushioned chair of the chief warden. His abilities seemed limitless. Equipped with ears like the tyrant of Syracuse, plus eyes of a Lyceus, no barriers stood in the way of his march upwards. And then his nose; not even St. Hilarion could smell out evil like he.

Just consider his latest feat. Five of the most notorious inmates planned an escape. To be sure that was a closely knit, taciturn gang. Not a syllable, not even a whiff of their intentions emanated from them. But, nevertheless, Sattler got wind of it. No doubt he had to engage his talents fully: namely, craftiness, mendacity, and treachery. But he managed to expose the conspiracy, thus preventing an escape. But no, it does not fully correspond with the whole truth, because one slipped through his mesh. He got out out after all.

When Sattler stood one morning at the corner of Peel and Ste.Catherine, the busiest crossroad in Montreal, he suddenly heard a hissing noise.

"Psst, psst," wheezed someone behind his back. "Don't turn around, keep busy, not to turn around," he was told.

It must be one of my informers, he mused. While pretending to be lost in thought, he poised booklet and pen.

"I am listening," he encouraged his informant.

"Garneau, the formidable, is hiding on a small island on Lake Quareau, near St. Donat. A cabin stands there, it can be found easily, it is known as Fleming's Island."

René Garneau was the escaped inmate.

Sattler found the island without difficulties; it stood quite alone in the middle of a big lake. After a scouting trip, whereby he gauged location and access, he appeared one morning ready at the shore. He came well equipped, nothing was forgotten. In the rowboat lay a loaded rifle, beside it binoculars, moreover, two pairs of handcuffs hung at his belt. Nothing was wanting, except fortitude, as became soon evident. The boat was hardly rocking in the water, when serious misgivings plagued him already.

No wonder; a weird silence lay over the wild and lonely area. Not a human being was visible, even the birds had already aimed their beaks southward, to begin their long journey to greener pastures. What more, the loons with their foolish, boisterous cries had also disappeared. Only the duty-bound chief warden rowed all alone towards the island. To take someone along never entered his mind, because it would mean sharing his fame. Although the sun still stood behind the mountains, he could make out his destination in the break of dawn.

Once arriving he found the island forsaken. While he moored his boat he noticed more than ever the depressing loneliness. A bit raised stood a small well-kept hut, whose windows and doors were secured with wood barricades. Nothing stirred inside or outside, which seemed suspicious, since he could have sworn to have seen smoke over the island on his arrival. "He is concealing himself somewhere," Sattler thought.

In the meantime the sun had pushed over the mountains, which rendered the area somewhat friendlier, besides, Sattler more courageous. To give truth its due, his heart began to slide. He simply could not divest himself of a feeling that a disaster stood before him.

Not long after he recognised the source of his disquiet. Dense clouds of fog rolled from all sides towards him. Threatening, like giant drums they pushed closer, eager to crush everything in their path.

Then a sensation of horror gripped him, because here he was alone, far away from protective amenities, which allowed him to dispense chicaneries. The eerie silence, coupled with uncertainty because of Garneau, preyed terribly upon his nerves.

"Where does this fellow hide?" he muttered. "Inside the barricaded cabin, or somewhere outside?"

By now the fog came down heavily over the island. The shores became gradually invisible, only outlines of the mountains could still be seen with some effort.

Richard Sattler was overcome by fear, he felt himself surrounded by hostile, destructive forces. It was high time to pull back. The devil fetch fame and honour, his skin was at stake. Oh, for sure, he would have welcomed an additional feather in his hat, it would have been balm to his wife's heart had he delivered the feared Garneau, secured and manacled. But his wellbeing came first.

Driven by assumed dangers crowding his neck, spurred by misgivings nipping at his heels, he plunged towards his boat. He intended to grab the oars with one leap, then fly from the fog with powerful strokes. But before he made ready to jump, his eyes noticed a gruesome reality. His boat was gone! But that could not be! First, he had moored it carefully, yes, even pulled it up somewhat, moreover, not even a ripple disturbed the mirror-like water.

René Garneau! Only he could be the culprit. In spite of his panic, he could see through his artful game. He was intentionally baited to come to this remote island, so that he can be kept imprisoned, possibly even made to disappear over time. His sense of duty, well-known to all, had been contemptuously abused. It accorded scheming scallywags to commit a knavery which could become his doom. To look for his boat was senseless, it surely had either been already sunk, or it floated somewhere on the lake with Garneau as helmsman.

Driven by desperation he broke into the hut. Despite his quandary he fell from astonishment to amazement. Books, nothing but books lined every wall. One thing was sure: neither Garneau nor his henchmen would ever set foot over this threshold. Once seeing such an array of books, they would have retreated like the devil sprinkled with holy water. Therefore they must have stayed hidden outside where, lurking about, they stole the boat along with the rifle and handcuffs, whereupon they went their way laughing.

Before Sattler's eyes appeared the gruesome reality of obvious dangers. He began, like bereft of reason, to pitch violently around the island. He wanted, no, had to get away from here. But how without a boat? Screaming was of no avail, to even think of swimming deemed him preposterous.

As mentioned, Sattler lacked fortitude, he should have stayed home. Instead of calmly weighing the situation, perhaps looking upon the whole affair as an adventure, he raced, driven by that harridan anxiety, many hours from one end of the island to the other. So it went the whole day. But alas! the night. Pursued by grotesquely distorted faces, one after the other possesssing a likeness with the prisoners, he crawled whimpering into the remotest corner.

There he was found half dead the next day. His wife of course, apprised of his expedition, had notified the authorities already the night before.

For three days he stammered confused rubbish. Only after the lapse of a full week did he feel capable again to carry out his duties. Never in his life had he felt so sheltered as between the sturdy walls of the prison.

Only one thing disturbed him mightily: The disdainful, defiant stares of the inmates.

Twelve O'Clock Sharp

Some men only love once in a lifetime, like Henry Fuchs for instance. Much anguish might be spared them, as much as their women, if such persistent affections, perhaps relentless would be a better word, were guided by more common sense and less possessive romanticism.

Fuchs was no longer young, but not yet old, although he looked somewhat older than his fifty years. Mentally alert, physically trim and robust, he had acquired relative prosperity early in life in the rum business in Antigua. From sugar cane fields to a factory, plus retail outlets, the name Fuchs was well-known.

Ten years ago, when he married Maria Sarlos, he moved to a recently purchased estate at Dickenson Bay. Even a detractor would have been forced to admit: its equal could not have been found easily in the island or beyond. It was completely private, yet readily accessible by land and sea. Upon closing the sturdy gates far out at the road, one had the feeling of being alone in the world. A heavenly serenity surrounded the beautiful property, a tranquillity heightened by an awareness that, although separated from other human activities, it was not isolated.

Enough commotion or nightlife to satisfy any man about town was only around the big bend. A short boat ride or stroll on land conveyed one to a world of high society. The swishing and rustling sounds caused by gusty winds, as much as the rhythmic breaking of waves below, soothed rather than it irritated. Nights, though filled with shrill cries emanating from throats of tiny whistling frogs, bestowed an almost hallowed sense of being at peace with oneself and the world.

Today was Friday, work and duty had been laid aside till Monday morning. By this time, after four o'clock, Fuchs usually walked out the door to commence a ten minute boat ride to his home. He preferred to travel on water; it warmed the cockles of his heart, when swells of the friendly Caribbean Sea bore him along. He loved to be out shortly after sunrise, watching the dome shaped peak of Nevis rising out of the mist, while thanking his maker for another glorious day in the offing.

This afternoon, contrary to his habits, he tarried for a reason. Gordon Frost, a business acquaintance wanted to meet him. His face took on a darker hue at the thought of that man, whom he simply failed to countenance.

Frost was a large man, considerably junior to him in years and deportment. He prided himself to be a regular fellow, meaning completely devoid of any reserve. For months now he attempted to interest Fuchs in that insolvent Halcyon Beach Club, which he partially owned. No doubt it was a spectacular property, besides being just around the big promontory from him, but the drawback was named Gordon Frost.

Cash requirements were surprisingly low, almost minimal. Despite a considerable mortgage with flexible, if not friendly terms, it was nevertheless a palatable purchase. The mortgagee, Barclays Bank, intended to foreclose mainly on account of Frost, the general manager. Of course they had a right to do so, had it for years, because of default in payments. Frost, they contended, made a conscious effort to turn the once exclusive resort into a third rate amusement park, a meeting place for the ragtag and bobtail.

Furthermore, the property's unique appearance began to suffer. True, money was scarce, but lending more stood out of the question, as much as tolerating the slide to seediness. They did not trust Frost, all his assurances failed to obliterate the fact that their ideals were derived from different sources. His had followed him all the way from New York; theirs never left this strange and beautiful island.

Frost, the regular fellow, as he labelled himself, made friends readily, but enemies even quicker. Actually a more apt description would be that he alienated people on account of an intrusive familiarity and lack of refinement.

"Come in, come in," Fuchs called out, when he heard a knock at the door, sounding more like a rap preceding a forced entry.

"Greetings, Henry," Frost bellowed through the half opened door.

"Same to you, Gordon," came a reply.

After a hearty handshake, Frost came to the point.

"I suppose you know what I want."

"I can guess," followed an acknowledgement.

"Well, were do we stand, are you buying or not?"

"I am not."

This abrupt answer made Frost prick up his ears, it almost sounded studied and defiant. He walked to the window, pretending to admire the view.

"Your last word?" he inquired while spinning around.

"Last and final," Frost was advised.

Silence then reigned for a few moments. For an instant a Mephistophelian leer crept all over Frost's face, which immediately was supplanted by a curious smile that made Fuchs feel uncomfortable. He was being sized up, glared at by ironic eyes, deep-seated under puffed up brows. Frost knew Fuchs well enough to realise that behind the staid facade lurked a shrewd business acumen.

Shaking his head he practically barked:

"Henry, you are a fool, if I may say so, a victim of an absurd obduracy. I'm completely baffled by such wanton disregard of a lifetime bargain. You have the resources ten times over, moreover, the implicit trust of the bank, so why do you refuse?"

Fuchs showed no inclination to respond, certainly not offhand. Maybe he knew not what to say, which seemed improbable in view of his reputation as a man quick on the uptake, and even faster on retorts. Unlike Frost, he was a reticent man, guarding his private thoughts with exaggerated zeal. Should he tell Frost the reason for his reluctance? Should he divulge his deep rooted distrust of him? Should he mention his belief that no matter how gilded this deal looked, the fact that it was connected with him tarnished all glitter?

But in doing so the question would arise why he made such claims, to which no ready answer existed. Not even the grapevine telegraph whispered about any shady dealings on the part of Frost. A ructious fellow he was, no denying that, but dishonesty could not be laid at his threshold. Fuchs' distrust could easily be termed a chimera, moreover, a design to do harm.

Meanwhile Frost had started his well-known 'stamp around the circle march', which meant to intimidate, but at the same time tread out any trace of flim-flam in Fuchs' head. Hiding his irritation, Frost inquired:

"Why so adamant suddenly. We had mulled this over more than once before, when every time you seemed, if not enthused, but receptive."

Then followed that leering look again, a sidewise glance that sent shivers through Fuchs' limbs. It seemed to bear a thersitical message of malevolence and intent to harm. Why this self-appointed friend, mere acquaintance to him, should resort to such disquieting shenanigans, manifested by ominous mimicry and threatening contortions, Fuchs could not imagine.

Benefits to shareholders in case of a sale would be minimal, moreover, none existent upon foreclosure. Therefore Frost's frantic effort to make him the new owner, appeared mysterious on the surface.

Just as he attempted to muster enough initiative to ask some pointed questions, it dawned on him; of course, that was it! Frost expected to retain his position as general manager, should he acquire the resort; therein lay the motive, not in his pretence to make him the sole beneficiary of a steal, as Frost termed it.

Fuchs wished his visitor anywhere except in his office, for he started to behave like an ungrateful guest. But Frost showed no intention to depart; quite the contrary, he poured himself a drink and sat down. Facing Fuchs squarely while nodding his head knowingly he raised his glass:

"Cheers, Henry," he said with pursed lips and a wry face.

His manner expressed a mixture of thinly veiled threats accompanied by a sardonic grin, and poorly disguised gloating.

"What a bumptious fellow this is," thought Fuchs, "he is up to no good."

He resolved to have less and less to do with this second-hand Falstaff. True, it would not be easy in a confined area like this small island to carry out, but with his wife's assistance it might be possible. Her sympathies for Frost he could never fathom. He was neither agreeable to look at, nor pleasant to listen to. To be sure he did possess a certain vitality which could waft away the gossamer of dark moods, which he also could bring on.

Fuchs was just about to announce his intention to leave, when Frost's demeanour changed drastically. It took on a puckish air, openly malevolent and sneering, to an extent that bewildered Fuchs enough to stall. That was a mistake however, it conferred nothing but grief on him. A devastating revelation followed, that changed his life. It tore his faith in marital notions to shreds. No doubt Frost relished what he was going to say, he practically smacked his lips a few times before he came out with it.

"Henry, what is the real reason for your absurd rejection, which defies every bit of common sense? Tell me, has it anything to do with your wife?"

Without raising his head Fuchs replied:

"Hardly; she, by the way, would welcome an acquisition on my part. As you know she frequents the club more than once a week."

"Come off it, man, you know what I mean," Frost blurted out.

"You are talking in riddles, besides, I must leave this instant," Frost was advised.

"Oh, you must, do you? Well, since you insist on playing possum I will tell you straight out: you reject the deal because of us, your wife and me."

Fuchs' head darted up. He asked sharply:

"What are you saying?"

If looks could cut, his would have pierced through glass. The withering stare gave Frost second thoughts, he grew less audacious. Although Fuchs guarded his privacy with Cerberian fervour, and was equally secretive about his past, some parts of his bygone days were known. He had served as a high ranking officer in the German Air Force where honour, according to him, counted more than wealth and popularity. Moreover, where insults and questionable conduct were settled in a manly fashion. He was reputed to be ruthless in such matters; duels, it seems, were no rarity with him. His aim was deadly, Frost had heard, which apparently was demonstrated several times in his younger years. It was also, the grapevine had it, the reason for his departure from Europe.

Never before had Frost seen a face being transformed so suddenly into a mask of suppressed anger and anguish. As if iron had entered his soul, it flashed through his mind. Seeing Fuchs rise and approach, made his heart pound and quickened his pulse.

"You tell me what you mean," Fuchs demanded in a voice accustomed to be obeyed.

He seemed different, a total stranger stood across from him, a man exuding danger. Fuchs drew himself up in a manner that made the taller Frost quail. He sat down, while his studied glances, meant to disquiet and intimidate, changed quickly. Though still retaining a measure of malice, they became more conciliatory. Avoiding Fuchs' penetrating eyes, he said:

"I thought you knew."

"Knew what?" Fuchs barked.

"That we were lovers once," Frost announced as if under duress.

Fuchs was stunned. Not in a hundred years had he thought such a thing possible. It seemed unthinkable that the lovely, soft and timid Maria could have been intimate with this selfish voluptuary, a veritable Braggadochio who openly boasted about his numerous conquests of native women. It shook Fuchs to the core, but he hardly flinched. Years of severe training rushed to his assistance, they helped him to check his emotions. Pride forbade to make further inquiries, even though Frost's revelation gave rise to awful suspicions, especially in view of their continued friendly relations.

Fuchs was a kind man, a good friend, sensible in all respects except love and women. Chivalrous notions seemed forever to mar his judgement of women. For that reason he married late; none of his female acquaintances met his rigorous requirements for a wife. Some deemed him too flighty, others too strident. Most, however, he found unworthy to become Mrs Fuchs, because of a presumed lack of faithfulness. He would never admit it, but Maria Sarlos was chosen more out of necessity than love or conviction of marital fidelity. Since he was advancing in years, besides being in the midst of accumulating a substantial nest egg, he hankered for female adulation.

Indeed, Fuchs was a remarkable man, just a fool when it came to relations of the heart. But he surely was not a temporizer. Instantaneously he realised what had to be done; his demeanour towards Frost changed abruptly. He visibly relaxed, which did not remain unnoticed by a grateful Frost. When a smile lit up Fuchs' face, a sigh of relief escaped his breast.

"Gordon, forgive my obstinacy, I see now how silly it is to reject your proposal. I shall look at it closer. Be so good and collect all pertinent information for my perusal. We should meet at the house to discuss it further. However, that will be delayed, since I shall be gone on business for a while."

"How long?"

"Two weeks at the most. Myself or Maria will contact you upon my return."

"Can I tell the Bank that you are seriously interested? Remember, they are threatening with foreclosure."

"Yes, you can."

Utterly relieved Frost jumped up and shook his hand.

"That's more like it, old boy, believe me, this transaction will benefit both. Can I have another drink?"

"Only if you pour me one too."

Fuchs lingered on the way back. Sunset was still an hour away, it would leave enough time to settle his nerves, which only an iron discipline prevented from dithering beyond control. The news was shattering enough to make his hands shake, especially when he recalled Frost's sneering insinuating glances, implying that there might still be something between them. The mere thought took away his breath, it required great willpower to contain his errant emotion. He paid no heed to the changing sky westward, where the sun approached the blue water of the Caribbean Sea. Yet instinctively he accelerated the boat. A subconscious yearning urged him on to reach the house before sundown, where they sat most evenings, wrapped in silence, high above the breaking waves, waiting for darkness to envelope themselves and their thoughts.

As the fiery sun disappeared in the water behind the horizon, a power greater than reason drew them closer together. By the time the peaks of Nevis took on ghostly shapes, they sat clasped in each other's arms, absorbed in themselves and the sounds and smell of the soft Caribbean night. It had become a ritual for him and Maria, like a mute thanksgiving at the altar of happiness.

"Not tonight," murmured Fuchs, "perhaps never again," for these treasured evenings had been sullied forever; the soft caressing hands of bliss had grown cold and stiff.

He slowed down to avoid their nightly gathering, but also to gain time to think. In any case he felt averse to face Maria in this distraught state. Her finely honed womanly instinct, once awakened, was not easily stilled. She would see right through him before he had made three steps on land. His faltering gait alone would betray him, not mentioning his voice, husky from excitement, and hoarse out of embarrassment over his unseemly thoughts and sentiments. Anger pounced on him, a resentment that all his faculties were unable to keep in check.

Why did Maria do this to him? wailed his baser self to the sinking sun. What has she done? asked his more reasonable alter ego derisively. So it went until naked rage overwhelmed him, triggering a seething hatred towards his wife and Frost, but most of all towards himself. One moment he railed against Maria viciously; the next he exonerated her abjectly, while castigating himself for his unjust and puerile behaviour.

She had never given him occasion to rue his decision to make her his wife, which he did about ten years ago in

Trinidad. The thought about her and other men had never entered his mind, until now that is. She was thirty years old when they met, a mature woman no doubt, but exuding a surprising aura of innocence, which thoroughly satisfied his romantic notions of women. She looked chaste and demure enough to kindle the fire of chivalry in his breast. Her ancestral home at Manzanilla Bay made a lasting impression on him; it had character and radiated lasting pride. Both had marriage in mind when they met, thus their acquaintance flourished quickly to friendship and romance. Admitted, sparks of love were absent, but a warm affection did exist.

Meanwhile darkness was setting in fast, lights started to flicker below the darkening sky. For some reason as the city lit up, Stan Markus came to his mind. He was a friend worthy of the name, a loyal comrade for many years. After all it was he who had introduced him to Maria, for he knew the Sarlos family quite well, ever since Maria sported pigtails and sat on his knees. That was it, a visit with Markus in Trinidad would help to salve his wounded honour, besides enlightening him about this alleged affair with Frost, that fast talking, self-centred Lothario.

When he mentioned to Frost pressing business abroad requiring his presence, he had nothing specific in mind. Now, however, he was glad he did, because an absence of a week or so would be beneficial in more than one way. It would distance him from the source of profound embarrassment, besides, obtaining information greatly desired. Frost's assertion might be nothing but grandiloquence, meant to injure his pride. It would be the height of gullibility to take the words of a vainglorious libertine for granted. Of course asking Maria was out of the question, it went completely against his grain.

Fuchs heaved a sigh of relief, he thanked his stars for the inspiration about Markus. If nothing else, it would keep his mind in motion, thus preventing his dreaded nemesis brooding to wind its tentacles around his thoughts. The path before him, still somewhat nebulous, no longer looked like a Serbonian Bog, from where escape is impossible. Frost's disclosure however, no doubt of scant importance to most men, unleashed the dogs of discord. Trifle or not to anybody else, his vaunted honour was sullied. "Laugh all you want," he muttered to the waves, "I will respond with actions befitting an officer and gentleman. A duel it shall be, nothing less, but after my return."

Maria stood on the wharf surveying the water anxiously. He could see her from afar in the diffused light of several lamp standards. His heart almost missed a beat at the sight of her familiar figure, whose womanly warmth he almost physically felt.

As every evening before sunset she had changed to formal clothes, a habit inherited from her mother and grandmother. It was part of their heritage, she averred, a Spanish custom adhered to by all their womenfolk. Her friendly face, bearing signs of a maturing character, appeared a bit strained, Fuchs thought. But, nevertheless, it radiated a zest for live, which invariably raised his spirits. Not today, however; before the rays of her smile could embrace him, he rebuffed them silently.

As he suspected, Maria sensed his inner turmoil before he set foot on the wharf.

"Henry, what happened? you look distraught," she inquired anxiously, unable to fend off shadows of concern that flitted across her brow.

"Nothing to worry about, I just received a message about some pressing matters, which I must attend to immediately. You know how I cherish our weekends together, but I must be off in the morning."

"Could I not go with you?"

"Not this time, darling, I'm just crossing over to Nevis and St. Kitts. Trips to the interior might be necessary, I fear it would be too rough and tumble for you."

When he noticed her pout, he added:

"It will only be for a few days."

"When are you leaving?" she asked still a bit peeved.

"Early in the morning," came his reply.

He was relieved because she made no fuss, for which he thanked his quick wit. Had he told her the truth about a trip to Trinidad where her parents lived, a more earnest remonstration would surely have ensued. Although uncertain whether Markus could be met as planned, he still desired to leave, be it only for a short while to collect his thoughts. The pretext of a possible business engagement that could prove difficult, served him well; it cloaked an obvious high-strung deportment, which he was unable to hide.

As intended he departed for Trinidad the next morning, arriving in Port of Spain before noon. Stan Markus, who had been notified of his visit, awaited him with open arms.

"Henry, what a pleasant surprise," he cried at first sight, while stretching out his hands.

"Are you here for a specific reason or just in transit?" he was asked.

"I shall tell you in a moment, but how about something wet first to unlimber my parched tongue?"

"Will lemonade do?" Markus kidded while grinning.

It was just a threadbare joke, that he could not refrain from using then and when. He knew his friend's pleasure well, having bent many an elbow with him, as much as he was cognizant of Fuchs' increased thirst the moment he stepped into the furnace-like heat, as he called it. Indeed, this assertion was not so far-fetched. Trinidad, less than five hundred miles south of Antigua, has a different climate. It can be called tropical in contrast to the other, smaller Caribbean islands. The constant heat, not cooled by trade winds once distant from the water, is quite oppressive. Perhaps the feeling of being in a mainland country rather than on an island, exacerbates this perception.

"Stan, I have a problem," Fuchs started the conversation.

"Well now, what hinders you to come out with it?" Markus encouraged.

Modesty and shame, Fuchs would have liked to confess, as he looked closer at his friend's kind, guileless face. Although older than himself, Markus' unlined countenance seemed surprisingly young. He radiated sheer health and good intentions from every pore. His whole being heralded the fact that there dwelled not a single mean bone in his body. Seeing the glow of good will on his friend's brow, as much as a spark of unadulterated benevolence in his eyes, made him waver. His concerns appeared suddenly trivial, if not ignominious.

"Don't worry, Henry, you can trust me," Markus interrupted his musing.

"I know that, Stan, it's just…well, just not easy to say what might better remain unsaid."

Markus could not suppress a smile hearing this vintage Fuchs remark. Not in vain did he openly call him the sage of Gotham, he thought, while waiting patiently for his friend's next words, who seemed plagued by a momentous decision. Indeed, he was.

As mentioned Fuchs was a good man, noble in spirit and just in action, but a fool in matters of love and women. Like a Spanish grandee once felt obliged to redress real or imagined slights upon his honour, particularly in matters of matrimony, so he too felt compelled to demand satisfaction. More than one notion raced through his mind now, chasing each other till only one remained; namely, to conceal his reason for coming.

As so often happens the fire of indignation, fanned to white heat by self-bestowed righteousness, cools off quickly under closer scrutiny. He once more congratulated himself for his presence of mind, because he realised that Markus would never be a party to his nefarious probing. Beyond a benign smile, accompanied by reproving glances, it surely would not have gone. He could just see how his friend would shrug his shoulders and change the subject. Therefore a subterfuge had to be invented quickly.

"It is not really a problem I am having, just a favour is needed," Fuchs started haltingly.

"From me?" Markus asked.

Fuchs hesitated a moment, he was forced to think fast.

"Yes, from you, and here it is: I will be away in Europe for some months. What I like to do, should you be willing, is to give you a power of attorney to manage my business till I return."

Markus raised his eyes in surprise. Not because of his friend's odd request, but more out of disbelief. He almost instantly suspected dissimulation by Fuchs, who obviously was troubled by weightier matters, but showed reluctance to be forthcoming. Smiling somewhat intrigued he said:

"I see no difficulties there, considering my acquaintance with your business affairs; I certainly accept willingly."

"I am relieved to hear it, the necessary papers will be drawn up before my departure."

"Is Maria going with you?"

"We have not decided yet."

After several days in Trinidad he returned home. Having spent most of the time with his friend accorded little opportunity to plan his next steps, not in detail that is. On few occasions he felt on the verge of confiding in Markus, to talk about sentiments that caused nightmares after dark, and paranoia during daytime. He was no longer himself, but rather a riven person, where sense and decency stood in conflict with irrational urges, nourished by foolish notions of romanticism.

Fuchs did not deceive himself, he realised there was only one way out: Either he or Frost had to disappear. May the enlightened scoff and laugh at such old-fashioned notions, he could not help it, the trumpets of honour resounded in his ears, they had to be obeyed, no matter of the consequences.

No doubt Markus divined his friend's dilemma; however, an innate delicacy forbade him to ask probing questions. Yet he silently prayed to become privy to Fuchs' quandary, for he learned a long time ago that burdens get featherlight when shared. He could have sworn on the book of books, that this power of attorney was nothing but a pretext invented on the spur of the moment. Fuchs had come to seek his help.

Though saddened by his friend's evident predicament, he never broached the matter, for he knew his penchants well. Once he wrapped himself in layers of secrecy, no amount of effort could penetrate them. In hindsight he castigated himself mercilessly. He should have been more intrusive, even if it meant grabbing Fuchs by the lapel and shake his troubles out of him. But what good is retrospect after an irreversible tragedy? They parted outward jovial, but inwardly groaning under the weight of oppressive mores.

By the time Fuchs embraced his wife back in Antigua, his path lay crystal clear before him. Accepting the state of things was not an option. No power on earth could move him to accept Frost's proposal. Rather would he languish in hell than suffer the proximity of that Lord Strut. His strident ribaldry alone would chase him to no-man's land within a week. Added to it that insufferable slapstick behaviour, gave Fuchs the final impetus to act. He harboured no illusions about impending occurrences, after informing Frost of his decision, irreversible that is, of terminating all association with him. He could see and hear his intemperate tongue, spreading defamation, casting aspersions all over this and other islands. True or false, what should it matter. Once uttered they would become irreversible as a discharged arrow.

It would never end, neither Frost's skulduggery nor his and Maria's misery. True, his wife possessed a Latin temperament, which in contrast to his Teutonic disposition was able to meet such unscrupulous disseminations with invectives and derisive laughter, maybe even with a showing of her tongue. He smiled at the thought of it, while wishing he could react likewise. But that was not in the cards he realised, much less pulling up stakes and replanting them elsewhere.

Maria seemed overjoyed to see him, it made him forget his troubles. Not for long, however, since a peculiar tension in his wife's demeanour disquieted him. She appeared wooden, in contrast to her normally unaffected self, somewhat rigid and studied. Even that usual volubility of hers, so difficult to keep in check, was missing. She carefully minced her words. Some trouble perhaps, he thought, encumbered her mind. Insignificant to a more calculating person, but unsettling to her ingenuous nature. As a rule he would have chaffed her with a tinge or two of sarcasm; but not today. Considering the recent unpleasant events he felt disinclined for banter; moreover, his suspicion was aroused instantly. For that reason he said nothing, knowing in any case that before long she would unburden her mind, because once her emotions were stirred, she was unable to restrain an urge to be communicative. Indeed, that happened.

Hardly had they sat down under the fragrant jasmine tree, when she steered the conversation towards the topic of her discomfort. Somehow he was unable to shake off a feeling of being furtively observed, appraised might have described it better. That in itself mattered little to him, far less than signs of mockery accompanying these oblique glances, as if she were revelling in his evident uneasiness, the source of which she divined perhaps.

"How was the trip, darling, everything in order?"

He could have sworn that he was being twitted, judging by a wry expression, suppressed to be sure, yet indubitably present.

"All things considered it can be termed successful," he answered, not altogether untruthful, because the journey helped to reach a conclusion.

Prior to arriving at the front gate, a plan was conceived which he deemed feasible as much as effective. Dealing henceforth with Frost had been declared anathema. How to prevent his expected backbiting stood within the realm of possibilities. He harboured no illusions about Frost's slanderous tongue and malicious intent. He would whip up a torrent of past experiences with Maria Sarlos which, by shaking the tree of innuendoes, suggestive stares and gestures, would imply their occurrences right to the present. He could see his satirical leers if someone should inquire whether hanky-pankies still existed. Should that not suffice as an answer, well, a wink or two might leave no doubt. No, that would never do, Frost had to be silenced.

"I was at the club yesterday," Maria announced, while observing him from the corners of her eyes.

"I see," he said with forced nonchalance.

"I met Gordon."

"Well now, that was to be expected," he remarked in a voice husky and a bit sharp.

She looked at him fully.

"He told me everything," she blurted out.

He very nearly jumped from his seat, only his training as an officer prevented it in time. Wiping his knitted brow while complaining about the excessive heat, he stiffened noticeably. It brought a barely suppressed ironic expression to Maria's face.

"What do you mean by everything?" he managed to ask with feigned indifference.

"Now, Henry, don't play possum with me, I'm referring of course to your upcoming partnership," she chided a bit piqued.

"Oh that, it will not really be a partnership, but merely a transfer of shares," – and even this will never happen – he barely refrained from adding.

By obeying a spontaneous presentiment, he checked his tongue. Maria's face fell, as if disappointed.

"That is not what he thinks," she advised.

"What does he think?" he asked.

Looking at her husband inquiringly, she said:

"If I understand him correctly, you have an arrangement whereby he retains his post, plus receives an appropriate compensation for his shares."

Surprised and perturbed he stood up. Pretending to scan the blue sea below, he kept his face averted from his wife's inquisitional stare. She obviously expected an explanation, which he felt averse to give. He never before experienced a desire for secrecy with her, it was an impulse that amazed and appalled him. Turning around he asked:

"Was that all Gordon said?"

"Yes, it was all," she replied without flinching.

He found that difficult to believe, considering her unwonted sarcasm and appraising glances accompanying this assertion. She makes sport of me, but not as before with well-meaning chuckles, friendly pats and a peck on the cheek, he thought. No, not this time. He sensed a change in their relations, a divergence from their common goal. Something inside her had turned, not wholly perhaps, but sufficiently to put him on guard. No doubt he too looked at her with different eyes; with good reasons, he thought. True, their dispositions were dissimilar, no denying it, yet it never created a conflict. To the contrary; it provided them, especially Maria, with a source of friendly rebuttal. Whenever she could not maintain an argument, she would say:

"It's in our blood, it is different, that is why we are unable to see it the same way."

"Oh nonsense, all blood is the same," he would retort.

"No, it's not; mine is warm and red, whereas yours is cold and colourless, like the ichor of gods."

They both invariably laughed, for different reasons perhaps, but laugh they did. But not today, he surmised, maybe never again.

"Tell me, Henry, what exactly have you in mind concerning the Halcyon and Gordon?" she wanted to know.

Fuchs hesitated while listening to an inner voice that exhorted him to be cautious. He resented yet obeyed that Cassandra whisper. Feeling rather awkward as much as guilty, he resorted to a prevarication.

"Your question will be answered as soon as we all meet to discuss and resolve the matter. Your presence then would be appreciated," he advised.

She looked up surprised, thinking at first that he was kidding, for she never attended his business meetings. But no! he seemed not only serious, but framed by a puzzling dignity, exuding an air of unaccustomed solemnity; he evidently meant what he said.

"When will this happen?" she asked with little enthusiasm.

Her long intensive stare seemed not to affect him, he remained his inscrutable self.

"The moment Gordon has all necessary documentations together," he answered.

"You know of course, Henry, that I will have nothing to contribute at your meeting," she protested.

"Nevertheless, your presence is important, just wait and see."

That sounded ominous, more like a warning than an invitation. She shrugged her shoulders and said no more.

Indeed, it was paramount that Maria should be there. Not so much to witness a transaction, which would never take place in any case, but to become privy to a revelation that might change their lives. Frost needed to be taken care of before the sluice gates of his malice opened. Fuchs realised that he took an awful risk relying on intuition so incompatible with his pragmatic nature. Comparing Frost with a fanfaron might prove fallacious, moreover, resulting in a devastating aftermath. Should he turn out to be a brave man, well, a different plan had to be instituted then. But he did not believe so, all signs pointed towards a swaggering bully.

Fuchs was certain that underneath that fire-eater cloak dwelled a quivering coward in mortal fear of being unmasked, which he intended to do. Fear not, he silenced nascent doubts, Frost is just like Bombastus, who pretended to carry a vicious devil in the pommel of his sword which, if released, would wreak havoc upon anyone found disagreeable to him. But once his bluff was called, he would pull in his horns and disappear.

So he saw Frost. Loss of face to him, he figured, would be unbearable, it might seal his vindictive tongue. Coming Thursday the meeting was scheduled, on Frost's request late at night, after the club's closing hours.

Days since his return from Trinidad passed slowly for Maria, evenings became outright burdensome. The evident change in her husband's deportment darkened her moods. His sudden taciturnity, especially in matters concerning Frost or the Halcyon Club, frayed on her nerves. No amount of prodding and teasing loosened his tongue. He just smiled enigmatically and remained silent. They still sat together at times outside above the shimmering moonlit water, watching the fiery sun disappear amidst the swells of the Caribbean Sea. But not like usually close together, or embracing, but keeping a distance between each other.

Fuchs seemed in high spirits when he returned on Thursday afternoon from work. A bit tense perhaps, but nevertheless exuding an air of confidence. Maria observed him occasionally rubbing his hands together, like a man having finally solved a long vexing riddle. She was miffed, for she felt deliberately excluded from his source of merriment. Her husband kept her intentionally at the perimeter of a scheme that she began to dread.

It was now past sundown on that momentous Thursday. Maria was left in the dark about her husband's intentions, still questioning him however, but now as before not receiving a satisfactory answer.

Frost should arrive shortly after eleven o'clock, surely filled with hope and brimming with expectations that she prayed would be satisfied. They walked around the garden, under blooming trees, surrounded by inimitable sounds of a

Caribbean night. But they were oblivious to the signs of that bewitching world of sweet fragrances and haunting noises. They did not hear the rustle in the palm trees above, nor the rhythmic break of waves below. Something more incisive troubled their minds. They felt awkward, like strangers striving for something to say. Their valued intimacy, so important to both, reassuring in hours of doubts and stress, having reached over the years a healing quality, had lately become unsettled.

Clouds had gathered, dimming their once bright and unconstrained relations. They now acted timid when approaching each other, as if expecting to be rebuffed. Conversation, hitherto relaxed and playful at times, became measured and desultory. Guards were raised quickly for no reasons and without warning. Questions received increasing evaluations before calculated answers followed. Fuchs eyed his wife at every opportunity, clandestinely of course, looking for signs that might confirm or allay his suspicions. She liked Frost, that much was manifested in many ways. Strange to say, however, she also treated him with puzzling condescension, as if thereby punishing a resented preference.

Maria was unable to contain her emotions any longer, a deep sigh escaped her bosom:

"Henry, why all this secrecy lately, you seem so changed that I begin to worry," she said.

"In what way, darling?" he asked a bit brusquer than intended.

A guilty conscience rendered his countenance a shade darker and made his voice sound rasping. Halting her steps, trying to stifle rising anger, she forced herself to sound casual:

"Now, Henry, quit dissembling, it neither befits you, nor is it necessary; remember I am your wife."

Her remonstrance irked and shamed him simultaneously, for on the one hand he felt justified to be secretive, while his sense of decency rattled his conscience on the other hand. For years they had lived hand in glove, thus this sudden reticence appeared odd even to himself. Nodding, he admitted:

"You have a point, Maria, let us go inside the house, where it is more comfortable. There I will tell you more."

After they had sat down, Fuchs started to talk, albeit not immediately. Why he hesitated would have been difficult for him to explain. Somehow his wife of many years, so dear and trusted, appeared to keep two faces under one hood. She was tense, understandable so in view of his wayward behaviour lately, yet she also seemed indefinably calculating, for reasons he could not even guess, at least not until his intentions concerning Frost were manifested, which he started to do:

"Here is what I have in mind: Tonight Frost will be advised unequivocally of my position concerning him and the Halcyon Club."

"Which is?" she inquired in a voice unfamiliar even to herself.

"That under no circumstances shall I deal with him."

"You will not purchase the club then?"

"Yes, I will; in fact the necessary papers were signed down at the bank today."

"What about Gordon's shares?"

"They are worthless," Fuchs advised with more than a ring of satisfaction in his voice.

Noticing her frown, as much as her rebuking glance, he added:

"I realise that this appears to contradict my earlier attitude; however, the emphasis lies on the word appears. I must stress that no promises were made to Frost. His assumption of staying on, plus receiving money for his shares, were hopes against hope, fuelled by intimidation, and flying on the wings of blackmail. These wings will be clipped tonight."

"I don't understand," she confessed.

He contemplated her more intensive, searching for signs that might reveal her thoughts. Inscrutable she had never been. Her emotions, if not expressed in words, were invariably manifested by gestures, or demonstrated through facial changes. Had he not known different, he would have thought her unduly apprehensive. However, that could hardly be, for his wife was not easily frightened. She had proved her mettle dozen times. Be it out in wind and weather amid a raging sea, or forcing down snarling dogs, she seldom quailed.

But tonight, indeed, since his return from Trinidad, she seemed fraught with anxiety. Fuchs explained:

"He thinks I am in his clutches, but as the saying goes, he reckoned without his host. When I refer to blackmail and intimidation, I am alluding to his love affair he apparently had with you before our marriage."

Maria grew visibly alarmed, hanging her head she whispered:

"I should have told you, Henry. Every time I tried my tongue grew furry, and my throat started to congest. Shame prevented me from making you privy to the darkest episode in my life. That long and intermittent affair is the only skeleton in my closet. But the past can not be undone."

He signalled his understanding.

"Quite true, say no more. I never pried in your past, and neither did you in mine. I will not deny, however, hearing it from Frost did affect me adversely. He flung it in my teeth, like a weapon that surely would force me to my knees. I resent that, particularly if accompanied by leers and innuendoes, which the most obtuse imagination could not miss. Indeed, it fanned a smouldering resentment and moved Frost squarely in the cross hair of my antipathy. Yet even without that, I, along with others have determined that he is a blotch on the island, therefore he should leave."

"I suppose nobody can force him to go."

"Yes, the government can. He is an alien, unemployed after tomorrow, moreover, without visible means of support, not to mention the fact that he sticks in many influential people's craw."

Maria winced at the first stroke of the grandfather clock in the corner. She took a prolonged look at her husband. Over her unlined face hovered shadows which were never there before; they dimmed the light in her laughing eyes. Uncertainty crept all over her countenance, so friendly and guileless usually, but now distorted by doubts and dread.

"Did you know that Gordon has a violent streak in him?" she finally stated.

"He might have, but he lacks the courage to give it free rein, especially if he is uncertain of complete dominance."

She shook her head vigorously.

"Even so, he can be dangerous in more than one way. I know him better than any of you, he is unpredictable once he feels slighted. Don't underestimate him, Henry, he is not the coward you think."

"What do you suppose he will do?"

"Who knows, he might attack you."

"With his mouth you mean," he scoffed.

"No, physically," she stated somewhat annoyed.

A smile stole around Fuch's lips, followed by a grin of contempt which, by trying to suppress, made him look impish. He rose from his chair and strode out on the balcony. A puff of wind touched his skin, welcome as seldom before, since it removed some of the heat generated by a sudden inspiration.

His plans underwent rapid changes. He now saw a way out not only to rid himself and the island of a noxious fellow's presence, but simultaneously showing his wife the true nature of Gordon Frost.

Chuckling to himself he strode back inside where his wife sat on tenterhooks. One eye squinting towards the clock, the other directed at him, she gave the impression of a woman unsure of her emotions. Concern was written across her brow, while a flickering irritation showed itself all over her features. Trying to conceal his appraising glances, Fuchs remarked:

"You believe Frost is a brave man."

"I don't know about bravery as the word goes, but a craven he is not, besides being unpredictable when cornered," she cautioned.

"I believe he is a poltroon, a fact that will manifest itself tonight," he said deliberately, emphasising every word.

Hearing him say that brought a grimace to her face, which turned into a scowl at his next words:

"When I tell him tonight about my irrevocable decision, he will react like any other bully; that is bluster, and puff himself up like a Mazikeen ass; but I have the answer for him."

"What is it?"

He made no reply, but just smiled enigmatically, then rose from his chair and walked over to a gun case. Before Maria could say another word, two pistols lay in front of her blinking eyes.

"I hope they are not loaded," she quipped.

"They are indeed," he explained grinning broadly.

Maria examined him closer. There was something strange about her husband since his return, he showed scant resemblance to the man she had known for over ten years. His movements, so purposeful always, appeared to have become involuntary and hesitant lately. His countenance, as a rule collected and serene, showed traces of anxieties now.

A glance at the grandfather clock indicated that the tenth hour would soon be announced. It should leave enough time to dissuade Henry from falling prey to a folly that could plunge them into a heap of misery. Judging by his pinched face and the pistols on the table, loaded to boot, he was up to some mischief, which she intended to prevent.

"Henry, you seem awfully strained the last few days, I have never seen you like this," she observed.

He glanced at her briefly, but made no reply. Nevertheless, she insisted:

"As I understood it Gordon will be here before midnight, ready to celebrate."

"That idea will be frustrated before he takes a chair," Fuchs interjected.

She changed her tack:

"What are the pistols for?" she inquired.

"You will soon find out."

"They are loaded, you say?"

"They certainly are," he assured.

"Should they not be stored in a safe place?"

"No, they will remain here."

"To daunt Gordon, I take it."

Again he shook his head, then raised his eyebrows, for he had perceived a note of sarcasm in her voice. It miffed him a bit, but he continued indulgently:

"As I said before Frost is a nuisance, whichever way we look at it. We, a committee of influential men want him off the island. On his own volition if possible, by force if necessary. He will be given a choice tonight: Either accept a cash settlement and leave peacefully, or be recalcitrant and face deportation.

"What do you think he will do?"

"Take the money and run," came a terse reply.

Maria's head perked up, a censorious expression spread across her face. Fuchs did not notice it, for he was busy handling one of the weapons, which he did with the dexterity of a seasoned fighter. They were his duelling pistols of past glory, when men knew the meaning of honour, and women loved them for it. Times had changed, he realised; point of honour, once an ornament to any proud man, had become an object of derision. Chivalry had found a substitute in bumptiousness, so repugnant to any high spirited man, who grew up in an environment of aristocratic Prussian mores. Negating obligations enjoined on officers seemed sacrilegious to him. He felt like Galahad in full regalia walking among naked men.

Of course reasons to challenge Frost did not exist; he had neither offended nor threatened him. Yet lofty sentiments urged for a duel, if only to restore his self-esteem. The fact that his adored wife, sylphlike and ingenuous, was intimate with this bombastic voluptuary, put a permanent dent in his concept of romance and marriage, even though it happened before their vows were taken.

The clock began to announce the tenth hour. Maria winced at every stroke, signs of misgivings marred her friendly face. Glancing at the pistols, whose significance she could not even guess, she referred to them again:

"I should caution you once more, Henry, Gordon has an irascible streak in him, he is liable to fly off the handle when you apprise him of the latest news. I think you should put those guns out of the way."

Fuchs smiled almost ruefully while shaking his head, thereby expressing refusal.

"Leave them here, they serve a purpose," he advised.

"Which is?"

Fuchs did not elaborate immediately. A sigh escaped his breast, stemming in part from indignation, but also because he felt embarrassed. It should not be forgotten that he was incurably romantic, compromising a woman was unthinkable to him. He hawed, rose from his chair, walked around the table, and sat down again.

"As I said Frost will be gone soon, but in the meantime I don't cherish the thought of being anyone's butt of derision."

"In what way?" she wanted to know.

"After Frost practically hurled that discomfiting revelation at me, about your past relation with him, I found out that he bragged about it to many people."

"Let him, there is nothing to crow about, it happens every day," she remarked shrugging her shoulders.

"That is not all; these descriptions are said to be quite revealing," he proclaimed in an accusatory tone.

That remark seemed to amuse her.

"Who cares," she chuckled.

"I do," he let her know.

His husky voice made her start up. Observing him closer, a sparkle lit up her eyes that indicated suppressed enjoyment. Despite entangled circumstances, she barely managed to conceal a rising merriment. His lofty attitude, totally out of place in this relaxed, guileless environment, would have made her laugh had she not been aware of his sensitiveness in these matters. A sensibility which neither the caressing trade winds were able to temper, nor the natives' lighthearted ways, whose calypso drums, accompanied by songs reminiscent of Africa, failed to soften his fixation with honour. She could not comprehend such proclivities, much less was she prepared to accept them. She balked. For the first time in their marriage Maria felt the need to oppose her revered husband.

"Henry, what exactly have you in mind?" she demanded to know.

"As mentioned already, we want Frost off the island. He has done nothing beneficial, and nobody expects that he ever will. The choice is his. Acquiesce to our proposal, or be deported; however, not before he turns over all compromising pictures."

"He might refuse," she averred. "I mean handing over pictures and such," she added.

"In that case he will be facing a duel," came a laconic reply.

"With you?"

When he nodded silently she exclaimed loud enough to drown out the voices of the night.

"You are insane!"

He smiled indulgently.

"Hardly; but fear not, it will never come to it," he assured her in a tone more condescending than comforting.

She gazed at him long and hard. For a while not a word passed between them, during which time Maria's countenance took on a masked expression. Only her eyes were alive, they spoke louder than words, emitting a cloud of antipathy. But Fuchs either did not see it, or feigned unconcern about his wife's refractory attitude. Had he been more attentive, who knows, a lot of grief and humiliation might have been spared them. Then she made an astounding remark:

"Don't bet on it, darling, he might accept your challenge quicker than you think."

Rising to her feet she hurried towards their sleeping quarters at the far end of their mansion. Before she disappeared she announced over her shoulder:

"I have no desire to be present at your meeting. Have a nice evening."

Hardly had she entered the rooms, when she stepped out again through a side door. Urged on by indistinct images, resembling presentiments rather than clear concepts, she hurried towards the Halcyon Beach Club. One thing stood uppermost in her mind. A confrontation between the two men must be avoided, or at least postponed.

The hour was late. Knowing Frost, he most likely had reached a state of befuddlement, when any excuse to start a fracas would do. A glance at her watch indicated thirty minutes to eleven o'clock, leaving enough time to avert a calamity. Gordon never locked up before that hour, rather quite a bit later usually. With twinkling feet she strode on.

Covering the short distance in less than fifteen minutes posed no problem to a woman with sturdy legs. Frost must be warned; a duel, which he would not survive in one piece, was out of the question. Nothing but sorrow would be bestowed on all concerned, should it take place.

Her head was in a whirl, she dared not collect her thoughts, fearing resulting discoveries. Were her concerns directed towards the welfare of her husband, or that of her erstwhile lover? She preferred that answer to remain in abeyance. If only the two men could have been friends, how happy it would have made her, she thought. But knowing her husband's aberration, as she called it, in matters concerning love and marriage, that possibility was not in the offing.

As she hurried towards the Halcyon, Fuchs sat in one of the easy chairs outside. A rising anxiety sharpened his perception; sounds and sights took on a keener aspect. The rhythmic splash of breaking waves appeared to be closer than normally, he could almost feel the cool spray on his bare skin. Never in his memory did the mighty chorus of whistling frogs sound so piercing. Their voices bore a mysterious message meant for him to decipher. Even the rustle of swaying palm trees, always sounding playful and soothing, had acquired a sinister implication. Listening intently, Fuchs could have sworn that they whispered ominous tidings from their lofty heights. Clouds of dire prophecies seemed to fill the air, that made him shudder despite the warm temperature.

He could sense a turning point in his life approaching, whose direction he was unable to envision. Yet one fact cropped up repeatedly: Frost had to disappear from their midst, soon, to a far removed place. This coarse-grained American, prone to tattle about conquests real or invented, would always be a thorn in his flesh. Maria had gone to bed, he assumed, which might be just as well under the circumstances. The outcome of their forthcoming encounter, unpredictable to be sure, could easily turn out to be ugly. He would mince no words; accept what is put before you, or face the barrel of my gun.

A clatter at the gate ended his reveries; Frost had arrived, the booming voice left no doubt about it.

"Hello, Henry, I'm here," he bellowed across the garden.

It was now twenty minutes to midnight, all business should be concluded before the first stroke announcing twelve o'clock, Fuchs told himself.

Then everything happened rapidly. At one glance Frost detected the pistols on a sideboard near the table. With three vigorous strides he stood in front of it, where he took one of them without saying a word. Fuchs looked up surprised, then dismayed when he perceived Frost handling the weapon with astounding dexterity.

"What a nice piece," he announced all aglow.

"My, my, and even loaded," he added while whistling in appreciation.

As if on its own accord the barrel turned towards Fuchs with lightning speed. He chuckled:

"Henry, this makes me feel young again. Did I ever tell you about my moniker in my youth and early manhood? I see you shaking your head, I was called quick-draw Gord. From the Adirondacks to the Appalachians my fame as gun handler was universal.

"All bragging aside, I dealt with hundreds, if not thousands of handguns from the time I had outgrown diapers until thirty years later when I left the States. Balderdash, you will say, but hear me. I can load, twirl, aim, and shoot faster than Doc Holiday of the Tombstone era, and with equal accuracy."

Saying so, he twirled the pistol from finger to finger with baffling speed and skill. Whenever it came to rest, the barrel pointed squarely at Fuchs, a target preordained it seemed.

"I understand there is a manoeuvre afoot to have me deported back to the States," Frost remarked with forced indifference.

Receiving no immediate answer, he continued:

"Take my word for it, that will never happen. I shall either prosper in this island, or be buried here six feet under."

Waving his hand peremptorily, Fuchs ordered:

"First, put that pistol away; second, listen carefully. As of tomorrow you are unemployed, with no visible means of support. Your work permit has expired over a year ago, which of course cancels your right to live here. As you probable know, I have purchased the entire club facilities from Barclays Bank. You have no place in the new company, nor are you welcome here. However, I, along with others am ready to temper justice with mercy."

"Meaning?"

"We are willing to compensate you fairly, provided you hand over all pictures and letters pertaining to Maria."

Fuchs spoke with authority, showing little concern with Frost's thinly veiled attempts at intimidation. He knew the type, potvaliant and aggressive, but buckling at the first sign of resistance. Fuchs erred; his assessment would most likely have been confirmed without an element unknown to him. Frost was guided by desperation which soon manifested itself.

That unpredictable emotion, inducing some men to cower in fear, others to rise up in unwonted bravery, spoiled Fuchs' plans. Taking dead aim at him Frost snarled:

"Now you listen. I have nothing to lose, but much to gain."

"What do you mean?"

"I am wanted in the States for murder, sending me back there would seal my fate, for which reason I harbour no desire to ever grace Uncle Sam's soil again. Here is my counter proposal: You sign me in as a partner in your new company, a token move, nothing more I want. More important to me is an irrevocable guarantee of my present position for at least another five years. I promise to serve honourably under your leadership."

When Fuchs jumped up and barked:

"Nothing doing, not on your life," Frost pretended not to notice.

He cast a significant look at the clock, tapped his briefcase with his free hand and continued:

"Contract, proposals, pictures and letters are in there. Don't be a fool, Henry, sacrificing life and limb to be known as a knight of the cloak, earns you nothing but snickers and guffaws."

"I refuse," said Fuchs in a tone of finality.

"You see that clock in the corner?"

"Of course."

"What time does it show?"

"Ten minutes to midnight."

"As mentioned I have nothing to lose, contrary to yourself who has much to forego. At the first stroke of midnight I will pull the trigger. Have no hopes, I never miss."

Fuchs chuckled, it sounded forced, yet not particularly concerned.

"You are drunk, plus half crazed to boot. Put the pistol down before it goes off and earns you a heap of misery."

"Misery my eye. Once the circumstances are known, who knows, I might be in better shape than now."

"Circumstances?"

"You challenged me to a duel commencing at the first stroke of twelve o'clock. What was I to do? Sit there with chattering teeth, waiting to be shot down like a stray dog? No! and no again! I felt called upon to act. After all, major, your reputation as a ruthless dueller has travelled far.

"Tsk, tsk, tsk, I will say to the jury, I aimed to injure, but shaking to the core my bullet found his heart. I am disconsolate gentlemen, but he was the aggressor. Admit it Fuchs, your plan has backfired, you have no choice but to negotiate."

Fuchs stared at Frost intently. Thoughts raced through his head, ideas which refused to take shape in the glaring light of reality. What was going on? That disturbing question forced itself repeatedly onto his mind. Was Frost bluffing, perhaps carrying out a weird practical joke, or just having some sport in his befuddled state?

But observing the aplomb with which he handled the pistol, Fuchs concluded otherwise; it signified intent and ability. That in itself he found disquieting, but not as much as Frost's astounding awareness of his latest plans. Only Maria could have kept him abreast, he surmised, then quickly rejected that notion. For she was only told about it a few hours ago, during which time she lacked the means and opportunity to communicate with Frost. She did not leave the premises, or did she?

"Maria, Maria," he moaned silently.

His trusted wife, the sole heiress of his fortune somehow managed to inform her erstwhile lover of his intentions. Did she mean well, or had she become prey once more to the American's wiles?

Suspicion, that ruinous force, stronger than reason, corrosive like hate, surged up in front of his eyes. But there was no time to climb onto its crest, within two minutes momentous decisions had to be made. Rushing towards and trying to grab the other pistol on the sideboard would achieve little, he determined. Frost's hand holding the gun neither wavered nor bobbed, it was almost uncanny how steady that barrel was aimed at his breast. No doubt, the man standing scant six steps away was not an amateur; moreover, Fuchs felt disinclined to find out. A seasoned campaigner always knows when he holds a shaky hand.

"I will agree to your proposition under one condition," Fuchs announced.

"Name it."

"A proviso, sort of a rider must be added."

"Let's hear it," Frost exclaimed.

Fuchs had no distinct concept what it should be, yet the sudden inspiration served its purpose of gaining time, but more so to save face. He was glad that for once his tongue outran his wits.

"We need a partnership agreement," he added, still quite vague about such an inclusion.

"Accepted," Frost agreed, while putting the pistol away.

He trusted Fuchs, whose word he knew was his bond. After a bit of posturing here, more flimflammer there, all was resolved.

The arrangement turned out surprisingly well; Frost became a different man. Being freed from constant money worries brought a hitherto hidden strain in his character to the surface. His efficient ways, albeit somewhat irregular, no less his sense of duty, met with Fuchs' reluctant approval. His performance belied many preconceived views of friends and acquaintances.

Frost revealed himself as affable, tolerant towards the natives, and surprise upon surprise, he even displayed sort of a roughish charm. Gone were days of hurry-scurry, when he stumbled like an abbot of uproar from one crisis to the next. He was in good spirits, which could hardly have been said about Fuchs who, shrugging his shoulders, inwardly that is, accepted the prevailing state of affairs, yet did not neglect to keep his eyes open.

"It will not last," he said to his wife, "soon the real man will become visible as layers of veneer start to peel off."

He was wrong. Weeks turned into months while all indications kept on pointing towards success. Peculiar it might seem, but Fuchs never confronted his wife concerning that momentous evening. It would have appeared unseemly to a man of the old school, which placed refinement of feeling ahead of curiosity. She too never referred to it, albeit for different reasons.

"Why should I," she told herself, "was my action not instrumental to avert a misfortune, and did subsequent occccurrences not prove me right? The club needed a general manager, and, lo and behold! Gordon fills that position with admirable ability. So were was the harm done by my precipitate action?"

Not a fuzz of it could be gleaned anywhere with ten fine tooth combs. Tarnished honour, jaded knight-errantry, sentiments of a bygone era, prevalent in old, tired countries? It all meant piffle to her. She was unaware what had occurred between her husband and Frost that night. Both men were rather evasive about it, for reasons she could not guess, nor felt inclined to think about. They let it be known that negotiations, fractious at the outset, ultimately reached an amiable conclusion.

She accepted their explanations with a smile and a grain of salt; probing deeper never occurred to her. Leave well enough alone was her rule of conduct, especially in view of the men's behaviour. Their attitude towards each other, not exactly genial to be sure, was hostile even less. Frost evidently tried to please her husband who, albeit reluctantly, acknowledged the effort.

Although she could hardly be called sophisticated, nor was endowed with psychological insight, Frost to her mind endeavoured to make amends through his actions for past wrongs. Fuchs in one way welcomed the arrangement, he saw a man at the helm of day to day operations, whose insight knowledge about the facilities and the industry could be termed matchless. His lack of intuition concerning the island's unequalled allure, however, left much to be desired. Yet surprising to many who knew him, he displayed an astounding compliance. His amenability elicited more than a few comments:

"It's a Gordon we never knew," said some.

"Henry must have an ace or two up his sleeve," announced others.

The short of it was this: While not exactly one of the Nine Worthies of London, Frost dug right in and did his best. As mentioned Fuchs remained wary, but not unforgiving. His upper class Prussian upbringing perceived a certain novelty in Frost's do or die stance that night. Was he bluffing, or had he seriously considered pulling the trigger? Who knows, and who cares. He kept his mouth shut, he performed his work exceptionally well, and besides attracted a host of American tourists.

Fuchs had to chuckle whenever he recalled that memorable night. Talking about pulling the trigger. Ha, what a feat that would have been, for the safety latch was engaged, a fact the tall talking, nimble-fingered Yankee never noticed. Let Frost think he steam-rolled him, it certainly boosted his ego, which in turn made him more compliant.

The reason, the gun wielding Frost walked away with a contract in his pocket would have been hardly understood, nor believed by him or his cronies. Point of honour? Fuchs could hear them snicker, while raising their full glasses. Bosh! they would snort in unison as they banged the snifters down again. Yet that code of conduct, at which they presumably would have snapped their fingers, had saved Frost. The pistol aimed at him held no terror, it did not influence his decision; far less than the voices of a long lineage of strict, but principled men, which rang in his ears:

"A man down deserves a helping hand; never, never a kick." These voices rang above the noise of wind and waves. Sending a man into the jaws of a vengeful setup, called justice, would never have entered his mind.

Till now he had nothing to regret. As time passed the business heaved itself out of a sea of red ink, a fact in part attributable to Frost's endeavours. The man not only applied himself with astounding vigour, but at the same time kept his seedy inclinations in check; namely, the urge to boast and revel in libertinism. To be sure, reasons for this reticence existed, for an adjunct, verbal that is, had been added to their agreement that night. It was this: Frost promised to hold his tongue about those events, more so concerning his history with Maria.

"Should you break your word I shall deal with you in accordance with the mores of gentlemen," Fuchs advised.

When Frost demanded sneeringly what they were, Fuchs just looked at him. Frost never forgot those blue, steely eyes, inexorable as destiny, piercing and cold. Despite the gun beside him, he felt an apprehension creeping up his spine. Whenever temptation sprung up to him, that unwavering gaze dampened his desire to link arms with it. But human nature is difficult to suppress, it has a penchant to burgeon through cracks of the best plated armour. That was exactly what happened.

Six months after that night's incident a banquet was given in honour of Fuchs and his staff. The government sponsored it, and Barclays Bank covered all expenses. Many people attended; every dignitary, including the Premier and his sons, showed up to pay tribute to Fuchs and his staff.

They were in a festive mood, relaxed yet displaying a serenity of demeanour so inherent in the natives. To describe a winter evening at Dickenson Bay requires special ink and a pen kissed by the muses. The bay, half-moon shaped, ringed by a lush growth of swaying palm trees and fragrant jasmine shrubs, has one of the finest beaches in an area of incomparable strands. The shimmering water, never dark, always friendly, heaves and falls in a never ending rhythm. The sound of breaking waves, not at all obtrusive, contributes to an atmosphere of contentment and inner joy.

As the evening progressed spirits rose, feelings ran high, and conversations grew livelier, but no signs of boisterousness cropped up, with one exception: A small group of revellers, oblivious to their cheerful yet reserved surrounding, began to act up. They seemed unable to keep their emotions in check, and their tongues even less.

They were Americans, judging by accents and mode of dress. All of them evidently knew Frost from days in the States, which was attested to by narratives of episodes experienced together. Yet these reminiscences were quickly replaced by a different, more recent topic. Considering outbursts of disbelief here, uninhibited hee-haws there, it must have been of a spicy nature.

Indeed, it was. Frost by now had flung all caution to the wind. Aglow with Dutch courage, emboldened by the presence of his raucous fellow citizens, shed all vestiges of self-imposed restraint. Bottled up resentment, fuelled by his own inadequacies bubbling for months in a cauldron, stoked by envy, finally rose to the surface. Motioning his listeners in a conspiratorial manner to draw closer, he informed them of his latest adventure. It was done in state whispers, although his audience hardly extended beyond the one table.

For the first time in years Frost felt at home. To be once again among men and women of similar inclinations made him bold, especially since they had shared many a wild party in clamorous surroundings, sorely absent here. His proletarian tendencies rose at the same rate as his pretence at decency fell.

"You should have seen him squirm," he announced triumphantly.

His listeners evidently liked what they heard; encouraging calls from all sides attested to it.

"Let's hear more, Gordon, tell us all," a woman cried above the strains of a steel band in full swing.

Frost needed no further prompting, he had entered a path of no return.

"You should have heard his teeth chatter when he stared into the barrel of that gun. Forewarned by Maria, his wife, I knew exactly where it lay. Three decisive steps led me to it, one twist of the wrist brought it into my hands."

"Did I hear right, his wife notified you?" Patricia Barrow interrupted, casting a most suggesting glance around.

"Yes. She came panting down the pathway just as I finished my late supper. Still out of breath she divulged the whole scheme."

"He had a plan different from the preconceived one?" a man wanted to know.

"Exactly."

As Frost explained the gist of Maria's information, Miss Barrow nodded while saying repeatedly:

"Hm, the wife, I see, I see."

Larry Fox, known as the maverick from Sotto felt incumbent to interject with:

"The rascal! What a scoundrel!" from time to time.

Frost's narrative, given zest to by frequent guffaws, indignant invectives, and exclamations of approval or disapproval, began to catch the attention of others nearby.

What followed ended the festivities abruptly. The steel band was playing a famous home-grown tune, for which reason the proud musicians went at it with increased fervour, especially since they were reaching the end.

At that moment a woman, yelling loud enough to drown out the calypso sounds, wanted to know:

"Say, Gordon, didn't you have an affair once with Fuchs' wife?"

"What do you mean–once?" Frost shouted back, insinuating a dalliance still existed.

It was an ill-starred inquiry, furthermore a most unlucky reply, because the music had stopped prior to the woman's biting remark. Therefore these fateful words rang trumpet-like through the sudden stillness.

A hush fell over the gathering; all eyes wandered towards Frost and his companions. Shocked to have overheard what should have remained unsaid, some coughed to hide their embarrassment, while others cleared their throats in an attempt to look occupied. Nevertheless, furtive glances, willing or not, strayed towards Fuchs and his wife, sitting at the premier's table, chatting away seemingly unconcerned. Soon after the festivities ended.

Two weeks later four visitors appeared at Frost's door.

"Good morning Mr Frost," they said almost in unison.

"Good morning," Frost answered instinctively, before he realised that the men were messengers of evil tidings.

It was not quite daylight yet, but the shadows of the night were disappearing fast. Soon the sun, that never failing companion of this enchanting island, would bathe land and sea in a flood of light and breath of warmth.

The men looked ominous, why, he could not say offhand, yet their presence sent pangs of anxiety up and down his spine. Admitted, their demeanour, accentuated by formal attire, suggested refinement. But observing their eyes told a different story. They had a steely gaze, just like Fuchs' that night when he put him on notice.

Frost's apprehension grew at an alarming rate, he soon felt downright endangered, especially since his house stood half hidden from the road, for which reason help might prove difficult to come by. Chasing these visitors, intruders really, from his threshold was left therefore entirely to himself.

Drawing himself up to an imperious posture, he growled in a peremptory tone; at least he thought he did:

"What do you want?"

"Don't be hasty Mr Frost, let us first introduce ourselves," remarked the tallest of the four with a slight bow.

"Allow me, Rudi Bruchner."

"Horst Deggenweiler," another one announced.

"Franz Seeger," came next, and finally:

"Anton Wieser."

They could have saved their breath, because Frost paid no attention, his mind was otherwise occupied; chiefly with thoughts of self-preservation. They are assassins sent by Fuchs to exact punishment, he concluded. Yet immediately he dismissed that notion as incongruous with Fuchs' character. But a connection exists between these heralds and him, he told himself, only their mission remained to be revealed. It soon was. Words followed that took a moment to sink in.

"Please get dressed, Mr Frost," one of the men remarked.

"What are you talking about?" Frost roared.

"About affairs of honour, which require dignity and formal attire," he was advised.

"Affairs of honour?" he parroted.

"Exactly. You are fighting a duel."

Saying so, he and another man came closer. Both bowed with ducal grace while saying:

"We are your seconds."

"You are the devil's own who will land on the street head-first, if you don't get out," Frost snorted.

"You refuse to dress properly?"

"Get out, I said."

Brave words they were, uttered loud enough to make a lion bolt, yet totally ineffective. Still sputtering, he felt himself lifted off the ground and carried towards a boat moored no more than fifty steps away. Struggling, had he possessed the presence of mind to do so, would have achieved little. Eight strong arms held him in an iron grip; four resolute, single-minded men acted as if everything had been rehearsed. Crying out for help, an urge difficult to resist, Frost nevertheless suppressed in time. Rough-and-tumble men did not request assistance, especially from fellows whom they openly belittled and covertly despised.

"A fearless brawler showing the white feather?" they would have sneered, while hoping his abductors send him to the bottom of the sea. Besides, all happened so quickly, thus leaving little time for much more than threats and curses. In less than a minute they were heading in the direction of the Montserrat Channel. As they reached rough water, Frost was released from their hold.

Talking would have been futile, even stentorian lungs could not have drowned out the rush of the sea. Frost harboured little doubts about the instigator's identity nor his intentions. Eccentric, if not unbelievable it may have looked to someone unfamiliar with a traditionalist's mentality; yet Frost knew better. Undeniable Fuchs would be waiting, somewhere off the island, judging by the direction they were taking.

In no time there lay a considerable distance between them and the palm ringed bay. Westwards they sped at full throttle, cutting through waves which rolled at them with increasing force. Far ahead the dome shaped peak of Nevis loomed high in the light of the wakening day, forcing Frost to assume that they were heading towards the forsaken east coast of that island. From reports here and rumours there, he deduced it might be an ideal place where a man could disappear forever.

Yet soon he came to a different notion, after the boat took a sharp turn to starboard, leaving the cloud-capped peak of Nevis to port. More than one thought raced through Frost's mind; some comforting, others alarming. Was Fuchs seriously considering to carry out such a harebrained scheme? or did he just intend to make a show? Directing questions to his abductors led nowhere. First, the splashing noise around the boat swallowed every sound; second, they refused to respond. Beyond an inclined head, accompanied by sympathetic smiles, he could elicit no reaction.

Seeing their dignified behaviour raised his hopes, which were quickly doused by the memory of that glacial gaze, accompanied by an ominous message: "Should you break your word...."

Despite the increasing heat under a rapidly rising sun, he felt a chill in his bones. What did it all mean? Surely Fuchs would not be reckless to the extent of endangering a promising future, if not limb and life, just to satisfy an inane notion about honour and manhood; it made no sense. Yet the memory of those eyes, changing so suddenly from their wonted expression of benevolence to harbingers of an unrelenting menace, made him think otherwise.

They were now speeding towards a small island, rising sheer from the sea. Being the only piece of land ahead, Frost felt certain it was their destination. "Redonda," it surged through his mind, the forsaken and forgotten island inhabited only by goats.

The moment of truth had arrived; it was time to act. In a flash he understood Fuchs' intention: There would either be a pistol fight or a marooned Yankee. Neither option appealed to him, therefore a way out had to be found. One part of him still questioned the whole affair which smacked of wild and woolly pilgrims' tales, invented to beguile the weariness of a long trek.

However, such doubts, carried on the wings of hope, paled in the light of reality. Veering neither left nor right, they aimed straight towards that round piece of land, surrounded by a vast body of churning water. They were obviously nearing the end of their journey. The small island looked forlorn alright, worlds away from civilisation and the law's reach.

Frost grew alarmed, he was frantically trying to collect his wits. Escape seemed impossible, for the moment in any case.

Bailing out, while foolhardy to begin with, could have fatal consequences, considering sharks and other predators surely lurking below the water's surface. Taking control of the boat, a most desirable solution, might prove more than tricky. Fighting his captors looked like a losing proposition. Though of far heavier built than any of them, his intuition left no doubt about the fact that he would fare ignobly against even the smallest one who, like the others, exuded concentrated strength in body and mind.

Distress or fear can dull or sharpen the senses. It makes one alert at times, thereby honing perception and awakening slumbering instincts, like in Frost's case. Reason reassured him, yet intuition made him apprehensive, especially when looking at these men. There was something ominous about them; not sinister mind you, almost kind, yet still frightening. Even the odd smile which lit up their countenances, left no doubt about their intentions.

Germans they were, judging by accent and appearance. Strangers, Frost determined, who most likely came from far away to perform a duty, to fulfil an obligation owed to a compatriot, possibly a fellow officer. They had something in common, not only with each other, but also with Fuchs. But no matter what, Frost had decided there would be no duel. No one could force him into it, whether by the threat of ridicule, loss of honour, or other means.

As expected Fuchs stood at the water's edge, all by himself, at a well chosen spot on the lee between large outcrops. It was a natural mooring place, protected from wind and surf. Despite his plight Frost could not suppress a snicker at the sight of his boss, who was dressed fit for a parade. In a trice his subconsciousness raced across the Sargasso Sea, all the way to New York's Tuxedo Park to a country club amid a cultivated surrounding. There he remembered the worthies occasionally dressing up like that.

As mentioned, danger had sharpened Frost's perception. He saw with his eyes, but like a man affected by fever, discerned beyond mere sight. The man at the shore, his boss no doubt, looked different, transformed by powers unknown. True enough, his figure, erect as ever, showed no exterior sign of weariness. Yet his face, mirror of the mind, as much as the inner man so difficult to disguise, showed an anxiety which Frost had never detected before.

Did a nagging conflict rend him apart, perhaps abhorrence from a pretended courage which lacked genuineness? Did his conscience, the inner thought of an upright man, disquiet him? He must know quite well that he, Frost, stood not the ghost of a chance to reach first base in a duel, governed by strict mores, against a master of the pistol. Alone the ceremony, bordering on a ritual would stifle his will and lame his hand.

Mooring the boat proved more than a chore. Even though a rope was tossed into the hands of Fuchs, manoeuvring it to a safe position appeared to be an undertaking straining the ability of the five men. All hands were active, except Frost's, who wished with every fibre of his being that each and every rope should tear and pull the men into the briny sea.

Something is amiss here, he suddenly realised. Fuchs barked a few orders in German, which caused a flurry of activity leading quickly to disarray. Frost, although not understanding a single word, gained the impression that something unforeseen was going to happen. Two men had jumped out to assist Fuchs, who appeared to be losing his customary composure.

Frost dared not to admit the unthinkable; namely, that Fuchs endeavoured to create confusion by design. But why? It made no sense, yet it was undeniably so. Frost's subconscious acknowledged it instantly, his mind confessed it reluctantly. His head was in a whirl, more so when Fuchs suddenly leaped into the boat and seemingly ordered the two remaining men out.

From hereon everything happened too quick for Frost's perplexed mind to fathom. One thing became evident however; there was a vital part missing in these movements, a duel appeared to be no longer on Fuchs' mind who, without warning, faced him squarely. Not a word was said, only a smile stole around the challenger's lips, followed by a suggestive turn of the head.

Instinctively Frost's eyes wandered in the same direction, till he stared transfixed at what he saw. In a twinkle he understood: Fuchs wanted him to escape, his antics were meant to create an opportunity without compromising himself in front of his men. There in the ignition sparkled the key, waiting to be turned. In the course of another command in German, Fuchs scrambled out evidently to lend a hand.

Frost needed no second invitation, he recognised his chance of a lifetime. Whether engineered or providential bothered him not a whit at the moment. The engine was running, the gears had slipped into reverse before Fuchs gained a foothold on the ground. Roaring backwards, thereby jerking the rope from every hand, Frost soon reached a safe distance.

Retrieving the line, then pointing the bow due east, he pulled the throttle lever to its limit. Ahead in the glare of a high sun he could see the familiar contours of Antigua, whose shores he would soon reach. One heartfelt sigh of relief after another escaped him. Shaking his head incredulously again and again, he tried to make sense of it all.

Was a duel with full rigour intended but abandoned at the end? Or did the whole exercise serve only one purpose, namely, to teach him a lesson and possibly frighten him into silence from here on? Whatever aim Fuchs was pursuing, he had succeeded in more than one way. He, Frost, would remember. Reporting this Mohockian escapade to the authorities never entered his mind. He and his cronies used other means to settle a score. First, however, he would have a heart to heart talk with Fuchs. There would be no beating around the bush concerning Maria and other ticklish topics.

Frost surveyed the horizon with eager eyes. He was making good progress, about half the distance lay behind him, leaving another ten miles to be covered.

"Less than half an hour," he shouted to the wind.

True, he would not quite make brunch, but lunch for sure, if, and if again the present speed had been kept up.

Within minutes he had to acknowledge a strange phenomenon which at first he poo-poohed across the waves, calling it a product of an overstimulated intellect. Soon, however, all too soon, a grim reality gripped his senses. The streamlined craft ploughed the waves with increasing difficulty, some unknown force seemed to hold it back. The engine now struggled in water, which a while ago it had cut through with ease. Frost's concern about fuel was quickly eliminated; one glance at the gauge put that worry to rest; the tank was still more than half full, sufficient to cover twice the distance. Cold comfort that was, and of short duration, for it was almost instantly supplanted by a most unsettling perception; his feet were getting wet. Worse than that, he felt water tickling his ankles.

"What on earth," he murmured.

It could, rather should not be, since to his knowledge these boats were equipped with self-draining devises, besides, having a raised sub floor. Then the engine's peculiar sound diverted his attention; it choked and coughed ominously, appearing to run on its last leg. A moment later he realised that he was sitting up to his waist in water, which started to wash freely over the gunwales.

"Time to baile out," a voice from within commanded.

As he climbed on the seat, Frost understood: Fuchs, the cool reckoner had duped him, he was ignobly deceived, tricked by a master schemer. No judge or jury would remotely pay credence to such an elaborate plot, therefore exempting Fuchs' base deed from punishment. He recognised his grave position. Reaching Antigua's shore surely stood not in the cards. His only salvation, remote as it were, might be a fisherman or sailor that passed along. Provided of course that the sharks did not get him first.

Later in the afternoon Fuchs turned up at the resort.

"Have you seen Mr Frost?" he asked his sub-manager.

"Not today, sir," he was answered.

"Should you see him, I wish to have a word with him."

"Yes, sir."

Next morning a report reached Fuchs' ears that a boat, almost completely submerged in water, had been sighted.

"It must be ours," he declared without hesitation.

A salvage party equipped with pumps and buoyancy material was soon on its way. Under Fuchs' direction the craft, recognised as theirs, was raised sufficiently to be towed. A connection between Frost's mysterious disappearance and the salvaged boat, began subsequently to circulate. To be on the save side, Fuchs made a report to the police, who showed up the following day. The chief, a man with extensive experience, nodded his head:

"It all falls in with Mr Fuchs' theory: Frost went out too far in a craft he was not known to have used before, and drowned in rough water."

A Lesson

On a late afternoon in January 1891 feverish hammering could be heard near the banks of the Fraser River. Despite high winds and driving rain the gallows had to be finished before nightfall. All hands were busy, for above the snow-covered mountains the evening colours had appeared. Anxious glances were cast over shoulders towards the river, tossed up by contrary winds, rolling irresistibly seawards. All signs pointed to a continuous rainstorm coming from the Strait of Georgia.

Tomorrow was an important day. Slumach, a Katzi Indian, was scheduled to be hanged, weather permitting or not. His execution had been postponed twice already: Once, because the hangman, blind drunk, fell into the icy water of the Fraser where he nearly lost his life in the impetuous current. The second time Slumach outwitted the expertly tied and tested rope; he suddenly became ill. Sick men in those days were not executed, they needed to be sound as a bell.

Tomorrow should be the day, all signs pointed to a favourable ending. Slumach showed symptoms of good health; the hangman had pledged not even to smell a cork three days prior to Slumach's death walk. Therefore the only thing trembling in the balance were the gallows. But with much heave, and more ho, the workers managed to drive the last spike before darkness descended.

Next morning the first spectators showed up at the gates, prior to the crack of dawn. Slumach was led down the slopes

ten minutes ahead of the fatal hour. Two sturdy men guided
him towards the gallows. They were neither armed, nor laid a
hand on him. Despite his robust build and fierce demeanour no
one worried about a possible escape. Let him try, was the
prevailing attitude, we will fix his hash in a twinkle. These men
were of a school which considered wrestling down and
overpowering a prisoner as part of the job. Besides, matching
one's strength with that of another man always tickled their
sporting instincts.

On Slumach's left tripped a praying priest, whom he
entirely ignored. On his right strode a bailiff holding an open
umbrella over the doomed man's head to protect him from the
rain. The executioner appeared to be in fine fettle. He and
Slumach knew each other well; they could look back on more
than a few adventures experienced together. Many a day and
more nights were spent in each other's company, carousing,
hunting, or prospecting. Untold hours they sat in the ubiquitous
taverns of New Westminster, clinking glasses, egging each
other on to raise Cain. There existed not a whiff of enmity
between them.

"Nothing personal, Slumack," he said as he shook his
hand; then added:

"Have a nice trip."

The next moment the noose lay around Slumach's neck.

"Any last wishes?" the bailiff asked.

He had none.

"Some last words?"

"Yes."

"Go ahead."

"The devil fetch you all."

Just as the executioner reached for the handle to open the
trap door, Slumach raised a hand while beckoning to his
nephew with the other. Bending his head as far as the noose
allowed, he whispered something in his ear. A moment later he
swung in the morning breeze.

Slumach's reputation grew after his death; his name
acquired notoriety beyond British Columbia's borders. Not
because of the murders he committed, of a woman to boot,

even less for swinging in that morning breeze, but chiefly on account of strident rumours about a fabulous gold discovery. 'Slumach's bonanza' it was called, a veritable Eldorado judging by the descriptions. Where exactly this fabulous hoard lay seemed not to be known, yet it must have existed.

The grapevine telegraph kept humming about Peter Slumach, the nephew and inheritor of the secret mine. He could forever be seen walking the streets of New Westminster with bulging pockets, seldom sober, always boisterous. Many a man, and woman for that matter, received standing offers to carouse with him, at which time they were regaled royally.

Every month or so he disappeared for several days. On his return gold nuggets once more jingled in every pocket. Quite a few men tailed him; all lost his tracks, their eyes never feasted on the rich veins in the forbidden mountains. Some returned with puckered brows and dismayed countenances, maintaining to have been scared away by shots from ambush. It was a wild region, still is, wild and inaccessible. Rattling hail, crackling cold even in midsummer caused several fortune hunters' untimely end for which the younger Slumach received the blame.

Peter Slumach's inheritance brought him nothing but grief. Like the hoard of the Nibelungen, it turned out to be a bane. Over time he degenerated into a loafer and drunk. Trips to the mountains became rarer; they proved more strenuous than he appreciated. In his near constant state of inebriation some ticklish moments ensued. To survive in that lonesome, inhospitable region, a man needs all his faculties intact. Weakened and confused by repeated swigs from an ever-present bottle, Slumach slipped occasionally, stumbled into steep gulches, or lost his way in broad daylight.

Once he was saved by sheer luck when he was found unconscious by two scouts who had followed his tracks, and resuscitated him. After that he changed his mode of operation to less dangerous enterprises, by fobbing off plans of his fabled mine, which were crude and divergent. He was much abroad, on the lam as it were, to avoid the purchasers' wrath, in case they compared notes.

Some years had passed since the uncle's meeting with the hempen collar, years in which the legendary discovery took on enormous proportions in people's imagination, but also went on extensive journeys. Upriver to the mouth of the untamed Thompson it wandered, all the way to Kamloops where the initial murmur soon attained stentorian strength. The grapevine grew; its tendrils pushed along the banks of the Thompson River, right into Ashcroft where it reached the attention of two German tourists.

A barren region that is, nearly treeless, arid in summer, hardly less dry in the winter. Few roads, pathways, or other amenities could be found in those days. Slumach's fabulous mine, originally said to be located in the Pitt Lake district, somehow managed to relocate to an area north of Ashcroft, between Deadman and Bonaparte River; home of rattling snakes, howling coyotes, and screaming eagles. A more desolate place could not have been imagined, yet insistent stories circulated that an immense treasure lay hidden there.

Some reports, oral and written, sounded credible enough to light a fire under the soles of adventurers, or men motivated by greed. Why Horst Koppel and Rainer Munk ended up wandering around that no-man's land, neither one could have said; yet both learned to regret it. Did it happen out of boredom to satisfy an adventurous propensity perhaps? Or fortuitously? One fact could not be denied; they were losing their characteristic gaiety at a rapid pace. Both seemed to be plagued by a growing anxiety, an inexplicable discontent that had no name. One as the other were well-to-do bachelors, neither prone to fret nor shy to laugh, and healthy besides.

Their initial contentment, bordering on jubilation at times, was on the wane for no visible reasons. The resort, remote, yet not lacking amenities, situated amid a vast wilderness, possessed a charm not easily forgotten. Strolling around, or roving on horseback amid a world of fragrant sagebrush, watching the bunch grass bend in the wind, while listening to the rustle of ponderosa pine trees, could surely reinstate a man's lost equilibrium.

Yet the contrary happened to Horst Koppel and Rainer Munk; they were in the throes of losing theirs. The reason? A mutual resentment, unthinkable among good friends, started to rear its ugly head; it eroded their contentment rapidly. They no longer perceived the unfamiliar beauty around them, but only each other's faults, real and imaginary. Resentment needs constant nourishment; it is as ravenous as a running sore that flourishes amid rancour. They were too busy observing each other with disapproving eyes to pay attention to their wondrous surrounding. Debilitating strain started to show; something had to give, a diversion was needed directly; it came as if ordered.

One morning, as Munk and Koppel sat at the breakfast table, morose to the marrow, Jon, the Indian guide and friendly cowboy, handed them the local newspaper. When Munk glanced at it listlessly, something caught his eye which made him snap out of his lethargy.

"Here, read," Munk invited his friend mockingly, for he was aware that Koppel knew no English.

"Stop that nonsense, you know very well how limited my English is," Koppel snorted.

Munk regarded his companion with a smirk on his face as if to say: "Limited? hm, I would call it nonexistent."

Nevertheless, he pointed to an artistically framed write-up, captioned: 'Slumach's Bonanza', under which an eye-catching Stetson tipping prospector led a mule towards that always present, ever elusive mother lode.

"I will translate the article," Munk offered.

"Go ahead," replied Koppel, gaining interest by the minute.

"It's a long story, let me read it first, than I will sum up the principle points," Munk offered.

"What is it about?" Koppel wanted to know.

"A fabulous lode, not far from here, from what I can see."

"Lode?" Koppel queried.

"A gold mine, seemingly richer than the mythical hoard of Columbia's Chibcha Indians, it says."

"Never heard of it," grunted Koppel, then added:

"What else does it say?"

"As I said, let me read it first."

"I will go for a walk in the meantime," Koppel suggested.

It was a resplendent day; not a cloud marred the wide-open, blue sky. Stepping from the covered terrace Koppel felt the burning sun on his skin. Despite a feeling of vexation, the vista unfolding before his eyes captivated his emotions. He was unable to ignore the allure of unobstructed views, clear skies, and unpolluted air. An incomparable atmosphere surrounds the lonely resort, amid an unbroken stretch of land; wild, yet not savage, smiling rather than snarling. A world away from civilisation, the entire place possesses a serene nobility, bestowed by the land and genuine folks.

"This place is good for the soul," Koppel remarked several times a day.

"It heals the scars of the mind," Munk agreed.

"You will have to drag me back on my feet," the friends averred.

These sentiments, felt and expressed initially, ceased to be heard. Praise was now supplanted by silent rancour that no amount of subterfuge could hide. Did the eerie stillness of the area disconcert them? its vastness or feral sounds perhaps? Or were they in fact adversely affected by the attendants' artless manners, whose bucolic demeanour contrasted sharply with the studied, cold efficiency expected?

"No, no," Koppel said to himself, "it must be the unwonted heat."

Munk greeted his returning friend with the words:

"Even a map has been included."

"Tell me all about it," Koppel requested.

"According to this report a prospector, known as Ohm Hansen, discovered Slumach's Lost Creek Mine some decades ago, not too far from here, actually, as I understand. Running low on stamina and out of provisions, he was forced to return to Cache Creek. Though not before making a map of the area, showing landmarks plus estimated distances. His intention to return refreshed and better equipped received a serious blow; he became sick and died. Among his belongings, so it says, this map was found. Here, take a look."

Of course the newspaper dallied with the facts a bit, tenuous as they were to begin with. The editor moved the mother lode from the original site over one hundred miles southwest, closer to his hometown. Who should blame him; then after all what purpose does a rural paper serve which fails to accentuate local attractions that confer colour to the area?

Ohm Hansen, a loafer beyond comparison, witty and entertaining, a weaver of tales of the tub, maintained to have found Slumach's mine, which he would soon exploit, perhaps starting tomorrow. But tomorrow never came; yet kingdom come did. When he failed to show up on the streets of Ashcroft for two days in the row, inquiries were made. He was found to be ill; a week later his obituary appeared in the newspaper.

After his death his reputation underwent a metamorphosis, graduating from scamp to paragon, imbued with virtues a pioneer of the badlands could have been proud of.

Did the visiting Germans give credence to the report? probably not. Nevertheless, they resolved to search for the legendary treasure. They instantly recognised an opportunity to escape the quagmire which engulfed them by the hour. The dislike for each other, inexplicable and fearsome, inched closer to the borderline of hate.

Declining a guide, mules or horses, but accepting with thanks the resort's proffered equipment and provisions, they set out in the morning. Jon, the Indian guide, had a word with them out on the grassland.

"Don't wander too far off, stay within sight of the ranch," he exhorted.

Munk, desirous to be on the way, raised a hand to silence him.

"Yes, yes, we know," he declared.

Jon, on his horse as usual, opened his eyes wide; he appeared to be genuinely concerned. He guessed where they were going, or aimed to go; to a place they could not reach, for little Utopia did not exist. The mine, as much as the plan were fictitious, meant to confer an aura of mystique, so eagerly sought by foreign travellers. The idea to relocate Slumach's legendary mine upriver proved beneficial to the area's image; it boasted tourism.

Jon, guide and cowboy, possessing the keen eyes and insight of his progenitors, had reasons to worry about Munk and Koppel. His finely honed perception divined their inner turmoil; his sensitive ears could almost hear the crackling tension between them. He recognised the signs of impending disaster. Amid the barren hills, a true wilderness despite its friendly aspect from afar, disharmony can have devastating consequences; it is like a volcano ready to erupt.

Glancing from Munk to Koppel contemplatively, he dismounted, then handed Munk a leather bag.

"This might come in handy," he said.

Mounting his horse again, he rode towards the ranch.

When Munk opened the pouch, he found a notebook, pencils, plus a compass inside. As he retrieved them and opened the booklet an inscription caught his eye which he slowly deciphered. Ignoring his friend's impatient scowl, he read it twice. The pucker on his brow smoothened gradually; a wry smile lit up his face, indicating pleasant thoughts.

"What are you reading?" Koppel demanded to know.

"Some notes on safety."

"Like what?"

"Well, you heard the Indian, he exhorted us to stay within the ranch's range of vision."

"Not likely," Koppel remarked.

"That is what he suspects too, consequently he jotted down some pointers."

"Tell me about it."

"To record every landmark in the little book; be it a tree, brush, or rock. Besides taking frequent compass readings, he urged to estimate the distances between these entered points."

"It's not a bad idea, I leave it in your hands," Koppel observed, for he was not technically inclined, or adept in mental exercises.

They travelled light. Being assured of sunny days and clear nights, tents were not requisite; sleeping bags would do. They carried sufficient water and provisions for five days.

It was still early morning, a glorious one at that, when they pointed their steps northward. The sun, though high above the hills, lacked the sting of later hours. By noon the heat would be oppressive, they realised, particularly if the wind failed to appear. But now they felt at ease, elated almost; so much so, that Koppel started to hum a tune.

Walking at a vigorous pace, they soon lost sight of the resort and the towns in the valley. Turning around repeatedly, Munk felt a strange sensation crawl up his spine. A yearning expression entered his eyes, like that of a castaway watching his ship disappearing on the horizon.

Koppel pretended not to notice, yet the humming sounded affected; it became erratic, then stopped. He too was visibly shaken. Seeing however his friend making entries in the booklet, reassured him somewhat.

One thing they could not deny: they were alone, isolated, forsaken as never before. Each other's company conferred little solace; to the contrary; it added an element of further anxiety.

The terrain acquired a more forbidding aspect by the minute, at least in their perception. Missing signs of human habitation made them apprehensive, inciting their minds to evoke images barely resembling reality. The region had not changed, scarcely in any case, but imagination, however fanciful, can acquire symptoms of facts. The grass, whether true or not, looked more withered; the sun bore down with twofold intensity; shade dispensing ponderosa pine trees showed signs of stuntedness, besides being scattered at greater distances. Even the sough in their tops sounded ominous. Wherever they turned wretched desolation met their eyes.

Munk was beset by a further predicament; namely, the presence of his friend, who was not overly blessed with grey matter, which he complemented with brawn. Koppel was a hefty fellow, endowed with physical strength nearly twice his own. It had earned him the sobriquet 'Strongback', in memory of Fortunio's servant.

Now, a man favoured with Herculean attributes should be a welcome companion in the wilderness, one might think. Then why was Munk apprehensive? What caused these scruples directed towards a man notorious for a placid disposition? True, he appeared to be somewhat irritated lately, but a kind word or friendly glance from his partner would have chased that vexation across the vast, semiarid land. What then engendered Munk's anxiety? Ugly thoughts, no doubt directed against Koppel whose existence he feared might be divined and interpreted by him.

Endeavours to suppress them met with scant success; they grew more antagonistic, acquiring a voice even that surely must be heard by his companion, he believed. Just the same, Koppel ought to be taught a lesson; this was the opportunity to do it, another propitious occasion similar to this might never again present itself. To humiliate Koppel, his friend of many years, meant more to him than finding Slumach's bonanza.

This notion, latent for some time, received impetus through Jon; the Indian's exhortations to register every landmark, compass point, and distance in the little book. That was why he smiled. An idea had been born which, however, lacked a trigger to launch it. To his eternal surprise Koppel provided it; it took a while to sink in.

By late afternoon he still wavered between annoyance and sympathy. Readying his tongue one instant for a sharp rebuke, which he swallowed every time out of commiseration with Koppel's apparent discomfort, he watched him suspiciously. Was he putting on an act deemed diversionary? Did he mean to annoy him, or was he just venting his frustration? No, Munk decided. What took place before his eyes could neither be considered a diversion nor vindictiveness; Koppel had a problem.

By the time the sun disappeared behind the Camelsfoot Range, he virtually stumbled over the sun-bleached ground. Disoriented, and fatigued in body and mind, he more often than once tripped over his own feet. It suddenly dawned on Munk what he witnessed was indeed no feint, but a serious flaw in his friend's character.

Koppel possessed no stamina, and even less heart; a fact that manifested itself through his promptings:

"Time to go back, Rainer, I have had enough."

Hearing it for the third time, Munk lost all patience; he roared:

"Go back, go back! Giving up on the first day already? You must be daft!"

"Very well, I will go alone then," Koppel countered defiantly.

"Oh, you will, do you? Tell me what direction shall it be?"

Taken by surprise, Koppel made no reply. Turning indecisively every which way, he stuck out his hands:

"That way," he offered.

"Ha, ha, ha, what a dolt you are. You make the angels weep. Go ahead! but first draw up your last will and testament, for your chubby face will not be seen again."

Halting for a moment he could not help adding:

"Certainly not in one piece."

It was a cruel remark meant to dissuade his friend from acting foolishly; moreover, to emphasise a single fact: his dependence on him and the little book. Then it dawned on him; the book! there was the missing link necessary to teach his companion a lesson for life. It was high time to show him up, take him down a peg or two, cure him from the erroneous notion of being a stalwart, worthy of acclaim.

The fact was this: Koppel needed his acquiescence to return safely, or alternatively obtain the book of directions, be it by stealth or force. Since no amount of cajolery or intimidation could induce him to comply, Koppel had no choice but to resort to skulduggery. He, he, he, what a surprise he will get when he opens the booklet. Munk had to restrain himself from slapping his thighs in anticipated joy and justified gloating. The resulting shame would surely redden his cheeks for years to come. Deserting a friend, leaving him at the mercy of bears and coyotes on a whim? What a story that will make.

The second day arrived. The cooler air and absence of that cruel sun enhanced Koppel's disposition. He became playful, unwontedly waggish, besides, signalling that returning was no longer on his mind. Munk's smirk grew broader as his vigilance heightened. He needed no animal entrails to read the immediate future: Koppel's demeanour said more than an open book written in large print.

"What a gawk," Munk repeatedly muttered under his breath. "What a duffer to imagine that this transparent ruse could deceive me."

His eyes spoke volumes. Try as he may, Koppel was unable to avert them from the little manual, which they followed as if glued to it.

All day the sun, blazing and unmerciful, made the sparse grass crackle, and the scattered sagebrush sigh. The heat by mid-afternoon took their breath away, not a cloud marred the sky. The wind, hot and dry, picked up sand and dust, which gradually filled the air. Koppel had reached the end of his tether; he refused to go on.

"Give me that book, I want to see where we are," he demanded.

"Almost there, Horst, another hour or two. Here, I will show you."

With these words he pulled the booklet from his pocket, which he held in one hand and tapped with the other.

"Remember, everything is recorded in there. Finding our way back will be a matter of course."

"Let's turn around," Koppel urged as he approached Munk, ostensibly to glance at the manual.

"Not yet. I suggest we set up camp for the night, take a long rest, and go on for a couple of hours in the morning. Should we not find the place, say, by ten o'clock, I am ready to turn back."

"Well, I'm giving up now. For the last time, give me the book. I just want to take a quick glance before I turn back."

Shrugging his shoulders, resigned to give in, he handed it to his friend with the words:

"If you insist, here, take a look."

Koppel hesitated, nonplussed over his friend's sudden change of mind; he stood there motionless for an instant. He paid no attention to Munk's curious demeanour, who seemed to enjoy himself. There was laughter on his face, and an impish sneer on his lips.

Recuperating quickly from his astonishment, he snatched the manual away with one hand and gave Munk a violent shove with the other. Turning to his heels, he hurried towards an outcrop nearby. Eager to put some distance between him and his companion, he neither stopped nor turned around to see whether Munk followed him.

There was no need to worry about that, for his friend, being pushed, staggered backwards, slipped and fell, thereby straining his ankle. Crying out in pain, clamouring for his companion's help led nowhere. Koppel almost tripped over his own feet in an endeavour to get away.

"Horst, come back, I'm hurt."

Receiving neither an answer nor a glance, he waited.

"Horst, I am unable to walk."

Upon hearing that, Koppel halted his steps.

"Unable to walk? hm, hm," the ever-present tempter sibilated. "There is your chance! take it, take it!"

Struggling to his feet, Munk, unable to make a single step, smiled despite an excruciating pain.

"Just as planned," he muttered under his breath.

When Koppel scurried away again, he hollered after him:

"Where are you going?"

Receiving no answer, he added:

"You are not trying to abandon me perchance?"

"Go to hell," Koppel cried back.

"Ha, ha, ha, you are going in the wrong direction," Munk jeered. Consult the book, man, open the book," he admonished derisively.

"You are not answering, my loyal friend. Ha, ha, ha, ho, ho, ho, what an incorrigible fool you are to think I had not seen through you years ago. What's the matter, Judas, the cat got your tongue? Take a look, open the manual. Tell me, you almighty donkey, what does it say?"

Koppel, feeling a presentiment creeping up his spine, stopped and opened the book. Leafing through it perfunctorily, his hands grew restive and his heart started to flutter. Shaking his head in bewilderment, turning page after page with nervous haste and trembling fingers, he expressed astonishment through clenched teeth, fighting back the groping tentacles of doom. He riffled through the booklet again and again. The vexation, darkening his mien, quickly turned into abhorrence. Munk's jeering utterances exacerbated his consternation; it disturbed his sorely needed power of concentration.

The entries made no sense. Page after page appeared to be nothing but haphazard jottings. Scratching his head, rubbing both eyes, he looked closer, then recoiled. For the myriad dots and dashes seemed to take on shapes of mocking, snarling fiends. That was it! All descriptions, distances, and compass readings were done in Morse, totally alien to him. A fact his friend was well aware of, since it was a subject that earned him many a raillery.

There he had it in a nutshell: Munk had set a trap in which he blindly stumbled. What an ignominy for a supposed stalwart, walking in the footsteps of Brother Faithful. How could he raise his head again back home where he was known, wanted to be known, as a latter-day flower of chivalry?

There was that raucous horselaughter again followed by scathing taunts:

"Hahaha, why so quiet? Has my loyal friend lost his voice? Come now, read, read aloud what is written there. Now then, I'm waiting."

Stung to the soul, in a dither, Koppel made an effort to collect his thoughts. The conclusion that without Munk he may never see his homeland again, pushed to the foreground. But now he hated his former friend with a passion; harming him stood foremost in his mind. Doing that, however, would be synonymous with cutting off his nose to spite his face. Had Munk kept quiet, a tragedy might have been averted. But he did not, possibly could not leave well enough alone; his sneering howls still filled the air.

"You oaf, you dumb Lord Strut, this will teach you a lesson; brawn does not reign over brains, the reverse is true. Now, be a good boy, come back and give me my book."

This request, expelled in a challenging tone, pregnant with disdain, nettled Koppel beyond endurance. Approaching menacingly, he told Munk roughly to shut up, or else.

"Nothing else, hand over the book, I say."

Koppel, having reached a state of no return, took the manual between his powerful hands and began to tear it up. Incredulous, aghast and wide-eyed Munk called out:

"Goodness gracious, what are you doing?"

"Teach me a lesson, are you?"

"No, Horst, stop! you are insane. We will perish without the book, give it back."

"Humiliating me, making me lose face? Here is your book."

With these words he tore it to pieces which he flung in Munk's face. Realising the next instant what he had done, blaming Munk for his desperate act, he lunged at him in a towering rage.

Jon, the Indian guide, grew worried after the two Germans had not returned by the end of the fourth day. Expressing his concerns to his superior, he was advised that there are no grounds for anxiety.

"These Germans are resourceful, they always find their way back," he was told.

"Let's wait another day," he added.

Jon, being an unobtrusive man, offered no objections.

Two days later the manager sent out his scouts.

"Keep it on the quiet, don't alarm the guests," he cautioned.

On horseback, armed with first aid equipment they sat out at a trot. They found Munk prostrate on the ground, dead as a doornail. No trace of Horst Koppel was found.

The Arch-Canadian

*F*rank Mason considered himself a true Canadian. He professed to love children, honoured women, and inveighed against foreign influences which, according to him, descended like avalanches over the country. He lived in a time when men were still men, and women enjoyed it. Mason called himself generous, sophisticated, and tolerant.

Foreigners, however, he could not stomach, least of all Germans. Associating with them, the foreigners, transformed his affability into grouchiness. To him Canada harboured too many aliens, whom he named displaced persons. Even in a small city like Clifton there passed not a day when these intruders did not cross one's path. Their atrocious double Dutch could singe anyone's ears, he proclaimed. Even a good-natured man like himself could lose his patience at times at the exposure of such dissonance.

The city of Clifton was still young, barely seventy years old; furthermore, founded and built up almost exclusively by immigrants from Europe. Such facts, however, bothered Mason not in the least, he bent and kinked them as the need arose. His motto was: "Foreigners remain aliens five generations, at least."

"Take me, for instance," he announced at every opportunity, "a Scot of the old block, a true descendant of Highlanders, who originally settled in Nova Scotia."

"We Canadians," one could hear him say again and again, especially in the presence of apparent aliens, "are far too indulgent with immigrants. Just look how we are being increasingly dragged down by these jabbering migrants. One can not even be understood in our homeland anymore," he avowed.

Once his suspicion was aroused that someone might not be a true blue Canadian, he habitually approached them to strike up a casual conversation under some pretext. Woe to the examinee who betrayed the slightest non-Anglophone accent. Mason seemed quickly to expand, upward and sideways, till he must have looked to the poor fellow like the giant risen from the bottle. People of colour hardly warranted Mason's second glance, for anyone could see where they came from; certainly not from Canada. Therefore he merely exercised his piercing sidewise glances on them.

Apart from that Mason could have been termed an agreeable man. He lived in harmony with his wife, meaning he usually bowed to her will. They were childless.

He was proud to be an average Canadian, a man of the people, in every way a regular fellow. These attributes, firmly anchored in those days in North America, were appreciated as a mark of the New World in whose light one felt at home. Thus they were defended, if need be with clenched fists.

Regrettably they were also increasingly exposed to dangers. But not as long as he and his burly pals had air in their lungs and power in their fists, they announced.

"They grow more disrespectful from day to day, they are getting downright intrusive," Mason declared at the beer parlour.

"I have noticed that some time ago," concurred Tad Brewster. "Just think of it, one of these tar-brushed chaps recently refused to yield. This guy steered straight towards me, sporting a mien I deemed dogged, if not menacing. I sure let him know who the boss is, ha, ha, ha."

"That's the way to go," praised his neighbour.

All then raised their glasses and vowed to continue to fight un-Canadian influences.

Mason did have a peculiar way of speaking, pronouncing at times words like a Britisher, for which reason he was occasionally asked:

"Where are you from?"

"From here of course," came a snappy retort.

"No, no, I mean originally."

"From Canada, can't you hear it?" he growled at the inquirer, whom he resolved to remember, sort of entering in his docket.

A few days ago Mason received a scant majority at the urns; he became the new mayor of Clifton. His joy over it knew no boundaries. A party was thrown, hands were shaken till the joints ached, and speeches were given until tongues stuck to the roofs of the mouth. In this general rapture he even temporarily forgot his vexation with foreigners. His wife, by the way, had exhorted him to be more tactful in that respect.

"You must heed your tongue a bit," she remarked after he had announced his candidacy.

"I know, I know," he agreed, albeit annoyed. "But finding it easy is a horse of another colour, in view of these people's cheeky behaviour. Just imagine, every runagate may now asked questions seemly for Canadians only."

"Oh well, a politician runs that risk, it can't be helped," she reasoned. "Someone posed a question? tell me, to whom?"

"To me, to councillors in general," came a morose reply.

"Who was it?"

"Who else but Ernst Kohler, that mouthy German with the atrocious accent. Three weeks ago that whippersnapper obtained Canadian citizenship, and since then became intolerable."

"Calm down, don't forget every vote counts at election time," she tried to soothe him.

Jumping up Mason blustered:

"That's the point, every vagabond can become a Canadian after five years, on paper at least, whether speaking English or showing respect for the culture of our country."

His wife kept silent, which seldom occurred. For she knew her husband well, who in all things showed indulgence towards

her, except in matters concerning aliens. Reminding him of
Canada's bilingualism, moreover, that citizenship in certain
cases may be obtained after three years residency, seemed not
be advisable. Such unwelcome facts poured nothing but oil on
an already flickering flame.

Mason turned out to be an exemplary mayor. Orderly by
nature, clear-sighted and endowed with a remarkable business
acumen, he had no difficulty to uplift the city's standing. He
travelled readily, a fact which some took amiss, whereas others
valued highly, because in their mind it lifted the town's
reputation beyond its borders.

After the second year in office he still sat firmly in the
saddle. The number of followers increased month by month.
He was uncommonly popular, praised above Olympus; indeed,
he was labelled a godsend. He sunned himself in the rays of
glory. The city's finances had improved considerably under his
stewardship. Green-spaces were expanded, new ones had been
added, moreover, an effort was made to improve the school
system; meaning a clamour was raised for more money. On
top of it, a day had been inaugurated in honour of women,
which fact alone would surely enhance his standing at the next
polls.

Mason stood pensively at the shores of Okanagan Lake.
As he reflected on past years, his heart swelled with
contentment about his achievements for the community, but
also for himself. He felt an urge to send shouts of joy across the
lake, but he checked himself on time. Just the same he turned
stealthily around, fearing that a stroller might have perceived
his intention. Just thinking about it brought goose pimples to
his skin. Such effusive outbreaks surely were unbecoming to a
real Canadian, especially if he occupied the mayor's chair.

"Only foreigners should be imputed with such
shenanigans," he grumbled.

Then he saw him! Mason at first stood rooted to the
ground. Recoiling aghast he disappeared behind the closest
tree.

"Gaining time, preserving composure," he instinctively mumbled.

Rubbing his eyes he carefully turned every which way, then ever so gingerly stuck his head out. Seeing the man again he had to rein in his feelings with all his might. It was him alright, he would have recognised that square head anywhere. Spellbound he watched the man starting to skip stones over the water. Flitching the bacon, that confounding Swabian called it. No doubt, it was none other than him. In front of his eyes pranced Ludwig Schimpel as ever before in the mood for silly capers.

An irresistible temptation to flee started to elbow itself to the surface; to run away in wild leaps and find shelter behind a nearby thicket. Just as he was preparing to do it, he curbed his urge, fearing dire consequences. First, it might attract Schimpel's attention; second, such gambols might be misconstrued by passing locals. After all the city's mayor, highly esteemed to boot, deserved attention as much as protection. No, being noticed was not advisable, any form of disturbance needed to be avoided.

Schimpel meanwhile had stopped skipping stones. Stretching himself, his glances wandered in every direction; his eyes even scanned the sky. How well Mason remembered those blue sparkling eyes in which all the world's imps used to dance. How often was he, Mason, ready to quit, run from Tillsonburg's vast fields, dead tired, parched by the burning sun; but one look in his friend's eyes, as always sparkling for joy, fanned the dust from his heart, and chased the weariness from his limbs. A sip of water, a few words in jest, and he was ready once more to tackle the rustling tobacco plants.

The object of his reveries had started to wander reflectively back and forth on the sand. Sauntering about, he came near the tree behind which Mason had sought refuge, causing a whirl in the mayor's head, and making his stomach feel hollow.

Lucky for him his temporarily lost presence of mind returned. Immediately he pressed closer to the huge maple tree, prepared to sneak around it if the need arose. His loose-fitting windbreaker which he had partially pulled over his head, saved him from recognition.

Schimpel stopped suddenly, he appeared to deliberate, during which time his eyes skimmed over the cabins across the street. Something evidently held his attention there, which suited the mayor immensely, since these cabins stood some way from his hiding place.

When Schimpel started to walk towards that spot, Mason expelled a sigh of relief; he felt save for the time being.

"Gaining time, maintaining composure," he exhorted himself again.

As luck would have it, there was no one else around; neither on the beach nor in the adjacent park. Mason felt an irresistible urge to follow Schimpel. With feigned unconcern, as if just lounging about, he followed at a suitable distance. He slowed down behind every tree, pretending to contemplate the surrounding absent-mindedly, hoping to deceive a casual observer, besides, making it more difficult to be disturbed. After all, even the mayor had a right to privacy at times.

Sidling along, endeavouring to remain unrecognised should Schimpel turn around unexpectedly, he remained on his heels till he disappeared in one of the huts. Mason took note of the number, repeating the digits till they became anchored in his mind. Then he withdrew with hasty steps, turning his head neither right nor left. Ignoring greeting passers-by, with a pallid face and tottering limbs he arrived at his home. He thanked his stars for his wife's absence, who luckily had been gripped by a yen to see her parents in far away Saskatoon.

After barring all doors carefully, and pulling down the shades, he sunk moaningly into a chair. His face lit up at the sight of an unopened brandy bottle, from which he took several copious gulps. Then he let his thoughts rove.

When did Schimpel show up? Did he just blow in, or did his presence serve a purpose? Just thinking of that name made his heart miss a beat. It resurrected a past which in his reckoning lay buried deep beneath the river of oblivion. Schimpel held his destiny in his hands, no doubt about it. Did he seek him out to cause grief, or was he just larking about?

"I must find out, today that is," Mason murmured, "for tomorrow might be too late."

He stood up. Unsure what fate had in store for him, he paced the floor, moaning and muttering:

"For twenty years I managed to obliterate my tracks, and now this – this simpleton shows up to spoil it all."

It wasn't easy to graduate from a stumbling immigrant to an accepted Canadian, a veritable Golgotha it deemed him at times, particularly in the initial ten years. Though he changed his name legally, acquired Canadian citizenship, plus doggedly emulated the mores of Anglophones, it took a long time to carry his intent to fruition.

Telltale signs of his origin, sticking to him like the mark of Cain, was the language of course. To obfuscate these lingering traces, Mason resorted to an age-old ruse: slurring words, and lisping as if befallen by speech impediments. Some were fooled by this subterfuge, most gave not a hoot, whereas a few took umbrage. With revulsion he recalled those ten, twelve years of Sisyphean toil, when he seemed to be climbing a never-ending stairway.

Finally he reached the top. Out of the blue after many years of torment followed his reward. One day, while talking to a seasoned Canadian about the influence of foreigners, the old-timer remarked:

"We Canadians, men like you and I, must oppose this inrush."

We Canadians! Did he hear right? We Canadians! Not all the Aeolian harps swaying in the wind could have produced a sweeter sound than these words: We Canadians! He was considered one of them. This recognition raised him above the apex of happiness; his confidence soared hereafter.

Buoyed up by a newly found assurance, he ventured westwards. His obsession, as Schimpel called it, with integration into a life terribly foreign and abhorrent to him, created constant friction between them. Exacerbated by his friend's scorn and criticism on that account, Mason decided to separate.

One day, while Schimpel gambolled in the back, he packed his belongings and left a message written on a piece of paper, which read: "I am seeking my luck elsewhere. Goodbye."

Casting a last glance around the room he saw what he was looking for; the little box containing their savings. Hesitating a moment, he took it and walked out. Allured by grandiose images, unpleasant memories of Schimpel nipping at his heels, he pushed on.

That happened twenty years ago; since then his life had changed drastically. Assailed by constant anxiety over his origin, to keep it concealed that is, enervated by pretence and the chase for recognition, he was ageing rapidly. In contrast to his friend Ludwig, who evidently had retained a youthful bearing.

"Ludwig Schimpel!" Mason expelled through clenched teeth. He should have left him drowning that hot summer day at the shore of Lake Erie. The reminiscence of that episode forced him to take another swig from the bottle. Yes, he should have left him there, ran away, pretending not to have noticed his struggle in the waves.

"Why did I have to save him? Why, oh god, why?" Mason lamented.

The revered mayor fell into a regular prisoner's walk. To and fro he strode, from wall to wall, tormenting his brains with dismal images. Revered? ha, reviled he would be soon; he felt already the welcome rug being pulled from under his feet. His ears tingled from shrill accusations, dripping with scorn, being hurled at him.

"Liar, swindler, faker!" they will say. He could hear them, even with both hands clapped over his ears. It did not attenuate the humiliating denunciations, for they came from within. He harboured no doubt about Schimpel's intentions. His secret, utterly ignominious in his estimation, so adroitly concealed, would be piper's news within a few days. Schimpel had sought him out for exactly that reason; to expose him to ridicule and disdain. Why else would he show up in this remote place? He must have noticed his picture in the newspapers.

Chuckling over pseudonym's transparency, remembering the theft of his money, Schimpel must be out to do mischief. He distinctly recalled that dreaded penchant for coarse pranks, and no less the inclination to gloat over someone's misfortune. Added to it an undeniable desire to get even, which Mason acknowledged, made a strong case for flight. He could never live down the shame of being unveiled, as it were, after the well advertised antagonism heaped on immigrants; especially Germans.

He must move away, this very night, far away to the north-country, where a man can still lose himself. Starting anew might be the only way out; under a different name, a German one, thereby easing his anxiety about a telltale accent which, despite Herculean efforts, he failed to overcome completely; for certain words did not roll over his tongue as intended.

Attuning his name to his speech would certainly remove a major worry, but might introduce ten others. What about his wife, the business, or the valued mayoralty? Besides, wouldn't his wife and others move heaven and earth to find him? Then the risk to be criminally charged had to be considered, which in itself sufficed to dismiss such notions as nothing but a wild-goose chase.

Bewailing his inescapable debacle he sunk down on a chair. Schimpel must be paid a visit, tonight under cover of darkness. First and foremost he needed to learn the purpose of his accursed presence. Perhaps his silence could be traded for a well paid government job, of course some distance from here. As he reproached himself once more over the rescue of Schimpel from certain drowning, he groaned:

"Confound that vagabond, I wish he were dead."

Yes, Schimpel's demise would ease his plight, for no one except him knew of his past. Not even his wife had an inkling about the name change from Franz Maurer to Frank Mason. Franzl, Schimpel always called him, which never failed to raise his hackles.

Schimpel dead? The very thought electrified him. Could not, couldn't an accident happen again which with a bit of help on his part might end fatally? Hm, wasn't that the silver lining on the horizon so direly needed? True, such thoughts were not entirely charitable, yet worth to be considered.

Another draught was in order to settle his addled nerves. Kobolds, one more mischievous than the next, assailed his conscience. Cajoling with sibilant voices one moment, taunting him the next, these whispers grew more insistent; louder, till the walls seemed to reverberate from insinuations which could no longer be silenced.

Mason listened with increasing interest. Unreceptive initially, beset by guilt, he ultimately overcame his compunctions. Indeed, a well-aimed shot, a bullet launched from behind some hedges would end his grief. Shocked by such ignoble ideas, he jumped up crying:

"No! No!"

But then vindication, that salver of an afflicted conscience announced itself. What right did Schimpel have to disturb his peace of mind? None whatever! How dared he endangering his reputation, built up with effort and nurtured laboriously? Such a man deserved the ultimate punishment. Ruining a citizen's life, considered to be a pillar of society, worthy of emulation by young and old, should not be tolerated. Preventive actions needed to be taken, he owed that much to himself, his wife and, yes, the entire community.

"Courage, it must be done," he urged aloud.

Casting a hurried glance at the clock, he expelled:

"Time to get ready."

The whole place would soon be in darkness. The lake's surface had already acquired a shimmering aspect, created by a full moon pushing over the mountains.

The Mason residence stood elevated on sloping terrain, somewhat secluded, totally surrounded by orchards in the midst of bloom. The view from all sides could stand comparison with the best in the country, especially in early spring. But presently that neither enhanced his feelings, nor shored up his mettle.

Ignoring the heart warming vista, shutting his ears to the myriad voices of nature, he removed the pistol from a drawer, which was always in there.

"Why a weapon in peaceful Canada, loaded to boot, in this serene surrounding?" his wife once questioned.

"My dear Ann, considering the transients, who can not even speak proper English, would I not be remiss in my duties if I kept no weapons in the house?"

She let it pass; but being neither dull nor gullible, besides, possessing a woman's insight, she gave little credence to his explanations. She sensed that the truth lay elsewhere. Indeed, it did; but the husband would have denied it even under torture.

The ever-ready pistol served only one purpose: to keep the ghosts at bay which guilt calls into being. Having done an injustice to many, be it in thought only, had besieged his mind with lurking dangers asking to be fought.

Night was rapidly falling; the time to act had arrived. He inspected the gun in his hands; then, with a grim smile pocketed it in his open jacket. It had to be done! Prior to leaving the house he put the bottle to his lips for a final swig. Pulling his cap down, turning up the collar of his jacket, he left the house. He no longer was steady on his feet, whether on account of the consumed brandy, or an arising uncertainty about his errand, he could not have said. One hand gripping the gun in his pocket, the other closed tight around the railing, he started to descend.

Halfway down, assailed by sudden pangs, he stopped. Did he really intend to slay his former friend? The gravity of that notion forced him to sit down on the steps. Looking at the ghostly shadows flitting across the lake, irresolution began to rise to the surface, changing presently to serious doubts. Because before his eyes appeared the lifelike shape of Schimpel, whose laughing face brimmed with a joy of life, forever alien to himself.

Chuckling involuntarily he recalled his penchant for pranks; not horseplay as he, Mason, imputed; far from it! His were innocent games of an imaginative mind, which unfailingly had annoyed him. It wouldn't anymore, quite the contrary.

To his surprise an inexplicable nostalgia seized him for these diversionary antics. What a larksome, unconcerned fellow Ludwig was, still is by the looks of it, Mason granted. A character more contrasting with his own fretful, grumbling nature, could hardly be imagined. Mason's resolve weakened to the point of no return.

"Impossible! I can not go through with it!" he told himself.

Come what may, let them deride, despise, and persecute him, he would not touch a hair on Schimpel's head; another solution must be found. But first he decided to go back inside the house, before someone saw him sitting on the steps like a vagrant. Besides, the still half-full bottle needed some attention.

With this in mind he rose. As he straightened himself up everything started to turn. Lights, lake and mountains appeared to be in a jumble. Then he tripped and tumbled headlong to the bottom. Somehow the pistol in his pocket, tightly gripped, discharged a bullet, which found Mason's heart.

The Prisoner

Some men are not susceptible to life's teachings. They learn nothing from experience, whether it brought them misery or joy. Hard times are accepted with equal equanimity as fortune's graces. They just go on as if their miseries and joys of the past had happened to others, not to themselves. Therefore they feel unaffected by them. No doubt such a disposition, considered a boon by some, by others a curse, influences life immensely. As in the case of Rufus Sargent, who called himself a realist, yet ignored reality's first doctrine; namely, that it can not be circumvented. He tried, which may be the reason why he is now languishing in jail.

An eight year sentence was imposed, the maximum under the statutes. Sargent's lawyer, Harvey Wilder, insisted that six years were attributable to his client's condescending personality, the rest to the offence. They were friends for many years, for which reason Wilder felt entitled to be blunt. He knew how.

"Show contrition, don't sit there like a hornet ready to sting," he berated his client mercilessly every afternoon on the way back from the courthouse.

"What should I do? tell me, come on, don't hesitate, just tell me," Sargent demanded to know.

Indeed, what could he be imputed with. His offences, more conceived than perceived, were difficult to name. His conduct in the prisoner's dock left nothing to be desired, certainly not to the uninitiated in court affairs where mores and decorum, unwritten to be sure, quite often influence decisions of guilt and sentence.

"Making judges, prosecutors, and juries feeling sympathy for you, is often instrumental in obtaining a lighter sentence, if not freedom," Sargent's attorney informed him.

"What is the insinuation here?"

"Rufus, your blasted aloofness sticks like a bone in the court's craw," Wilder snapped.

"What do you suggest? I can't crawl out of my skin," Sargent objected.

The lawyer heaved a deep sigh.

"You convey the impression of a colonial among vassals. Don't forget, your English airs are not exactly received with hallelujahs by the all black authorities and jury."

That was almost six years ago, now his mandatory parole hearing was coming up.

"Keep your tongue reined and your mien compliant," the attorney advised. "And for heaven's sake show remorse and deference," he added.

"You mean lick their boots?"

"Why not, if it means a remission of your sentence,"Wilder exhorted.

Sargent was an exemplary prisoner; co-operative, obliging, never shunning duties, always lending a hand where he could. Testimonials given by guards and the warden were generally favourable. True, they contained a hue here and there, caused by his reluctance to mingle freely with other prisoners, as much as his unyielding attitude towards improvement and rehabilitation programs. Apart from that, however, he was a model inmate.

But there was a fly in the ointment by the name of Sestus Webb, an old guard, black as ebony, malicious as Barbariccia, one of Dante's devils. About two months ago he came on duty from somewhere else. He was quickly baptised 'Old Rancour' by one of the younger, not yet browbeaten prisoners. A more cantankerous and domineering creature on two legs could hardly have been found in the island. Among other chicaneries he insisted to be addressed as 'Sir' by all the inmates, which Sargent steadfastly refused to do.

"You will rue the hour of your birth," Webb hissed at him repeatedly.

Webb's pleasure, as it were, consisted of charging inmates with offences which naturally would prejudice their paroles. Therefore most prisoners, especially older and hardened men, quickly learned whence the wind blew. They took care not to incur his displeasure, and consequent censures, thereby inferring inordinate powers upon this veritable Lord Strutt, who really resembled cousin Limp a lot more. He had a game leg, which elicited many a snicker and some hoots.

On the morning when Sargent laid eyes on the new guard he knew that his goose was cooked, for they had met before. Down at the harbour it happened, where Webb had worked as a security guard. Altercations between them were no rarities, though reasons for their occurrences remained nebulous. No doubt the roots of the ugly encounters sprouted in the miasma of Webb's myriad problems. Being physically handicapped, furthermore chafed by never ending vexation, he carried an additional burden; a beast gnawing at his soul. It was the feeling of inferiority towards white people that overshadowed his life. An urge to control and subjugate them fomented within his being. In Sargent he saw the embodiment of an archenemy. His innate equanimity, in Webb's mind a clear sign of superciliousness, drove him to distraction.

Webb's harassment came to a sudden end one fine morning, when Sargent confronted him amid his colleagues and friends, approaching the group in his inimitable way. Measured, yet somewhat rueful, he stopped when he was almost brow to brow with him.

"Are you a good swimmer?" Sargent asked in his clipped English accent.

Webb found himself in a twofold quandary. Bystanders prevented him to give ground, in addition his self-propagated reputation as a fearless pugilist demanded a manly stance.

"What do you mean?" he managed to say.

"Because you are going to take a bath, right here in the briny sea," he was advised in a manner not threatening but promising.

Some of his cronies could not suppress a titter, others egged him on. Sargent had not finished yet.

"You are a man, a cripple to be sure, however, that can not be helped. Up your dukes, let's get at it now," he encouraged.

But Webb entertained no such intentions; quailing visibly, he snapped:

"Be careful, you are going to get it."

Sargent smiled deprecatingly. Still polite, but in a voice dripping with disdain, he exclaimed loud enough for the whole surrounding to hear:

"You are nothing but a Jack Brag, my good man. I see that we must postpone your swim to next time."

With these words Sargent went his way.

From thereon he was left in peace, until now of course. Despite Sargent's relative youth he had led a turbulent life, vexatious beyond endurance at times. But he bore reverses, which would have smitten many a weaker man, with astounding indifference. Did he learn from these painful experiences? Had he grown more prudent or calculating, so as to avoid similar misfortunes? Not a bit. Shrugging his shoulders, shaking his head as if amused, he acknowledged fate's vagaries and carried on. Forward that is, till he stumbled once more into the outstretched arms of the next calamity. Like now for instance.

He realised beyond conjecture that Webb had to be taken care of, but how? As often before, he reflected coolly but inferred irrationally. Rampant emotions never entered his bloodstream, neither did logic. Another quirk of his character manifested itself, which helped to raise a minor affair into the sphere of distress.

Sargent abhorred complaining, and accusing even more. Any sensible man would have raised the matter with the prison board, who surely upon learning of their vexatious past might have acted promptly. Yet he never entertained such notions for a single moment. Informing lay not in his bailiwick. As always he held his own counsel till he arrived at a conclusion. It was a mistake, but Rufus Sargent knew no better, he had to follow his star.

Webb's iniquities were becoming insufferable. Noticing the prisoner's unwillingness to protest, he lost all restraint. He now tormented his defenceless victims with demands, rebukes, and outright threats. To these nefarious machinations was added a new element: Webb started to goad and challenge him.

"Are you a good swimmer, prisoner? Answer me, you worm: 'yes, sir, yes, sir.' Repeat that after me, I order you."

These were some of his vile taunts hurled at Sargent. Others, more insidious, at times outright threatening were also hurled at him.

One day Webb planted himself in front of Sargent's cell bars with a particular provoking attitude. The whole man was soaked with evil intentions. There he stood, like Milton's imp of darkness, sneering from cheek to jowl, leering at Sargent with a mixture of hate, fear, and guilt. He snarled:

"Are you a good swimmer, prisoner? I hear your parole hearing is coming up."

When Sargent simply ignored him, he stamped his foot and shrieked:

"Answer me, prisoner, answer me this instance or I shall report you!"

Screwing up his face, while moving closer, he hissed:

"Forget it, you don't stand a chance."

Sargent had turned his back, he showed no sign of either having heard or understood. But he had comprehended only too well. Webb needed attention, for he evidently had shifted into higher gears. A new element was added to his chicanery, that of a dare. For the first time when alone did he approach close enough to be touched. That seemed curious. Had he shed his fears, or could it be ascribed to mere coincidence? None of it. Sargent decided Webb wished to be attacked, or at least provoked to some sort of an attempt, thereby negating not only chances of being paroled, but having his incarceration extended by years. Parole in any case had turned into a mirage in view of Webb's subversive schemes, whose constant needling would soon stretch his nerves to the point of snapping. Even a dullard could contemplate the results.

"I must act quickly," Sargent mumbled to himself, while his tormentor still ranted outside.

As mentioned Rufus Sargent possessed a homing pigeon's instinct to fly in a straight line towards its destination. In his case right into the maw of disaster. He determined to escape. That should not prove to be too difficult, since prison security could hardly be called severe, neither were rules adhered to with much dedication.

To begin with, violent prisoners were rarities in Barbados; moreover, should they escape, where would they go? Anyone familiar with that windswept island would agree there are no hiding places to speak of. True, a man could camp out in sugar cane fields, provided assistance from nearby was accorded him, but only for a short while.

Leaving the island? Well-nigh impossible for poor and ignorant men. Therefore attempts to decamp were seldom undertaken, except as a lark or dare by some nimble youngster. Should a foreigner, like Sargent for instance, succeed to abscond and return to his homeland, they just shrugged their shoulders as if to say: "Good riddance."

"I am waving my parole hearing," Sargent announced to his flabbergasted attorney.

"For heaven's sake man, why?" exclaimed his defender.

"Two more years will not kill me. Then at least I am my own master," Sargent said in a tone of finality.

When Wilder made further attempts to persuade his friend and client, Sargent looked him straight in the eye without saying a word. His attorney recognised the signs. Rising he said:

"Well, goodbye then, let me know if you need something."

When Webb heard about Sargent's decision, he was surprised, stunned would be a more apt description. All day he was seen walking around in a daze, mumbling to himself, while shaking his head. To tell the truth he was worried, uneasiness was written all over his face. Sargent's silence confounded him, as much as his collected composure. He obviously had never lodged a complaint with the authorities, a puzzling fact indeed. It alone fanned the flames of his suspicion, which crackled even louder when he noticed the smile on Sargent's face, accompanied by a mysterious glint in his eyes. Both were not present before.

The whole man looked different, a glowing confidence lit up his face and lightened his steps. He gave the impression of a man in the throes of great expectations. His attitude towards Webb, although now as before standoffish, had lost its edge of enmity. He contemplated him with the smug countenance of a wolf who is about to devour his prey.

Webb did not trust Sargent, who in his conception concocted a scheme squarely directed against him. Racking his brain, however, brought him not an inch closer to an explanation. Nevertheless, the prisoner in cell number 14 became his proverbial incubus.

Two weeks later Sargent received a visitor. This in itself should not have raised a single eyebrow, yet it did more than that in the case of Webb, who had developed a keen sense of attentiveness where Sargent was concerned. Guilt had turned him into a doubting Thomas, suspicion had sharpened his eyes and ears. Every incident, ever so insignificant, takes on Gargantuan proportions for the man whose conscience is riddled with scepticism.

Sargent's visitor came to Webb's attention almost immediately. After a passing glance at the caller, alarm bells started to ring in his head, for the visitor resembled the prisoner in looks and stride. This fact unsettled the guard's nerves even more, thus aggravating the lameness of his leg, and adding a twitch to his face. Shortly after the visitor had left, Webb sidled towards cell 14.

"You had a visitor, I see," he remarked in a most inveigling manner.

Sargent made no reply, he turned around and remained mute. He was loath to show his face, for fear of betraying his emotions. Had the guard been able to see his countenance, it would have given him food for further thought, and grounds for greater apprehension. He refused to turn around, although ordered repeatedly by the guard to do so, not to show his feelings of suppressed jubilation in his normally staid face.

Webb's alluring voice, as much as an almost benign behaviour deceived him not one moment. In any case his Rubicon had been crossed; the matter of Webb versus Sargent neared its resolution. Strange to say, Sargent harboured no thoughts of revenge. Odd, to be sure, yet a fact. Retaliation for months of needless torment never entered his mind, since he decided to escape. To achieve this, outside as much as inside help was essential. Obtaining assistance from within the prison presented no difficulty.

Most prisoners showed a surprising eagerness to help. Some readily jeopardised their well-being by actively aiding an escapee, despite possibilities of reprisal and extended incarceration. Others played a more passive part; they acted as decoys for the guards' attention. In addition some guards could be persuaded to look the other way, for a consideration of course. Once an absconder had reached the other side of the walls, he needed reliable accomplices to take over.

The planning of Sargent's flight progressed well; it was scheduled to take place during the yearly cropover festival, an island-wide celebration commemorating the ending of sugar cane harvests. The resulting excitement, the schemers hoped, would dull the guards' vigilance, besides, engendering indifference.

Webb's shift at the jail ended at four o'clock in the afternoon, for the coming week in any case. He was beset by conflicting sentiments, and plagued by an inexplicable apprehension as quitting time approached. On the one side he looked forward to leave that dismal place behind, yet at the same time felt a strong desire to remain. This came as no small surprise to him and his colleagues, who shook their heads over such unfamiliar behaviour. They could hardly wait for their shifts to end, thus signing out late hardly ever occurred. In contrast to Webb who did it regularly.

Leaving the jail reluctantly as usual, after the end of his shift, Webb almost jumped back inside before the heavy door slammed shut. There, in front of his eyes stood Sargent's visitor, pretending to be fascinated by a blooming hibiscus tree nearby. The man, seemingly oblivious to the guard's presence, showed no intention to move aside. Deeply absorbed in what heaven only knew, he had planted himself in the middle of the narrow walking way. Debating with himself whether to return inside, or sidle along in another direction, he finally decided to walk straight ahead as intended.

"You are blocking the pathway," he tried to snarl, but only managed to grumble at the stranger, who was either deaf or just plain ornery.

He showed no inclination to give way. But he turned fully towards the defiant guard and said:

"Ah, Sestus Webb, one of the guards, if I am not mistaken."

While examining Webb unabashed from head to toe, especially his clubfoot, he announced:

"The name is Randolph Sargent. You got my brother inside. But don't worry, I will not hold that against you, far from it. He was always the black sheep in the family, up to no good, so I suppose he deserves his punishment."

Hearing that name, plus finding out the close relation with the prisoner, gave Webb an unpleasant jolt. His ears shut out everything else that was said, while his mind opened wide to let a surging apprehension enter. Looking around for support, that seemed nowhere near, voices rose within him, cautioning to mind his step; especially when he noticed a peculiar glint in the eyes of the man facing him, contrasting a courteous, if not friendly deportment. Looking at that unlined face, tanned by wind and sun, Webb clearly detected suppressed anger as much as unswerving determination.

The man before him evoked unpleasant memories that made him shiver despite the afternoon heat. He saw himself standing amid his cronies at the deep-sea harbour, where some years ago this fellow's brother humiliated him unforgivingly. He recognised the same deliberate stare boring right through him; moreover, he felt cowed by an identical demeanour, barely suppressed, to pounce on him. Seeing no other guards outside, understandably so since they had left on time, he gave Sargent a wide berth and hobbled on without turning around.

The following day Webb left the jail with the other guards, which earned him a certain amount of teasing. One of his colleagues nudged the other while saying:

"Pinch me, Justin, I am seeing a ghost?"

"What's up Sestus, going to a tryst?" another asked amid laughter.

"Who is the lucky gal, Lothario?"

Webb only glowered at the gibers and said nothing. But he stuck to his new schedule from thereon, making sure to leave the building in the company of other guards.

Brother Randolph never missed a visiting hour, furthermore always remained the allotted time. Webb found that strange, for he recalled the brother's expressed indifference towards the man in cell 14. However, he heaved a sigh of relief when after a full week there was no sign of the dreaded man anywhere outside of the jail. He felt safe, but not for long.

Looking through the window one morning, whom did he notice sauntering up and down the pathway? Randolph Sargent! This made a stir with the neighbours, who could not remember seeing a white face in their vicinity before. When Sargent espied the dumbfounded Webb at the window, he waved and sang out:

"Ah, good morning guard, a fine day it is going to be."

Webb did not believe so, even less when he noticed being followed all the way to work. Not conspicuously mind you, far from it, their paths just seemed to cross here and there by accident. Webb silently cursed his lame leg, putting him at a disadvantage with the nimble and much younger man, who could run rings around him with bated breath. What galled him most was the white man's duplicity. Wherever they met, that sanctimonious foreigner acted surprised, but pleased. His heart seemingly bubbling over with joy, he hailed him from afar:

"What a pleasure to meet you again, sir," he exclaimed in a loud voice that made the birds take wing.

Upon arriving at the jail, Webb asked to see the warden, who received him not exactly with open arms.

"Good morning, Webb, what can I do for you?"

The guard hemmed and hawed for a while till his stern superior demanded to know:

"Well, what is it?"

"I don't know how to begin," stammered Webb, lowering his eyes to avoid the warden's rebuking scowl.

"Go on, I don't have all day," he was urged.

"I'm being followed," the guard blurted out.

His chief's annoyance quickly changed to perplexity and then to amusement.

"Right now, you mean right here inside the jail?"

"No, no, on the outside," he confessed sheepishly.

"What has that got to do with me?" snapped the warden with knitted brow and narrowed eyes, then he added:

"Isn't that a police concern, if anything?"

Discouraged, but driven on by a need to share his apprehension, his voice acquired a suppliant tone:

"I just want to report, sir, that it concerns one of our inmates."

The warden's head came up in surprise. More annoyed than interested he asked:

"Which one, and how can he follow you if he is inside?"

"The brother of Sargent in cell number 14 is trailing me."

The warden was unable to suppress a grin.

"Is that not the one heaped with sheaves of complaints?"

"Yes, sir, everybody grumbles about him."

"Not so, Webb, you are the only one," he was told by his chief, who had little use for the limping guard, whom he considered nothing but a nuisance.

He wished that busybody and whiner with a chip on his shoulders anywhere, except near him.

"We can't help you, go to the police," he was advised curtly, and then dismissed.

Encounters with Randolph Sargent became more numerous. They met on his way to work, in Webb's neighbourhood, plus the odd time near the shore where he did most of his shopping. Sargent's pretence that these encounters were fortuitous, made no inroad with Webb, who firmly believed they were schemes of a treacherous mind. If the intention was meant to disquiet him, well, he had succeeded. Should his aim be intimidation, again, he had achieved his goal. Webb indeed had undergone a transformation concerning the inmate in cell 14, whom he no longer harassed. Disparaging reports about him with higher-ups had also ceased.

Avoiding Sargent proved cumbersome. Dodges and ruses were ineffective. Hardly did he heave a sigh of relief, thinking he had given him the slip, when that accursed voice resounded from somewhere:

"Hello there, what a surprise, what a pleasure to see you again."

A visit to the police station bore no fruit, it earned him ridicule and rebuke:

"Has he threatened you, or became belligerent perchance? Not really, you say? Well then, there is nothing we can do."

"But he is a foreigner," remonstrated Webb.

Shrugging his shoulders the desk sergeant remarked:

"So are many others. Go, see a lawyer."

On the way out the policeman asked:

"Why do you think he is following you?"

Why, indeed. What should, rather could he tell the sergeant without incriminating himself. The truth? Not ever, it might drag him before a disciplinary panel, resulting perhaps in an indictment. After all, a man's freedom lay on the scales. Preventing his parole gratuitously by means of manufacturing evidence, could be construed as a serious matter. He therefore gave no answer; mumbling something unintelligible he left the building.

Stepping into the afternoon heat of Bridgetown, the often mulled over question arose again: Why did Sargent neglect to file a grievance against him? That fact, mysterious and inconceivable, caused greater uneasiness within him than he cared to admit. But now, considering the brother's machinations, the reality must be faced that something was being plotted, nefarious to be sure, and squarely aimed at him.

July had arrived, the crop-over festival drew closer, soon it would be in full swing. Amid the rising heat and sultry air, rehearsals took place from North Point to Crane Beach. Tuning of steel drums had begun throughout the island. A peculiar medley indeed, sounding dissonant when first heard, yet quickly acquires a trenchant resonance, sought after and longed for. Soon that haunting rhythm obtains a symbolic quality reminiscent of these enchanting islands, similar to the piercing cries of whistling frogs after sundown. As one hears these sounds, the mind conjures up rustling palm trees swaying in the wind, coral sand beaches as much as warm smiles and lilting voices. Unending fields of sugar cane the memory calls into being, standing tall, undulating, and whispering louder as harvest time approaches.

Sargent's escape was arranged, the appointed time being in three weeks at eight o'clock sharp. The moon, most likely behind clouds in any case, would then be on the wane. Guards on duty, along with other islanders should be in a festive mood. Their attention would be diverted by the omnipresent sounds of blood stirring calypso, their thoughts directed towards love and sweet moments of a tryst.

A week went by, nothing much happened in the jail. Final preparations for Sargent's jailbreak were pretty well made. Brother Randolph had arranged everything down to the last detail. A large motor yacht was moored at the exclusive St. James Club, ready to whisk them down to Trinidad, and then across to Venezuela. Since extradition agreements with these countries did not exist, they felt save there. Not that Barbados was likely to exercise them anyway, considering costs and inconveniences.

A week before that eventful day, guards and inmates became aware of a surprising change in Sargent. He began to lose his customary good cheer, as much as that famous optimism, uplifting in such a sombre surrounding, contagious to many. His stride, always purposeful, had lost its bounce and direction; he now shuffled more than he walked. His head frequently bent, shoulders more often stooped than straight, he stumbled around the playing field where until recently he was the star of every game, hurrayed and cheered on for his daredevil performances. But there he now stood on the outside, paying scarce attention to the action on the field, lost in thought and deeply troubled. What had happened? the others wondered.

He was the only white man in the jail, which made him not only conspicuous, but also sort of a ward to some inmates, and guards for that matter. A few older ones asked almost shyly:

"Rufus, are you not well, can we help?"

Stung to the quick, for reasons no one understood, he barked:

"Why don't you mind your own business."

But calling to mind their genuine concern, he added apologetically:

"It is really nothing, a bit of indigestion I think, it will pass."

"Small wonder, considering the grub dished out to us," someone remarked obligingly.

They let it go at that; however, no one believed him. Among themselves they spoke of more profound causes that might explain such a rapid transformation from brimming vitality to signs of decrepitude. Subtle inquiries, gentle nudging, as much as amiable hints led nowhere. A clam could not have been tighter than this formerly loquacious Britisher. Indigestion indeed! they demurred without reserve. They talked, surmised, and conjectured. Yet none guessed the truth, in fact it would have bewildered and shocked them. Even at the end when reality stared them in the face, truth remained elusive as ever.

Sargent found no rest. The days were bearable, but not the nights. Plagued by unrest, he hardly slept a wink. An inner turmoil had gripped his very being. Images, inexplicable but scary, flitted before his eyes. Dangers seemed to lurk everywhere, nebulous, possessing neither form nor name. This was the third night prior to his planned escape. How sultry the night air was, Sargent thought. Never in all the years did he experience such oppressive heat, making him sweat from every pore of his skin. He could not understand this suffocating dampness, since nights were invariably cooled down by the ever present trade winds. His cell, considered palatial compared to most others, had a window, plus a self-propelled fan at the ceiling. True, the opening in the wall was secured with iron bars, but it allowed air to move in freely.

Sleep was out of the question. Bathed in perspiration he fought rising waves of panic, which he tried to stave off with comforting thoughts: "You are just overly excited, that is all," he told himself. Indeed, who would not be in a dither at the prospect of approaching freedom? Imagine for a moment, in less than a week he could see himself loafing at Maracas Bay, burying his toes in the white sand only darkened by the shadows of palm trees.

Money created no difficulties, his affairs were in capable hands, his brother's that is, who managed everything well. Yields from their investments should provide them a life of comfort. Returning to England, or Europe for that matter, never entered his mind. Leaving the Caribbean he considered synonymous with self-imposed mortification. The charm of these islands, sought in vain anywhere else, had ensnared him. The ways of the natives, untrammelled yet dignified, had become part of him, as much as the sights, smells and sounds of a world obviously created by angles.

The heat became unbearable, his cell acquired the attributes of a sauna. Tossing from side to side, tumultuous thoughts assailed him, while unsettling perceptions floated through his mind.

Suddenly he became aware of weird noises reaching his ears. Leaping from his bunk he turned in every direction, frantically trying to locate their source. They were voices, he decided, raucous and ominous, evidently directed at him. Stepping closer to the barred opening, he imagined that they emanated from the wind-stirred treetops in the yard outside.

But that could not be, since these stately palms were straight and high, making it impossible to climb them. Besides, who would be out there after midnight. Yet the voices would not go away. Rising above the rustling in the trees, they became more strident and urgent, as if abetting someone nearby to action. Between fits of snickers and shrieks of laughter he heard teeth gnashing and throats growling. What did it portend? Were there forces outside, ready to pounce and chase him through the night, if ever he should dare to step beyond the walls? He was unable to make out a single word, though the clamour continued unabated till the first signs of morning appeared in the sky.

In the afternoon during yard sessions Sargent felt himself unable to avert the eyes from the palm trees.

"What are you staring at, Rufus?" more than one inmate wanted to know.

"Nothing," he grumbled.

These trees were impossible to scale, it flashed through his mind, it would be absurd to think so. But somebody, something was up there last night. Among other things he possessed excellent hearing, as much as a stout heart. Those fronds, he said to himself, now swaying gracefully in the wind, dallying with each other, bore a sinister secret.

Sidling up to an inmate who occupied a cell next to his, Sargent started a conversation. After a few moments he ventured to remark:

"I say, Clancy, that was quite a night."

"How do you mean?" came a surprised response.

"Well, the heat for one was unbearable," Sargent said.

"I did not notice it," the other remarked.

"Did you hear the racket outside?"

"What kind of racket?"

"Loud voices, plus sounds I never heard before," Sargent explained.

"No, I heard nothing."

"I guess it was the wind rattling and rushing," Sargent mumbled to himself as he walked away.

Spending time among other inmates proved salubrious to Sargent. His confidence gained strength that waned quickly however, at the thought of his impending liberty. One more day would see him bidding this place farewell. Tomorrow night, under the cover of darkness, he would walk out of here into the free world. What a memorable hour that will be, a day to celebrate the rest of his life. But were was the joy? He searched in vain for signs of elation, but found tracks of apprehension instead. Now, that was strange, considering an imminent license to act in accordance with one's will, and do what enters the mind. Why then was he not enthralled?

He skipped over these questions quickly, as if in fear of an answer. Admitting it or not, these dank confines, encircled by gloomy walls and spiked fences, had grown familiar, if not intimate. True, it was a constrained world, but home to him. The unvarying routine possessed a soothing quality, but regrettably also weakened his spirit and eroded his mettle. The fiery man of years ago existed no more, he underwent a lamentable transformation. Unknown to him, Rufus Sargent had disappeared, leaving only his skin behind into which a timorous caricature of himself had crawled.

Darkness followed on the heels of sunset, as always in these regions. Sargent's nerves were in a frazzle. He listened intently, his ears glued to the bars for sounds that he hoped would remain absent tonight. Sleep had to be postponed till early morning, for he realised there was no chance of finding rest prior to daybreak.

All was quiet outside, only the rustling in the trees and the frogs' sharp whistles were audible. There was no indication of last night's torrid heat or suffocating mugginess. He nearly dared to hope that this would not be a repetition of the previous night, where oppressive heat and ghastly events almost robbed him of his reason.

A notion sneaked closer, more of a whimsical wish to be sure, that what he had experienced last night was but a chimera, a horrible fancy of his overexcited imagination. This helped to mitigate a rising desperation, it allowed him to lay down. Not to find sleep, but just to rest his weary bones and tortured mind.

He must have dozed off for a while, therefore remaining oblivious to the darkness outside. He received a rude awakening however, that gave him a jolt, which almost threw him off the bunk. All hell had broken loose again. But this time the clamour seemed closer and more menacing. Not only did mocking cries assail his ears, but also taunting calls, daring him to step outside. The temperature and humidity in his cell had risen to alarming proportions, forcing him to gasp for breath and pound his chest.

Amid this terrifying, blood curdling din, Sargent suddenly realised what had to be done. Leaving jail tomorrow evening was no longer an option. He would be persecuted by these avenging voices the rest of his days. Though he did not admit it loudly, his subconscious concluded that much. Fear, never ending apprehension would be his companions, calling into life this nerve-racking cacophony. Like the dreadful tinnitus that dwells in the head, but rings in the ears, it would slowly drive him insane. No, the idea of breaking out tomorrow, or at any other time, had to be permanently discarded.

But how could he live down the resulting shame? How indeed could he face the men who helped him, in particular his brother, after such a despicable betrayal? A craven he would be called, some doing it aloud, others in thought. A shameless poltroon, false to the core, thoughtless and a schemer, they would pronounce him. His mind found no rest, clambering atop the wings of indecision, he hovered between despair and hopelessness. There seemed to be no way out, he saw no escape from an inexorable dilemma; yet he finally did. As the clamour in his head reached insufferable degrees, he suddenly found a solution.

Next morning, just before sunrise doors started to clank amid calls to wake up. To the guard's surprise nothing stirred in cell 14, which he found highly unusual. Sargent always sat fully dressed at his small table, either reading or writing; but not today. Rattling his truncheon across the iron bars, the guard bellowed more insistent:

"Get up, Sargent, what's the matter, too much carousing last night? ha, ha, ha."

Not a sound nor any movement could be detected. Another guard, noticing the hubbub, stepped closer to investigate. Looking up he cried out:

"My god, look, look at the ceiling!"

They both did. There in the first glow of the morning hung Rufus Sargent. His predicament was solved.

Moro's Apples

*L*eon Moro rubbed his hands gleefully, a broad grin spanned his still handsome face.

"How stupid the police are," he announced to the low mountains above. Below him flowed the historic Richelieu River, which alone might know his secret. He had grown wealthy in five short years. His wife no longer called him dodo-head; far from it, she now referred to him as my dear Leon, or my honourable friend.

When he started to make proposals some years ago, offers on blooming orchards surrounding their dismal homestead, she curled her lips up to her nose, but said nothing. How someone, poorer than Lazarus of old presumed to make even a token down payment, should any vendor be silly enough to take him serious, she was unable to fathom.

After he purchased and fully paid for Legare's fabulous twenty acres, Marie's withered love underwent a miraculous revival. Her former good-for-nothing husband changed in her estimation to a scion of industry. Honouring and loving him seemed natural, to say the least, for a woman blessed with a man that knows a thing or two.

So it went for a spell. Offers were made, rejected, accepted, and consummated, till almost every valuable piece of land nearby came in Moro's possession. As always he paid cash, provided clear title could be obtained. To be sure, many eyebrows were raised; questions, some quite pointed assailed him, particularly by the authorities, which was no surprise in view of an ugly incident a year before.

Lukas Loti, a dealer in jewellery was found one morning lying under an apple tree, not far from Moro's ramshackle house. He was quite dead, strangled in the phansigar fashion of India: that is efficiently and silently. He never stood a chance; there was no sign of a struggle, no cry in the night was heard. Someone, in all likelihood known to Loti, after meeting or accompanying him, throttled the unsuspected dealer with the dexterity of an Indian thug. Surprisingly there was no mark on Loti's neck, nor any clues or witnesses.

How a robust man, sure and nimble on his feet, could have been strangled so unnoticed, moreover, so deftly without leaving welts or fingerprints behind, remained a riddle to the police. Had they been aware of thuggee, that infamous art of doing someone in swiftly, silently, and untraceable, the investigation would have been crowned by success perhaps. Searching for someone having spent time in India might have proved less of a chore than groping along their chosen trail leading nowhere.

Moro surveyed his ever expanding estates with pride and satisfaction. Orchards upon orchards extended under the rising spring sun. Spraying time was approaching, he recalled, which led his mind to that young and eager Harvey Ramuz, who was gaining quite a reputation around here. Recommendations from all sides came to his ears; glowing appraisals, songs of praise were even sung by that pinched Bourget, his remote neighbour. Every time when they met he said:

"Mister Moro, I can truthfully tell you that my apples are crispier and juicier since that young Montrealer sprays our trees. I am thanking our master above for his presence."

Bourget was the first to succumb to Ramuz's sales campaign, whereas Moro so far withstood all his imaginative promotions. He could hear his wife stirring in the house, mind you, not the lopsided shack of years ago, oh no! they now lived in a splendid structure called from Sorel to Lacolle 'La Manse'.

The memory of the police forced itself again upon his mind, which made him chuckle. "How clumsy they were," he informed the river below, that never slowed down in its march, or rather flow of destiny. Between its banks it carried the fierce pride of French Canada, down from the Gaspé coast to the United States. Sometimes this pride was wavering, now and then cowed, causing rifts and anguishes, but it never disappeared completely.

As his fortunes rose, the authorities came down on him with a vengeance. They rode up all the way from Montreal across the mighty St. Lawrence. Self-assured, puffed up by their sense of power, they tried all customary, but ever hackneyed ruses and transparent tricks.

"Where did you obtain the money to suddenly acquire all these properties?" they thundered.

It should be noted that Loti was rumoured to always carry jewels of great value on his person.

"From an inheritance abroad," he unfailingly advised unperturbed.

A thousand questions they asked him, threats alternated with cajoleries, but it was to no avail; a connection between him and the peddler could not be discovered. His refusal to co-operate with them to trace the source of his legacy fuelled their suspicion, but it furnished no cause for indictment. Chagrined the police finally gave up, they left him henceforth in peace.

That was six months ago, they had not bothered him since.

"Leon, Leon," he heard his wife calling.

"What is it?" he wanted to know somewhat irritated to have his train of thought interrupted.

"Don't you see who is coming?"

He looked up and down, but saw nothing except the joy of his bosom: that is rows upon rows of apple trees. They were all his, well, almost, only Louis Bourget, that old grumpy descendant of a string of habitants, refused to sell. But he would get to him in due time, no doubt about it.

Then he saw who was approaching. Harvey Ramuz, the young sprayer waved to him with his usual exuberance. Moro realised instinctively that he would give the young man an order to proceed, but not without playing hard to get.

"Good morning, Mr Moro, I hope all is well with you and your wife."

"Well, well, look who is here, I wonder what he wants," Moro said turning to his wife, who meanwhile had appeared all spruced up.

"It's that time once more, sir. Since I am in the neighbourhood I took the liberty to show my face again. Of course as always, I'm at your service."

"Hm, I am not sure what he means," Moro said with feigned seriousness to his wife.

"Ha, Mr Moro is as always inclined to jest," he informed the smiling woman.

"Are you here to tackle old Bourget's trees?"

"I am, yet this very day. So tomorrow I should be free to take care of yours."

"Ho, ho, not so fast young friend, not so fast," countered Moro with raised hands.

After a little cat and mouse game an agreement was reached. Moro accepted Ramuz's proposal for two reasons; first, his apples last year were not quite to snuff; second, a quarrel with Montague, the sprayer, ensued on account of it. Of course Moro was oblivious of the fact that Ramuz had tampered with Montague's tanks the night before. So it was finally settled; Moro's trees would be sprayed by Ramuz beginning at sunrise the following day.

After he had left, his wife looked quizzical at her husband. It annoyed him, that's why he grumbled:

"Have you never seen me before? My, the way you stare at me one would think so."

"That Ramuz, do you think he can be trusted?"

"And why not? Has he not done a lot of work in this area already? all satisfactory to my knowledge. Come, Marie, what is it that you actually mean?"

She hemmed and hawed visibly ill at ease, all the while evading her husband's reproving glances.

"Nothing really, Leon, it's just that I have my doubts about this fellow."

"Not another of your premonitions," he quipped.

Her answer was an inscrutable smile, so she thought; to him, however, it seemed transparent as clear glass.

Spraying went ahead without a hitch, it took all of three days. After completion Ramuz seemed in a hurry to leave, indeed, he almost did so without his pay. He left his equipment in care of Bourget, who treated him more and more like a son.

Afterwards Marie walked through their orchards every day, which surprised her husband, since it stood in complete contrast to her previous habits. Was she looking for something in particular? perhaps searching for a quiet spot to meditate, or simply going for solitary walks? He could not even hazard a guess, nor would she have known the exact reason. She just followed an urge to be among the freshly sprayed trees.

"What's up, Marie, have apple trees become fascinating to you?" he inquired in a mocking way.

"Not really, Leon, I just noticed that I gained weight during the long winter, exercise should get me back in shape," she explained without looking at him.

A week later she noticed a curious phenomenon; the bark of many boles was peeling off, in particular on higher ground. However, she said nothing for fear to become a target of his merciless derision. Next day all trees in the higher regions were affected, some stood completely bare in the shimmering sun. She now hurried down to tell her husband, and should he scold and laugh to his heart's content.

From thereon things happened rapidly, the fact could no longer be denied: every tree suffered from a rampant pest. Some already stood in the last throes of decay. Marie Moro said it first:

"That miserable scoundrel, he ruined our trees, all ten thousand of them."

Her husband was too stricken to say a word, he just leaned against one of the rutting trees and groaned. It was self-evident: Ramuz had poisoned their orchards. But why? Then something puzzling happened. When Marie cried at the top of her voice:

"Police! fetch the police immediately!" Moro hushed her and held her back.

"Wait, Marie, let me think," he almost entreated.

His head was in a whirl, thoughts of the past obtruded themselves, memories of a strange land leaped at him. His mind raced across the continent, over the vast Pacific, to regions in the shadows of the towering Himalayas. There he met Lukas Loti a long time ago. He was a young man then, reckless and fearless, without a treacherous bone in his body, just full of vim and brimming with the spirit of adventure. True, he stumbled into many scrapes, committed questionable deeds, but all the while he remained decent.

But back in Canada this changed. As it happens so frequently, advancing years carried a corroding substance, which gnawed through the sterling qualities of his youth. Increasing age ate away his idealism till under the pretext of undeserved indigence, he joined the ranks of the corrupt. The willingness to commit deeds for gain, foul or otherwise, developed in due time, only opportunities were lacking – till he got wind of Loti's return. Moro racked his brains to find a connection between Ramuz's knavish act and his acquaintance with Loti, without discovering any. Yet it did exist, also not visible on the surface.

Of course he knew about the diamonds. When the authorities in Paradesh caught up with them, Loti somehow managed to get his precious stones out of harms way before their arrest. In contrast to himself, who was caught red-handed. He lost all, including his freedom of five years.

Finding Loti was not difficult, everybody on the lower St. Lawrence knew him; that is everyone walking in the shadow of the law. Moro was circumspect in his approach, none saw him in the presence of his Paradesh acquaintance, because from day one he harboured unworthy thoughts, especially after he became cognizant of his purported wealth, of which Loti seemed quite unostentatious about.

He slipped a note for his attention, furtively to be sure, at one of Loti's haunts, asking for a clandestine meeting up in St. Hilaire. – I have buyers for all you know what; bring them along. He signed the note Paradesh, which was their password of old.

All went as planned for Moro on that fateful night, with one exception: there was a witness.

Ramuz was a young boy then, barely fifteen years old. His uncle Lukas was all the family he had left. He followed him like a shadow, at the same time learning much about the trade. When they approached the meeting spot, well hidden behind a row of hedges, his uncle bid him to stay behind:

"Stay hidden till I call you," he commanded.

The quietly spoken elder's words were law to the lad, he always heeded them instantly; but not this time. With pounding temples he crept closer to the spot where his uncle had just greeted a man. Young Ramuz heard and saw everything. The silent night allowed words to reach his ears, which were filled with gladness and assurance. Under a rising moon his eyes witnessed an impulsive embrace. All is well, he thought, therefore creeping back to his assigned place seemed advisable, lest he arouse his uncle's ire.

But at the same time things began to happen, so fast, to leave no time for evaluation, let alone to step in or cry out. Suddenly he saw a lightning movement. Arms came up with something shimmering like a scarf, which the stranger slung around his uncle's neck with a single motion. Not a sound was heard. Before he could muster enough will to intervene, all was over. His uncle lay on the ground, his assailant hurried down and disappeared in a nearby house. Ramuz, whose name was actually Marcel Loti, finally found the strength to come to his uncle's aid; albeit too late.

The boy knew instantly what had to be done; he directed all thoughts and energy towards that aim. Nothing was left in the lurch. First he got a good look at the stranger by daylight, he made sure to know the name of the man who had emptied his uncle's pockets. He did not, however, come in possession of all the gems, far from it. How could Moro have known that a boy, hiding behind hedges a mere hundred feet distant, horded the most valuable ones on his body. Of course he knew nothing of the uncle's habit to use his nephew as a decoy, as a mule as it were, that carried the most precious stones sewn in the seams of his baggy clothes.

Young Ramuz said not a word to anyone, except Enzio Cottroni, his uncle's closest associate, and also his godfather. The ancient Corsican code was going to be his guidance, his duty was written in the sunny skies of a proud land. True, he was a mere boy, but time and nature would take care of that.

He waited around Mont St.Hilaire to see his uncle claimed by local friends from Montreal. Afterwards he began to plot his course. Police or other authorities did not exist for him, they never for a moment obscured the road ahead. He changed his name to Harvey Ramuz, cashed in some precious stones, and moved away. But not before saying goodbye to his godfather Cottroni.

"Marcel, my boy, shall I take care of this affair?" he asked.

"No, sir."

"You will manage it for yourself?"

"Yes, sir."

After a silent embrace the elder said:

"You know the pipeline."

The boy nodded and left.

That was six years ago. At nineteen years of age a plan had ripened in his head, it was time to start its implementation. He proceeded with great circumspection to preclude any hitches, as much as not to arouse suspicion. Obtaining the necessary pesticides proved rather difficult. He wanted to do a thorough job; not a twig, not a leaf of grass should ever grow there again.

He had to travel far to strange and forbidden lands to obtain such substances, but he finally succeeded. This liquid of hell resembled regular pesticide in colour and smell, rendering it therefore indistinguishable from them. Even a careful observer would have pronounced it identical; but of course had he sprinkled two or three drops on some growth, any growth, its vastly different nature would have quickly been revealed. Ramuz knew its devastating effect only too well, that's why he disappeared without a trace.

His godfather, however, received a message via the pipeline which only said: "Done." Enzio Cottroni smiled; he was satisfied with his godchild.

Misjudgement

*P*ierre Lamont stared already for days through the peep window in his cell. Steadfastly he directed his sight through the sturdy iron grating over the Ottawa River. What captivated him there would have puzzled even an imaginative observer, because little could be seen except stones and withered grass. Hardly a tree grew on that desolate terrain, not even shrubs thrived on the neglected wasteland. As far as the eye reached, neither settlements nor farms were visible. Only the odd dilapidated hut leaned lopsided in the wind; it was a depressing sight.

But Lamont seemed to think otherwise, he could not separate himself from the view. The guards looked at this harmless pursuit with jaundiced eyes. They first tried with humour, then malice, but finally by means of authoritative force to prevent it. All was in vain; his wistful eyes remained glued to that rocky, unsightly strip of land beyond the restless river. It bothered the wardens to no end. Under the pretext that he was hatching some plot, they started to agitate against him. Lamont either did not notice, or just gave it the cold shoulder.

So it went for some time, back and forth, till a regular tug of war ensued. While the wardens leafed eagerly through the book of rules, in the hope of finding means and ways to a solution, Lamont seized every opportunity to plant himself in front of that peep window. They called it spite, clear defiance, which no self-respecting guard could lamb-like put up with. Something had to be undertaken against such presumption.

Could it not be achieved with deviousness, then force had to be employed. They found no peace any more, it turned into a driving thorn in their flesh. Particularly the chief, an uncouth, ambitious man, took considerable umbrage. That an inmate should glare day in day out at a godforsaken desert he could grudgingly accept; but never the resulting enhancement of his spirit. A pleased inmate would simply be intolerable. No, it may not be! before Lamont returned from his isolation cell, preventative measures had to be taken, so that other, behaving inmates would not be infected by his nonsense.

Now, what induced Pierre Lamont to stare enraptured every available hour at the shores beyond? The opening was small, the stooped position highly uncomfortable, moreover, the view was dismal. Indeed, what had he discovered over there? Did stringent reasons exist why he incessantly combed that insignificant area with his eyes?

Maybe these bare rocks contained a secret which could reveal itself at any moment; or bore the wind over the wilted grass an exceptional message? Nothing nearby warranted such persistent vigil at the barred hole; no, just his inclination to malevolence was responsible, plus of course a distinct recalcitrance. Because when he noticed the indignation of the wardens, manifested through gestures, insinuations, and pointed remarks, he tripled his efforts. One could safely call it such, since his back was already stiff from bending, and his feet hurt from so much standing.

But he did not desist, their vexation became his encouragement. The more dogged they proceeded against him, the more persistent he got absorbed in his observations. The little chicaneries, including more serious bullying, he bore with equanimity. Their cuffs and challenging jostling he accepted with smiles. Nothing robbed him of his composure; the thought of their annoyance and chagrin made him impervious to this meanness. Not even when he was pulled with rough force from his station did he, to everybody's surprise, raise a defensive hand. Why should I? he thought, after all, they were in his pocket, their legs were being pulled.

The wardens did not relent. In their reckoning Lamont had thrown the gauntlet defiantly at their feet. Nothing could convince them that a prisoner, young and impetuous to boot, would day after day spend so much time at an uncomfortable lookout for pure joy. Either he hoped to escape with the aid of allies from the other side, or he played a spiteful game with them. Chief Gilbert maintained doggedly that, while showing his teeth and clapping his thighs sore for fun and amusement, he led them ignominiously around the nose. Their initial benevolence transformed itself gradually to vindictiveness. The tolerantly treated Québecois became now a butt of rude jokes, which soon turned scurrilous.

Under the pretense of discovering a detailed plan whereby he intended to escape, no doubt with the aid of accomplices who were in the midst to prepare all steps at the Quebec side, they approached the superintendent. He stands continually at the little window, they explained, ostensibly to transmit signs to allies, moreover, to receive communications from them.

The superintendent, a sensible man, smirking secretly, nodded his head a few times sympathetically, but no actions were taken. He knew his wardens inside out; they once again nursed a grudge against a prisoner, nothing else, he surmised. To contemplate an escape from that secure cell? Let him, the superintendent chuckled, as the last petitioner closed the door on the way out. Just let him, he will not get far. The requested transfer would in any case have been of little expedience, because all isolation cells afforded a view over the Ottawa River. In six weeks, he advised the next day, he could be housed in another cell of their discretion.

Six weeks? not a chance, that would not do, such a period deemed them untenably long.

When increasing mistreatment, even the craftiest machinations showed little effect, except earning them scorn and disdain, they decided to proceed in earnest. They put their heads together, partook at meetings, talked low at the dining table, till finally a solution was found. From then on the atmosphere throughout the jail changed; it became more relaxed.

Two days later, when Lamont as usual stood at his post, his eyes almost popped out of their sockets. Three figures moved around one of the ramshackle huts which without effort he recognised as men. This change suited him well, then despite his joy over the wardens' chagrin, the peekaboo had slowly become monotonous. With awakened interest he therefore followed the movements over there.

Suddenly he was blinded by a ray of light, which forced him to close his eyes. What now, he thought while opening them again. Once more something flashed before him, now repeatedly, furthermore at set intervals. Once short, then long, as if governed by meaningful timing. No doubt, those men behind the wooden shack tried to catch his attention. Why, for what reasons Lamont cared not, then he was thankful for the diversion. Interested how it would continue, he looked on.

The blinking did not subside, it rather intensified. Oh well, he thought amused, they are having fun. Then the realisation struck him: these signals were meant to convey something. When he associated the signs with Morse signals, it dawned on him that it could only be Gil Lecomte, recently released counterfeiter from his hometown Quebec City, who once worked as wireless operator with the coast guard. Gil intended to send him some news through the means of the Morse code. His joy, however, received a rude damper, because he understood not a syllable of this code. But this did not deter him, his reputation to be resourceful was not just empty tittle-tattle.

When shortly after one of the wardens came along, he approached him with the demeanour of a mendicant friar. In no time the conversation drifted to Samuel Morse and his tricky alphabet, which Lamont would have liked to learn with a burning fervour. No problem, he was assured, the superintendent will be glad to hear of it. Within a scant hour the desired information lay in his hands.

Lamont went to work with the ardour of a zealot. Pen and paper in hand he waited for a sign, which took not long to come. Painstakingly he noted all signals, again and again for the better part of an hour. Then he started translating them, which took the rest of the day. Finally he deciphered their intricacy: an escape was devised to the last detail. It should happen next Monday, shortly after midnight. He needed to feign violent stomach cramps, after which everything would fall in place. This communication was given in French, wherewith it was hoped snoopers would have a more difficult time.

At the stroke of twelve o'clock Lamont began a heart-rending moaning. From there on things fell in line, everything functioned like clockwork; in any case till the moment when he clambered ashore on the other side. Neither Lecomte nor his henchmen were visible, only a deathlike silence all around greeted him. Calling out was out of the question, but then it was not necessary, because behind one of the huts a dim light started to flare up. It shone in short intervals, actually more like a reflection. With his young, healthy legs he ran towards it. He did not get far. The first shot hit him between the shoulder blades; the second one somewhat lower; the third he heard no more.

The ensuing investigation disclosed the fact that Lamont almost succeeded to escape. It was a close call, only the watchfulness of Chief Gilbert and some of his deputies thwarted his flight. Repeated urgings to halt, the same as warning shots, remained unheeded; he ran towards one of the shacks without stopping. After a weapon was noticed in his hand, there remained no choice. The shooting, although regrettable, was necessary.

The superintendent read the chief's report with knitted brow and puckered lips, but he said nothing.

Snarl Tiger, Snarl

*U*lal Dhali had learned about tigers and snakes before he could walk. From the day his spindly legs supported his skin and bones body, he was on the prowl for them; not the tigers, but snakes. Tigers he avoided, although the prices paid for a decent specimen, especially by zoos, were quite an allurement. Poisonous snakes fell into a different category. Killed and delivered, they fetched a bounty; small, yet welcome where short commons reigned.

Almost every day he scoured the area for them. He grew quite adept at ferreting them out. So much so, that over the years the ministry cited him several times for special services rendered. He even caught the eye of the minister, who ordered a plaque to be issued to the youngster, praising him for his indefatigable work.

"Tell us your secret," he was asked.

Well, what the authorities did not know, and no one could guess, was the fact that Ulal bred the snakes, which he turned in for head money. Sochurekis were his favourite trade. It is one of the smallest, yet deadliest viper on earth. Their venom kills, or lames for life. He learned to handle them so adeptly that, although more aggressive than the black mamba, they had not left a scratch on his skin.

One day Ulal wandered through the jungle on the lookout for them, when all at once a din assailed his ears, which instinctively made him scurry behind some dense underbrush. Listening with a leaping heart he made out voices, shrill and insistent, trying to drown out the snarls of an enraged beast. He knew that ferocious growl, fuelled by savage fury, heightened by panic. A group of men had cornered a tiger, that was it. He remained cowering in his hiding place till silence reigned. No amount of curiosity managed to entice him to rush, for he was aware of a wounded, or provoked tiger's uncontrollable wrath.

Approaching with the innate caution of a feral being, he saw the spot where the path made a sharp turn. Signs of a fierce struggle were everywhere. Trampled down bushes, flattened brush and turned up earth gave evidence of a spectacular encounter, in which the tiger got the worst of it, judging by appearances.

Ulal stood in awe, ready to bolt at the slightest sign of danger. Tiger and men were gone. Although beyond his range of vision, he could hear them far down the path. The men were laughing and singing amid a tiger's roars, followed by blood curdling growls, which the combined fiends between heaven and earth could not have imitated. He recognised the signs; the tiger, a man-eater no doubt, got his punishment.

"Serves him right," Ulal muttered as he turned, ready to go back.

Just then something caught his eye; there was an almost imperceptible movement at the clearing's edge. A small animal, looking at first sight like a kitten, cautiously made its way into the opening. Quite curious now, Ulal turned fully towards the little creature. He mused:

"It couldn't be a cat, which in less than a minute would have been torn to pieces. Oh, I see, it's a tiger cub, still blind by the looks of it."

Sidling up to it for no particular reason, an idea suddenly struck him, a notion heartily condemned later. In fact, it adversely affected the lives of many people. That, however, lay in the future. Right now he thought of his uncle, the venerated chief of Tagish, whose fondest wish might soon be fulfilled. Chief Wangiri, a surrogate father to him since the death of his own, was bent on obtaining a tiger cub, to be trained in the fashion of the Khans of Tatary. There, before his eyes groped the object of his uncle's desire. He decided to catch the helpless whelp.

Helpless? Ulal discovered something different. Though still blind and scared, the little rascal proved to be neither meek nor defenceless. Such hissing, spitting and scratching, one couldn't have imagined from a small, just born animal. Ulal finally managed to subdue the struggling ball of fury, which for a while strained every muscle in his small body to escape.

"Go on, sputter, kick to your heart's content, this very day you will make uncle Wangiri happy," Ulal remarked.

Moved by gratitude, he was about to pat the struggling cub, but decided against it. His steps lightened by his uncle's anticipated joy, he hastened towards the village.

Chief Wangiri's delight knew no bounds. Moved to tears of joy he announced a regal feast to be held in Ulal's honour. First, however, appropriate quarters had to be erected for the little imp. They all knew how quickly tigers grow, hence a suitable compound was built without delay.

From the start the chief and Timbur, so he named the tiger, got along famously. When nearly grown to maturity he showed an astounding devotion to the chief. Though quite ferocious generally, he literally licked his hands. The time came when Wangiri entered Timbur's enclosure without trepidation.

"Soon I can take my tiger out for hunting," he announced.

"You are all invited to watch. Look well, and remember, spread the word in every direction. Fame awaits us, Tagish will be entered in the books of annals."

Hearing this, some chuckled, others snickered, but most nodded approvingly. Chief Wangiri paid no heed to his detractors, for he felt the hand of destiny patting him on the back. Most villagers, though deeming his assertions tinged with talkee-talkee, nevertheless continued to respect and trust him implicitly. The old man, a formidable warrior in his younger years, was considered to be a sage.

"Ask Wangiri," exasperated fathers told their errand sons.

"Let's consult the chief," perplexed people advised.

"Wangiri shall decide," disputants cried.

He was not only venerated, but held up as the epitome of prudence.

"He seldom errs," it was said.

"He knows the mind of men and beast."

Yet, he was tricked by a tiger. It happened towards the end of the summer monsoon, which from the beginning behaved erratically. Indeed, the weather, as a rule predictable in that region, alternated between fickleness and caprice; so much so that the best of augurs felt stumped to make a forecast.

The season did not, as expected, arrive tentatively, but assailed the highlands with full force at once. The wind's direction changed virtually overnight, lashing heavy rain across Nagaland. None of the villagers had anticipated such a rapid turn of events. Invariably weeks pass, if not a month, before the full cycle of the season is reached.

Not this year however, far from it. From the day when the monsoon changed direction, it rained day in, day out. The relentless downpour caused the matted grass walls and thatched roofs to absorb buckets of water. The heat too inflicted a measure of discomfort on young and old. Constantly soaked to the skin, either from perspiration or rain, people experienced the full extent of misery.

Halfway through the season a pungent smell saturated the air. Nagalanders, not known for their squeamishness, turned up their noses in disgust. The abominable weather was not their sole source of discomfort, which acquired a greater degree due to the scarcity of game. To make matters worse, a rinderpest broke out. Men, women and children raised a chorus of lamentation, when it became known.

"Hardship is knocking at our doors, we can see hunger lurking on our doorsteps."

Indeed, food grew scarcer, while anxieties mushroomed. All eyes turned towards the chief, pleading silently for help.

"Your wisdom alone can save us," their worried countenances expressed.

Wangiri, though not quite ready to act, nevertheless contrived a plan, which he laid before the counsel of elders.

"Our plight will soon be over," he announced.

"How so? crops are failing, game has fled, and cows are dropping like dead flies," he was reminded.

"My tiger will find the elusive quarry," he promised.

Hearing this, even doubters and detractors moved their heads as if to say: "A fanciful scheme is better than none at all." The idea found general acclaim, it sure warranted a try, they agreed. The chief advised:

"Prudence must be our guidance, hence time is needed to make the necessary preparations. Let's say, in ten days we start."

"Why so late?" Tewahli inquired.

"The tiger must be initiated first," Wangiri answered.

Then he explained:

"Timbur never hunted, neither for himself nor on his master's behest. To be sure, he is a model of obedience within the compound, but how wide-open terrain affects him remains to be seen. Consequently some outside training is required."

That made sense. The elders nodded and left, assured that their sagacious chief had matters well in hand.

Now, the village of Tagish counted among its inhabitants the regional wiseacre. Old, shrivelled, and crotchety he was, yet reputed to burst with wisdom up to his gills. He visited chief Wangiri as two of the inevitable dawdlers left.

"Wangiri, I hear you want to use your tiger for the chase. Good idea, very laudable, if you are serious, of course," he commented.

"I am."

Clicking his tongue, then smacking his lips, the wiseacre moved his head and raised both eyebrows in a way that exasperated the chief. Words that followed annoyed him even more.

"Wangiri, you need advise. But first let me tell you about Umat."

"Who is Umat?" Wangiri interrupted.

"Was, chief, was. It happened a long time ago, more than fifty years, when Umat, noted throughout the Naga Hills as 'Know-it-all' met his fate."

"What are you saying?" Wangiri asked visibly annoyed.

"This Umat, like you, trained a tiger for the chase. All went well up to the first hunting trip. When he whistled, the tiger came hopping; at the command, run! that huge cat ran faster than sound; when his master ordered to stop, the brute came to a screeching halt."

"So, what went wrong?"

"The tiger had lost his instinct. As mentioned, he conducted himself well in and outside the enclosure. But hunting? not that mollycoddle. Anyway, when the time seemed ripe to seal his fame, Umat invited an elite of warriors and hunters to witness a singular performance. A sumptuous feast was scheduled after the first hunt ever with a tiger."

"It was not a success, I deduce."

"Miserable failure would be a better description. I was present. Although still a stripling, I considered myself to be a keen observer. That beast made Umat look like a braggart fool, it showed not the slightest intention to hunt. At Umat's cries of 'tallyho! tallyho!' the tiger merely blinked and inclined his head as if to say: 'What's gotten into you, master?' Then he yawned and stretched himself out on the ground."

"I am surprised to hear it," Wangiri remarked.

"Not I. Overfed and pampered, the tiger had lost the desire to hunt; for himself and for his master. What that beast thought, I can not say, but the villagers' reaction I recall vividly."

"No doubt, do tell me about it," the chief encouraged.

"He was derided mercilessly, mocked by children, taunted by youngsters, and ultimately chased out of town. Now to my advice. Curtail the tiger's ration down to starvation limits. Do it gradually, day by day, till the beast learns to beg for more."

"Timbur will balk."

"Let him. A lean tiger will be more eager to please. After each satisfactory run, reward him, not before."

At first the chief scoffed at the old man's counsel, whom he deemed ignorant anyway, despite his claim to sagacity. Yet thinking about it for awhile, it started to make sense. "Besides, what have I got to lose," he told himself. Of course the growing food shortage also needed to be considered.

The following days Timbur's ration were diminished gradually. Little did Wangiri realise that by doing so he poked his head in the proverbial hornets' nest, from which, like many a greedy bear, he would be unable to extricate himself again. It took several days, however, to manifest itself.

On the new regiment's first day, not much happened. Timbur, after noisily devouring the reduced hunk of meat, looked inquiringly at his master: "Where is the rest?" he seemed to ask. On the second and subsequent days the situation became precarious, then risky, and ultimately outright ugly. Timbur did not accept the incremental reduction of his daily fare demurely. The old wiseacre's prediction held true in part only. Hunger made the tiger more compliant, but also irritable. Besides, it stirred its feral instinct. Wangiri, surrounded by a sea of anxiety, paid little heed to a dumb animal's antics, as he labeled them.

It turned out that the tiger neither acted prankish, nor could he be called dull-witted. On the fifth day Timbur's behaviour changed drastically. As always when the chief approached, he emitted sounds of welcome, consisting of soft grunts and inviting purrs. On the surface he appeared tractable as ever, but his movements, invariable lithe and confident, were strangely angular. Also his voice had an ominous undertone. Nevertheless, he licked his chief's hands submissively as expected; but that was before devouring his ration. After the last morsel disappeared in the ravenous maw of the tiger, he uttered a loud whoof, then growling menacingly he grabbed the chief's hand; not playful as before, yet neither with any measure of force.

After that incident calamity's silhouette loomed in the mountains, but no one saw it. That evening, as darkness descended over the afflicted highlands, Timbur kicked up a row which drowned out the jungle's myriad voices, and set the inhabitants' teeth on edge. It wasn't a roar really, but a nerve racking din, eerie and abnormal for the lord of the jungle. Timbur gave it no rest. Bawling one moment like a being with a wounded soul, bellowing the next in a manner of an enraged bull, his unearthly calls resounded through the night.

Came the next day the tiger had shed all vestiges of docility. Snarling like a fiend unleashed, he glared at his approaching master. A demoniacal glint illuminated his eyes, it could no longer be denied: the magnificent beast's baser nature had gotten the upper hand. Startled, the chief stopped in his tracks. It saved his life, for the raging, belching brute hurled himself forward, as if intending to attack, should he enter the enclosure.

Chief Wangiri, though old and not so nimble anymore, did not flinch easily. In his breast still beat a stout heart. Never since childhood had he shied off from a fray, nor was he inclined to do so now. His slumbering fighting spirit reared its head; he would teach the beast a lesson, starting right this moment. Boldly he stepped towards the fuming tiger, who seemed startled by this brazen move.

"Down, Timbur! down!" the chief hollered at the top of his voice.

That command, till now obeyed before fully pronounced, failed to show any success. Repeating it in a more imperious tone, merely fanned the tiger's wrath.

"I will starve you into submission," the chief threatened, while walking away.

A pitched battle of wills now ensued. Wangiri resolved to match his mettle against his ornery pet, which roared and growled every hour of the day, and throughout the night. Although his compound stood some distance from the village, the inhabitants soon started to grumble. After four days and nights of this inhuman clamour, their gore rose. At daybreak the next morning a group of warriors presented themselves at the chief's hut. Out of their midst stepped Hamun, the venerated elder.

"Wangiri, the tiger must go," he announced.

Taken aback, but also feeling guilty and sheepish, the chief remonstrated:

"Wait a few days, his good manners will be back."

Hamun showed no willingness to yield.

"Let him out today, or we will force the locks and do it ourselves before nightfall," he reiterated.

It was an audacious request to make to one's chief, who harboured no doubts about their resolve. It was not meant as a threat, necessity dictated that the tiger be removed for more than one reason: shortage of food, and abundance of noise.

With a heavy heart, somewhat contrite, but no less angry at the world, Wangiri walked towards the enclosure. Wary in mind and sluggish in body, he plodded through the rain. His fondest hopes were dashed, a most precious expectation turned out to be imaginary. What should he do, or rather what could he do? Keeping the tiger, his pride and joy was not in the cards. Feeding him any longer full rations seemed untenable, considering the scarcity of game. Keeping him underfed would surely prove disastrous, more so if he took him out to hunt.

While racking his brain to find a solution, he came into the tiger's field of vision. Hardly had he done so, when an odd sensation gripped him. Glued to the ground, with dilated eyes and pricked ears, he tried to ascertain what was happening. At first he refused to acknowledge the phenomenon before him, yet it could not be denied: the raving beast had become a peaceable lamb. Crouching low, moaning piteously like an ingratiating dog begging for mercy, the huge cat, ferocious like ten demons a moment ago, wanted to make amends. It took a while to sink in, to realise and acknowledge that his struggle was not in vain; Timbur was ready for the hunt.

"I have won the contest," he whispered with tears welling up in his eyes.

Still a bit apprehensive, the chief mused whether to go inside directly, or rush back for some meat. The tiger's submissive attitude, which was manifested through beseeching expressions and wooing utterances, decided his actions. Never had he seen such joy in his pet before as when he approached the gate and opened the locks. It was the end of chief Wangiri; he became Timbur's first prey.

Emitting a bloodcurdling roar, followed by vicious snarls, Timbur pounced upon his master, who neither had time to cry out, nor possessed the presence of mind to jump back and secure the locks again. With one swipe the brute's powerful paws severed Wangiri's vocal cords. Then his deadly jaws opened wide and closed on the chief's neck with a crunching sound. In a few seconds beast and man disappeared in the jungle.

The Hermit

*T*he message that changed his life reached him on a raw September afternoon. The wind, gathering strength by the hour, moaned through the treetops. It was cold and snowing. Up in the Standard Mountains of British Columbia winter starts early, snow accumulates fast, it can fall any time of the year.

Brent Shehan, the sole inhabitant of a vast wilderness traversed by torrential creeks and rivers, seldom received visitors. That suited him fine, for he was fed up to the teeth with people. In fact, he had turned his back on them many years ago.

Edward Tanner, known as 'Eddie the mouth', had just arrived from the valley. He was one of the very few men welcome at his camp.

"What's new, Eddie?" Shehan asked.

"Gold is on the rise. As of yesterday it sells for six hundred and fifty dollars an ounce."

Shehan, seldom up to date in these matters, whistled appreciatingly:

"Good news old chap, I'm on my way to riches."

Rubbing his hands gleefully, he reached out and produced a vial nearly filled with gold nuggets. Shaking the glass in a roguish manner, he exclaimed:

"Here, me son, are five ounces, multiply that by six hundred and fifty, what do you get?"

Eddie scratched his head, for unlike Shehan, a certified accountant, reckoning was not his strong point. Shehan, though quite aware of that, never let a chance go by without having a bit of fun. Pursing his lips, Eddie offered sheepishly:

"I don't know exactly, but I gather it will tide you over the winter."

"And then some," Shehan chuckled.

After more small talk Eddie burst out:

"Sid is in jail."

"Sid Logan?"

"So I hear."

Bolting upright, Shehan cried:

"Sid in prison? where, what for?"

Taken aback by Shehan's vehement reaction, Tanner answered:

"He is held in solitary confinement in the New Westminster penitentiary; what for, I don't know."

"Who told you that?"

"Marc Wissel, down in Revelstoke. You might remember him, he used to be a teacher in Salmon Arm."

Receiving a nod, he continued:

"Wissel returned from the coast a few days ago, where he read an article in the Vancouver Sun; picture and all, describing Sid's situation. Of course he recognised him instantly, since they prospected together near Walter's place in the past."

Shehan couldn't help glowering at Tanner, although he realised it was unfair. However, his reproachful attitude relaxed when he noticed Eddie's hurt expression. The generally placid demeanour of the corpulent grocer underwent a drastic change. He appeared to be wobbling between an urge to say more, and an impulse to swallow what lay on his tongue.

Feeling sorry and guilty, Shehan was about to tender an apology, when Tanner started to hem and haw, while fidgeting repeatedly. It annoyed Shehan.

"What's the matter, Eddie, you got the jitters?" he mocked.

"Sid is going to hang," Tanner announced.

That remark brought Shehan to his feet again. Raising a hand, shaking his head in disbelief, he remonstrated:

"No way, Eddie, you must have your information mixed up."

Miffed, Tanner pulled a clipping from his pocket, which he thrust at Shehan.

"Here, read it yourself," he commented, quite peeved by now.

He resented Shehan's attitude, hostile he called it, for no reason at all. Thanks should be his dues for keeping him posted. Besides, he sold his placer gold, stocked his favoured provisions in his store, plus personally made deliveries, trekking through the most inhospitable terrain imaginable. All in support of this strange man's quirky propensity towards people and civilisation, which he abhorred and shunned like the devil shuns holy water.

Tanner, a good-natured man, albeit inclined to prattle, perceived Shehan's treatment like a stab through his artless heart. He was made to feel guilty for Logan's plight. He knew Sid Logan, probable far better than Shehan. Some years back he sold him many sides of bacon, sacs of flour, plus tins of coffee and sugar.

In those days, Logan, a secretive, taciturn fellow, prospected up and down the Selkirks, right to the Great Divide. He sure was, most likely still is an odd fish, Tanner mused. Veiled in clouds of mystery, cloaked in layers of rumours, Sid Logan walked in the boots of a modern day Midas, who staked more sure-fire claims than anyone else.

One of them was the successful Mars Mining Property, now defunct and occupied by Brent Shehan. Tanner recalled the ballyhoo surrounding the mine, owned partially by Logan, its president. Out of the blue, practically over night, the facility was closed. Why? people asked. The industry expressed astonishment, the workers wailed in dismay, searching for reasons, yet finding none. An odour of suspicion rose, thicker than morning fog. Accusations were made. The local newspaper, true to form, cast aspersions wrapped in innuendoes blindly aimed. The abstruse man, known by many, yet familiar to few, left the area without saying goodbye.

Some years later, on a gusty spring day, Tanner's store received a visitor. Springing to his feet, stretching out both hands, Tanner cried:

"Sid, how the devil are you?"

Then hearing the man speak, he stopped dead in his tracks. It was not him, but by golly his twin brother, Tanner surmised; yet the stranger set him quickly right.

"I am Brent Shehan, the manager of the Mars property," he announced in a tone of finality, which brooked no further inquiries.

Realising his mistake, but incredulity mirroring in his eyes, Tanner offered an apology:

"Sorry for the mistake. No offence, barring your accent I would insist you are Sid Logan; the resemblance is striking."

So it was, moreover in several ways, Tanner soon found out. After closer acquaintance another amazing analogy revealed itself. Logan's tendency for secretiveness was easily trumped by Shehan. That man turned out to be a veritable clam. Tanner, no slouch at pumping, extracted next to nothing from him; neither about himself, others, nor anything at all. Strange to say he talked freely, but the more he said, the less he disclosed. This much Tanner was told:

"Sid Logan sent me to make an inventory."

That and no more Tanner learned when he tried to draw him out. The question:

"Will you be here long?" earned him a withering look. With knitted brow and a pinched mouth Shehan replied:

"It all depends."

Eighteen months later he was still there with only a dog to keep him company, ensconced for life, so it deemed Tanner. A camaraderie developed between the two, falling short, however, of intimacy, rebuffed by Shehan. Tanner's confiding nature, his come-hither attitude cried foul when confronted by Shehan's offish deportment, whose exquisite manners attracted and repelled him simultaneously.

Nevertheless, he liked and respected the Irishman, who, willing or not, became privy to his life's story from birth to yesterday. Shehan's past in contrast, plus to some extend the present, remained a closed book to Tanner and others.

Tanner was not quite the gawk some believed him to be. Behind that unaccommodating front he recognised an uncommon character. He was willing to bet that Brent Shehan, the quirky recluse, was a good friend. As it turned out, he would have won the wager.

Shehan stood outside his cabin watching Eddie ambling back towards the road. His friend seemed irritated, judging by his movements and gestures. Shehan paid scant attention. Deep in thought, oblivious to the swirling snowflakes melting on his face, his mind travelled to the streets of Calgary. There he first met Sid Logan, an enigma, if ever there existed one. No soothsayer on earth, not all the oracles of ancient times could have predicted what was about to happen.

He had just lost his job again, the fifth within three months. A brilliant accountant, government approved, one is entitled to think should find and hold a position hands down. Why did he neither, in a burgeoning economy to boot? Indeed, a puzzling fact, a riddle even to himself. Not because he could no longer work at his profession, but why it got thus far.

Tremors, having arisen from nowhere made writing a chore. It wasn't so bad till he consulted a team of doctors. Parkinson's disease, they diagnosed. Symptoms were explained to him, as much as aggravations and time frames, which he felt a compulsion to heed.

Soon he was unable to hold a pen between his fingers, let alone write legible. That in itself would not have prevented him from earning a living, since hundreds of openings existed for a bright young man. The problem pervading his present dismal situation lay elsewhere; it was a growing resentment for society and people, which by degrees intensified till hate, born of fear, became paramount.

Such sentiments, gradually drying up life's juices, and making the spirit groan, overwhelmed him. Parkinson's disease, whose existence Shehan increasingly doubted, nevertheless took its toll. Deeper and deeper he waded into the proverbial Serbonian Bog. Lately he felt a sea of misery rising to his neck. Then he met Sid Logan. As he sat brooding on a roadside bench, oblivious to everything except his own wretchedness, he was suddenly hailed:

"What do you know, my Doppelgänger!" someone cried in his ears.

Annoyed, Shehan raised his head. He blinked, then opened his eyes wide. In front of him stood a man looking like himself. The resemblance, striking at first glance, became less distinct on closer contemplation, but it was still remarkable. They surely could have been mistaken for brothers.

Shehan, too listless to rise and scamper, let his head drop, hoping that the intruder would go away; for misery resents to be distracted, certainly not by good cheer. It is a Moloch, feeding on illness, disaster, and despair. Yet the man standing before him evidently had little sympathy for stricken souls and challenged minds. He invited him boisterously for a stroll to the miner's club.

"Leave me alone," Shehan moaned.

"Not a chance. Leaving my double wilting on a bench? not Sid Logan. Get up, we are going to hoist a few."

This was Calgary in the fifties, a Stetson tipping, good and lively place, taking its reputation as Canada's last frontier serious. Oil had been discovered in the Leduc area, changing land and attitudes profoundly. An excitement lay over the foothills that lightened people's steps, and filled the air with an intoxicating ozone.

Ranchers and cowboys a few months ago, petroleum magnates today, walked jauntingly through the streets of Calgary. Risks were taken, fortunes made and lost with neither a whoopee nor a whimper.

Sid Logan was in his element among these bold and a trifle haughty men, they were cut from the same cloth as he. Unlike this heap of misery, whom he was ready to take by the scruff of the neck and drag to the club. It proved not necessary, Shehan came along without further prompting.

It was a hot sunny day, barely a week away from the stampede, when the old friendly ways of the West are being revived for a spell. Sitting in a chair in the sumptuous lounge, Shehan thought more than he said. He still had the wind up; distrust made him wary, and vexation morose. He could not think of one reason why a man, successful by appearances in more than one way, should occupy himself with a seeming loiterer spending his time on a public bench. Nevertheless, he started to open up. Logan sure had a knack for drawing a man out. Being neither devious nor scornful, yet with an air of authority and brotherly concern, he asked questions. So he became privy to Shehan's grief. He scolded him:

"You are a fool, Shehan, a poor excuse of a man. Instead of moping and sitting around like a warmed up corpse, you should be pounding the pavement looking for something to do."

"Easy said by someone sound in body and mind," Shehan countered.

"Why, are you sick?"

"Can't you see it?" Shehan cried.

Saying that he stretched out both hands. To his surprise Logan laughed, he broke out in a regular guffaw. Shehan winced, he didn't want anybody's attention directed towards him. But none turned their head, or even batted an eyelash, for everyone in the club was familiar with Logan's boisterous outbursts.

"You want a job?" he asked Shehan.

"Yes, but I wouldn't last."

"Why not?"

"I – I can't, how shall I say it, I can't work with or near people."

Logan, giving him the once over, inquired:

"What about bears, can you abide them?"

With a pained expression, Shehan remonstrated:

"Don't scoff, I got Parkinson's disease, aggravated enough to be terminal."

"Piffle man, and piffle again, you got the willies, nothing more. How old are you?"

"Thirty-five."

"And you are talking about doom and dying. Man alive, don't you know where you live?"

Receiving no answer, Logan roared:

"In Canada's west, and no mistake about it. Wipe that hangdog look off your face and listen. But first answer my question."

"Which one?"

"Can you live and work among bears and wolves?"

"I don't understand what you mean."

In lieu of an explanation, Logan posed another question:

"Do you know the Selkirks?"

"No. What, and where are they?" he asked disinterestedly.

"Just across the Great Divide. I got a job for you there, it will keep you afloat, plus chase the bees from your bonnet. Are you interested?"

"I – I think so," Shehan replied not exactly enthused.

"Well, I will explain the details. Remember now, you will be all alone, your next neighbour is Ed Tanner, known as Eddie the mouth."

"How far distance is he?"

"Oh, a good twelve miles downhill."

After making himself absolutely clear, Logan asked:

"Is it a go?"

It was.

Two years had passed since then, it was the happiest period of his life. For the first time since childhood he felt at peace with himself. The rapacious beast ambition had been subdued. As the poisonous craving for admiration disappeared, so did Parkinson's disease. Within a month there remained not a hint of palsy, nor a tinge of anxiety. He felt whole, young and healthy, all thanks to Sid Logan, the most enigmatic character he had ever met.

Sid must be well off, Shehan thought, for not once had he asked for a report, nor questioned the amounts of money sent him. As per agreement fifty percent of the proceeds from equipment sales belonged to him, the rest went to an account in Calgary. The entire returns from placer mining were his. With the value of gold rising, his little hoard was worth a tidy sum. All thanks to Sid Logan, who now it seemed, would end his life at the end of a rope.

What a pity to see that happen to a man to whom one owes so much. Shehan felt troubled by vivid memories, pleasant, but no less disquieting. He would never forget that momentous encounter on the streets of Calgary, nor what took place in the miner's club. What an experience, what a man!

After stating his generous intentions, Logan wrote out and signed a most liberal agreement, which he handed him along with sufficient funds to get established. Still suspicious, yet more astounded, Shehan asked:

"Sid, why are you doing this for me?"

Logan, cocking his head, winked mischievously, then said:

"Because I like your Irish accent."

That was vintage Logan, he learned later. Everybody who knew him had stories to relate, attesting to his eccentricity and largess. True, some of these narratives sounded like tales of the tub, but only to someone unfamiliar with the man.

Eddie, in the meantime, had disappeared from his sight, he was alone again. Stepping inside the cabin he read the article once more. Then he sat down, propped his head on both elbows and tried to come to grips with the gruesome reality of Sid's date with death.

Six weeks from now, the man who made him a present of life, would lose his own. Sad it was, but unavoidable. Confused, downcast, and riven by contrary forces, Shehan slumped deeper. Notions raced through his head; some shameful, like the hope to end up with the property after Logan's demise; others, ruffling his conscience, bid him to help his benefactor. Contradictory voices filled his ears, appealing to common sense, urging to accept the inevitable with equanimity. But they were interrupted by indignant shouts demanding to be obeyed:

"It may not be, Brent Shehan, you owe a debt, you must prevent it. Find a way, find a way!"

How could he? Night was falling when common sense still wrangled with his conscience, which ultimately gained the upper hand. He would help Sid to escape. By what means needed to be reasoned out. He racked his brains for many hours, yet found no solution. Short of storming the jail single-handed, surely a harebrained idea, he couldn't think of any scheme to free his friend. A notion to bribe the governor arose, which was quicker repudiated than expanded. He finally concluded that nothing could be done on his part. To save Sid required a miracle.

Midnight approached when he suddenly bounded from his seat, crying out:

"I got it, I got it!"

Gripped by a feverish excitement he stepped outside. The pitch-dark night, soothing to calm natures, hostile to fractious ones, left him untouched. He was busy hatching out details of his just conceived idea.

Next morning he knocked at Tanner's door.

"I need a favour, Eddie," he announced.

"What is it?"

"Can I leave my dog with you until I return?"

"Most certainly. When will you be back?"

Shehan didn't answer immediately, he contemplated Eddie silently for a moment. Tanner couldn't help thinking that his friend was saying goodbye for good.

"It depends," Shehan answered.

Then extending his hand, he said:

"Take care, Eddie."

In Revelstoke Shehan sold all his gold. He uttered not a word about his intentions. To the gold commissioner, whom he knew, he handed an envelope with the words:

"Give this to Ed Tanner if I'm not back by Christmas."

On the same day he stepped onto a train heading west to the coast. "Six weeks," he muttered when alone, enough time to put in motion the boldest plan ever devised. His name would be remembered for decades. "A friend indeed," people will say. "A boon to any man." He could hear chuckles, but also curses rolling over the tongues of officials, who might perceive an escape from their stranglehold as a personal defeat. No doubt, they would clamour for retribution.

But what could they do to him? After all, laws that can be manipulated to punish, could also be wangled to protect. It won't be easy he realised, to get Sid out, yet meticulous preparations, steady nerves, plus a dash of good luck, should bring success.

Unfortunately there was a rub. The previous, all forgotten affliction, reared its head again. Fuelled by unwonted excitement, encountering rampant apprehension rather than combativeness, it soon acquired alarming proportions. By the time he stepped off the train, palsy had him in its grip once more. This would never do, he told himself, for it endangered his mission.

He therefore resolved to tackle the recurring malady, presumably conquered, right after suitable quarters were found. Renting furnished apartments proved not difficult. After a day's search he moved to a flat high above the historic Fraser River. Although the sight of murky water and muddy banks cast a shadow over his senses, he had chosen the comfortable rooms because of their proximity to the prison.

Shehan felt depressed by the drab surrounding, inhabited by cheerless people scurrying over never ending pavement. It was a sorry sight, which from day one awakened a profound nostalgia for the pristine Selkirks.

Brushing aside such sentiments, he led his thoughts to weightier matters; at least he tried to with various success. It proved not easy to do, for the former trouble played the deuce with him in a most remarkable fashion, causing uncertainty whether to laugh, scream, or cry. An experience, a conundrum really, drove him to distraction.

One day while puzzling over details of his slowly ripening plan, deep in thought for how long only heaven knew, he became aware of a peculiar fact, which he could not immediately name. Suddenly it dawned on him: his tremors had disappeared. Pleased, also baffled, he stopped what he was doing. As he watched his hands, waiting, growing tense, watching and waiting for what he could not say, rather dared not admit, the tremors returned. Tentatively at first, then as if obeying a silent command, they assailed him with renewed fury.

Shehan was not a stupid man; besides, the lone life amid undisturbed nature had taught him more than perfunctory wisdom. He began to understand a simple, though incredible fact: Although feared and hated, the tremors were subconsciously welcomed. It sounded far-fetched, nonsensical really, yet the realisation eased his mind and soothed his nerves.

So far he had not visited Logan yet, in fact he deliberately avoided the precinct of the prison. Meanwhile he learned a few details about his friend's situation. Murder in the first degree read the indictment, guilty as charged decided the jury. It appeared that Sid offered no contest, or rather tried to. But the judge, in accordance with the law rejected the plea. He appointed a lawyer by the name of Marc Bertram, whose offices were located nearby.

Shehan's first impulse, which he luckily suppressed, was to rush out and knock at Mr Bertram's door. Talking to the lawyer would have satisfied a burning curiosity, but at the same time might have jeopardised his intentions. His plan was hatched, implementing it required additional thought and effort.

First, his disguise had to be dealt with before the next step, finding an intermediary, could be inaugurated. The striking resemblance needed to be dealt with. It took a while to find a solution. At first he tried mascara and masks, which gave him a grotesque appearance. Looking in the mirror, he felt like the great serpent who swooned at the sight of its reflection in the water. But he finally hit upon a simple method that suited his scheme. Alone the drastic change in clothes should divert anyone's attention from the face.

The next step, a more difficult one, consisted of the procurement of a priest's habit, including necessary trimmings. It turned out to be an exhausting and bothersome job; so much so, that for an insane moment he considered abducting, and if need be murdering a clergyman to obtain his attire.

Desperate, since time was marching on, he tried rental outlets and pawnshops, where he received nothing but askance stares.

"It's against the law," one man told him.

"You need police clearance to wear it," another remarked censoriously.

When he told them he needed it for theatrical purposes, they shook their heads and bid him good day.

One rainy afternoon he walked aimlessly along Wharf Street, possibly the gloomiest section of the town. He passed a string of stores, dingy, but stocked liberally with vessel supplies, plus a variety of other merchandise. Across the tracks

the great river's turbid water depressed him even further.
Discouraged, occupied with dreary thoughts, he took scant
notice of the men, Asians mostly, who stood outside chatting
and offering their wares in colourful accents. The odd one tried
to engage him in conversation, but quickly swallowed his
words when Shehan's reprimanding scowl bore right through
his genuine heart. One fellow planted himself right in his path,
gobbling in his ears:

"Come, mister, inside, I have everything you want."

More intrigued by the Chinese's misuse of the English
language than his specious offer, Shehan halted his steps. Of
course that was grist to the chandler's mill. He knew the fish
was hooked, reeling him in should be a trifle. Opening the door
wide he entreated:

"Come, mister, I show you."

The place was chock-full with boat accessories, clothing,
and an array of curiosities. With a sweep of both hands the
Chinese exclaimed:

"Tell me what you want, I have it."

By golly, Shehan thought, I'm going to have a bit of fun
with this chap.

"You are sure you got what I want?" he asked with tongue
in cheek.

"Quite sure."

"I need a priest's outfit."

"Outfit, outfit, priest?" the chandler echoed, obviously not
quite comprehending.

Then his face lit up, his eyes wandered up and down
Shehan's body, as though taking his measurements. If the
unusual request astonished the dealer, he showed no sign of it.
Nodding his head he declared:

"I have what makes you look like a priest. Come back
tomorrow noon, all will be ready."

"Cassock, cross, rosary?" Shehan questioned still more than
a bit dubious.

"Everything. Tomorrow noon," he affirmed.

"How much?"

"Cost?"

"Yes."

Without blinking the Chinese replied:

"Five hundred dollars."

Raising his eyebrows, Shehan protested:

"That's a cut-throat price."

Untouched by the objection, the chandler repeated in a tone of finality:

"Five hundred dollars, come back tomorrow."

As promised, next day at the agreed hour, the chandler proudly presented the desired ware.

"Try it on," he recommended.

Shehan did, then grunted satisfied.

"It will do," he muttered, whereafter money changed hands.

Not a muscle twitched in the Chinese's face as he counted the bank notes.

"Thank you, come again," he remarked.

"Not likely," Shehan said under his breath, as he stepped outside.

"A priest is here to see you, Mr Bertram," the secretary announced a week later.

"A priest?" the lawyer parroted.

"Yes, a Father O'Reilly wants to talk to you about Sid Logan."

Hearing the name, Mr Bertram rose in a flash.

"Send him in," he said.

"Mr Bertram, I am Father O'Reilly from the Society of Jesus. I will come to the point."

"Please do," the lawyer encouraged.

"I understand that Sid Logan, known to our church, is in a predicament."

"In a manner of speaking he is," the lawyer admitted.

Eyeing him closer, the putative priest commented:

"I wish to help."

Puckering his face, Mr Bertram wanted to know:

"In what way? The execution is a foregone conclusion, I am sorry to say. Unless cogent evidence can be presented, proving Logan's innocence, it will not be stayed. All legal recourse has been exhausted. Also remember, Logan admitted his culpability."

"True enough, counsellor, I am not proffering temporal help, but spiritual."

"I don't understand."

"His soul must be saved."

"Well now, that's hardly within my precinct," Mr Bertram chuckled.

"Quite so."

Looking his visitor full in the face, the lawyer remarked:

"Why are you coming to me?"

"For a simple reason called expediency. Logan refuses to see me, or any other priest. In fact it seems that everyone, except you, his lawyer, were rebuffed with the words: 'They can go to hell.' But to reiterate, Logan, a Catholic, must be administered unction, be it by hook and crook."

The admission by a man of God to employ dubious methods if need be, elicited a wry smile from the lawyer. It also raised his sympathies for this unconventional Jesuit.

"What do you want me to do, Father?"

"At your next visit with Logan ... "

Mr Bertram raised a hand and interpolated:

"I had not planned another visit."

Seeing the priest's disappointed face, he hastened to add:

"Unless requested."

"May I take the liberty to do so?"

"For what purpose?" Mr Bertram inquired.

"To give Logan a message."

"Cocking his eyes inquiringly, the lawyer wanted to know:

"Why not go there yourself and have the prison authorities do it?"

"I tried."

"And?"

"They refused."

Mr Bertram found that strange, since in his experience jailers were always more than happy to oblige a priest. His presence soothed the nerves of the condemned, and therefore made him more tractable.

"What is the message?" he asked.

"Brent Shehan has died. Before his death he exacted a vow from me to find his friend Sid Logan, and relay a communication which only I can repeat to him."

Mulling it over for a moment, the lawyer said:

"Well, it seems innocent enough, I shall convey the message."

"When?"

"Coming Friday."

The lawyer considered his visitor closer, while trying to suppress a knowing smile. Being a member of the legal profession, Marc Bertram had learned to read between the lines, and assess beyond appearances. He suspected a ruse on the clergyman's part, a stratagem to gain access to Logan. Father O'Reilly left a strange impression on him. From an unseemly restlessness to the habit of sticking, hiding one could think, his hands up the sleeves of his cassock, he deemed him an odd man and no less a queer priest.

"I take it you expect an answer, Father?"

"I do. May I call on you again, say Monday morning to hear Logan's response?"

"That will be fine."

It was an unforgettable weekend, the most harrowing in Shehan's life. Needless to say, palsy, more than ever played havoc with him. But that was not all. Rampant uncertainty, as much as dread of the unknown plagued his days; nights were pure agony. When he lay down, exhausted, worn out by incessant fretting, the fiend that tramples pounded his chest and shrieked in his ears.

After a sleepless second night, he seriously considered abandoning his project; only gratitude prevented it. After all, one good turn deserved another. The man about to lose his life, had rescued him from the tentacles of a demeaning existence worse than death.

On Monday morning he heard the good news. Barely did he step through the lawyer's doorway, when the secretary announced:

"Mr Logan wants to see you, Father."

"When?"

"As soon as possible, today, if you can."

He needed no further encouragement. Expressing his thanks, he hastened outside and guided his steps towards the prison. No time could be lost, the hour of execution drew inexorably close. Barring a reprieve, Sid would breathe his last a week from now. However, if all went to plan, the noose might swing alright, but not around a neck. True, unforeseen events could thwart the project; but what of it? As he said before, what could they do? Hang Sid twice? punish himself? Maybe so, if a felony can be proved. Even then a short stint in jail would hardly kill him. Who knows, an escapade so daring and inventive, may rather intrigue than anger the prosecutor and judge. After all, chivalry hadn't completely died yet, and an appreciation of loyalty even less. A token sentence might be his lot, nothing more.

He dawdled not a minute on the way to the prison. Arriving there, a guard promptly led him to the superintendent's office, who greeted him cordially with the words:

"Take a seat, Father, we were expecting you."

Shaking his head in disbelief, he mused:

"We can't figure out Logan's sudden about-face, after refusing adamantly to see any visitor, let alone a priest. Even his lawyer had a difficult time getting through. 'He can go to hell or Connaught,' the guard was told at first. But he finally relented."

"I am glad he did. Now the Lord's work can be done."

"I suppose so; nevertheless it's a stunning reversal," the superintendent insisted.

"It happens all the time. Invariably the most callous criminals turn to religion when they feel the end nearing. We call it perfect contrition."

Call it what you want, the superintendent's mien conveyed, just let's get on with it; for he, like everyone in the penitentiary felt on edge. As always near an execution, a prickly tension pervaded every cell, corridor, and office. The inmates, through the grapevine telegraph, immediately know the name of the condemned, his crime, plus the date and hour of execution. They grow more sullen, truculent in fact, and unmanageable. Hence the guards become jumpier, scared actually, and tyrannical.

Consequently the welcome mat was eagerly rolled out for priests, whose presence had a soothing influence throughout; leeway towards them generally prevailed. The superintendent knew of occasions where they were granted special privileges, similar to a lawyer's. But not here, because the governor, Mr Carson, frowned on practices like private rooms to minister to felons, or any such tomfoolery. It was an obsession, an evil spirit coursing through his veins. 'Holdfast Carson' they called him, an epithet that buoyed up his self-esteem. Not once in his long tenure had his reputation been marred by an escape.

"I would rather be six feet in the ground, than see any of these villains abscond," he said to all and sundry.

The guards had no use for him, management even less. Thin lipped, lean and tall, walking like Lord Strut, he was inclined to be prim and patronising. Added to it a Prince Charlie accent, completed an object of general resentment. Indeed, many guards wished a prisoner would escape; not a few were willing to connive at it. So far, however, such sentiments were mere wishful thinking.

"Now, Father, there are certain formalities to observe. For one, you must submit to searches on the way in and out."

"I understand."

"You realise of course, there is a guard stationed outside, who has a clear view of the cell."

"Constantly?"

"Yes."

"But how can I take his confession then? Unfortunately I am hard of hearing, for which reason the penitent must speak up."

Signifying comprehension, the superintendent explained:

"Don't worry about it for now. Let's see how it goes first before we commit ourselves. A guard can always be asked to step back and avert his eyes. Don't forget, Padre, we, as much as you, have the prisoner's spiritual welfare at heart."

"His soul must be saved."

"Quite so, Father," the superintendent agreed, whereafter he called a guard, who arrived within the minute.

"Take Father O'Reilly to 0942," he ordered.

"Sid Logan?"

"Of course," he snapped.

At the sight of the putative clergyman, the gaoler seemed taken aback, but he said nothing. He was an affable young man, prone to be loquacious. After talking a bit, he remarked:

"Do I detect an Irish accent, Father?"

"You do, my son."

"Just like the inmate Logan, in fact you almost sound alike."

"Oh well, there are quite a few of us around."

Smiling shyly, the guard suggested:

"You even resemble each other to some extent."

"Well then, he must hail from county Armagh, as I do, we all look alike there," the priest chuckled.

Baffled, unsure whether being made fun of, the guard fell silent.

Shehan's nerves were in a knot, he realised that one more hurdle had to be overcome; a crucial one. If Sid recognised him and revealed the fact, the whole scheme would come to naught. As they approached the cell, he tipped his hat forward and adjusted his glasses. With that, plus the priest's habit and a frowning face, he hoped to avoid recognition. Besides, he assumed that the cell, like most, was dimly lit.

His anxiety proved groundless. With his back to the guards, his head inclined till the hat brim almost touched his chest, he stepped into Logan's cell. The prisoner said nothing, indicating that he was not recognised. However, Shehan knew as soon as he uttered a few words, Sid would take notice. He would prick his ears and ask questions. That possibility had to be forestalled. Taking off his glasses absentmindedly, Shehan laid them across his lips several times in a suggestive way. It was a clear signal to remain silent, which the prisoner seemingly understood. As the gate closed with an echoing clang, Shehan whispered:

"Don't say a word, Sid, it's me, Brent Shehan."

"What on .... " Logan blurted out before he managed to check himself. Suppressing further exclamations, he tried to collect his wits. Did the message not say that Shehan had died? Did he rise from the dead, stood a spectre before him, or was this a prank? Doubts, astonishment and consternation mirrored in his face. Though unable to determine what it meant, he decided to play along. Keeping a straight face, however, proved not so easy. Recognising Shehan as he came closer, he couldn't refrain from sibilating:

"You crazy Irishman."

Clearing his throat the priest announced in a prophetic voice:

"My son, I bring you joyous tidings, Jesus has found you, open your heart to receive him."

This of course was meant for the guard's ear, who stood outside glowering at the prisoner, whom he evidently disliked. Still not comprehending what Shehan the priest was up to, yet tickled by the novel diversion, Logan said under his breath:

"You silly paddi-whack."

Shehan had studied his role well. Assuming a cherubic face, he announced solemnly:

"I have brought you the New Testament. You should read it to gain salvation and freedom."

Opening a second bible, the priest read in a tremulous voice:

"Your love and faith shall prevail, you soon will be free again. There is a message in these passages for him who pays heed."

Logan sensed that within these pages cited, could be found a communication meant for him. Hence after the priest's departure he opened the suggested sections, where he found more than just marginal notes. Shehan's intentions, though expressed somewhat cryptically, were grasped nevertheless by Logan, who thought them bizarre and unworkable. A footnote made him chuckle; it read: 'Your response under Mark, the withered leaf.'

On the next and following days the mummery continued. The guards, three in all, each working an eight hour shift, reported the prisoner's redemption appeared to be slow, if anything it might be faltering. Not for lack of trying on Father O'Reilly's part, they admitted. He did more than his best, praying to heaven, beseeching the angels, and at times bullying the recalcitrant prisoner, to no avail. It was a comedy really, unfolding before their eyes, worthy of Aristophanes the

Athenian, a farce, which the guards took in, hook, line, and sinker. They never realised that a drama beyond their acuity evolved before them.

None had an inkling of being brazenly hoodwinked by this zealous, amiable priest whom everybody liked. They would have shaken their heads in disbelief if told he was a fake, for he appeared to be genuine beyond a doubt. Small wonder, since Shehan enjoyed playing the role, which seemed to be written expressly for him; so much so, that whenever he slipped into his frock and put on his Jesuit hat, all signs of palsy vanished.

"I have missed my calling," one of his footnotes read.

The guards were masterly duped. A regular uncensored correspondence flourished right under their noses, which neither one in the least suspected. They had no idea that the holy book served as a vehicle of communication. They changed hands at every visit within their sight.

The perception of the guards underwent a subliminal transmutation, it was bent and shaped cleverly. They were inveigled by a ruse as old as the hills. As a juggler deflects attention from reality by extraneous talk, gestures, and facial expressions in order to manipulate the spectators to accept his legerdemain, so were they steered onto a path of self-delusion. They became silent participants in his apparent struggle. Seeing disappointment spread over his good-natured face, darkened their countenances also. Hearing his voice choked with grief, awakened their sympathies.

"He has a long row to hoe," they said and thought, and only a few days to do it.

But he was a fighter, the priest, set to make a breach through fields of thorns and acres of thistles for this worthless criminal's soul. As their compassion for Father O'Reilly increased, by the same token the sympathy for the prisoner decreased. Two days ahead of the execution, dislike had taken on shapes of blinding hate, which skews discernment as much as pity dulls perception. A fact well known by the conspirators, who exploited it to the hilt.

Yet not all was staged. Part of the priest's woes were real, certainly at first, for Logan showed not the least will to co-operate. His rough and tumble nature balked at his friend's intentions, which he termed laughable, and in any case unworkable. Being an adventurer by inclination who possessed a pronounced tendency towards strife and danger, his predicament, as terrible as it was, left him unperturbed. A long, lone sojourn in the wild mountains of British Columbia, had taught him to accept fate with a shrug and smile. Besides, letting another man suffer for his sins, he considered anathema.

But those sentiments soon changed as his thoughts started to rove when alone in the cell. In the stillness of long nights a prickling sensation crept gradually over him. A baffling phenomenon it deemed him, but nevertheless welcome. Shehan's proposition, initially repudiated and derided, took on a different aspect. He started to reconsider this presumed wild-goose chase. Questions were asked, answers were given, in part by way of the book, but also by himself.

On the fourth night of Shehan's appearance, he felt a curious glow rising from somewhere, which alarmed and pleased him simultaneously. Growing more agitated by the minute, he rose from his cot and fell into a prison walk. As he strode from wall to wall, careful not to rouse the napping guard, he felt like a man on the threshold of great events, announced by the flourish of trumpets. A stirring excitement made his ears tingle and lightened his steps. It was hope, that smiling temptress, kindler of dreams, enemy of reality, which had him on her wings.

From there the world, as much as his circumstances, took on a different view. Scruples, a part of his character, disappeared behind clouds of vindication. Did he not rescue Shehan from an ignominious existence? Save him from the abyss of no return? Repaying the favour should be an obligation, a privilege really, even at the threat of punishment. After all, a short jail term, if anything, is not too much to ask for an eased conscience and clean slate. Besides he, Logan, by any measure not a poor man, intended to reward him generously. The Mars Mining Property will be his. With rising gold values, that should be ample compensation for his help.

Next morning, to Shehan's delight, he was informed in a whisper:

"I am with you."

Soon the guard noticed a changed atmosphere inside. Understandable, he thought, for the clock ticked on, spurring the Father to greater efforts of course. It could not be denied, judging by his voice, hitherto persuasive, yet never strident as now. His movements, generally poised if not elegant, became brisker. Gesticulations, measured to a fault so far, increasingly grew rough and abrupt. Patience, a trademark of the clergy, gave way to impetuosity. Mopping his brow he remarked:

"It is hot in here, exceedingly so."

Turning, he asked the guard:

"My son, may I remove my frock?"

"Most certainly, Father," came an obliging reply.

In a single movement the frock was taken off and thrown on to the cot. Exasperation lined his face as he turned towards the guard, who saw and recognised the signs. What he could not perceive, however, was the satisfaction that lightened the priest's heart. Another hurdle had just been vaulted, he knew things were falling in place.

On the way out, the guard commiserated:

"Father, you are trying to square the circle, give it up, let him roast in hell, I say."

Wincing, as if in pain, more to hide a smirk however, than because of suffering, he observed:

"You mean well, my son, but we can give no quarter to Beelzebub. Any man's soul is worth saving. We must leave no stone unturned to find the means to do it. I am confident we shall succeed."

"I wish you luck, Father."

He then remonstrated:

"You are worn with exertion, even your voice is failing."

"Tut, tut, that is nothing, just signs of a cold. By the way, are you working the same shift tomorrow?"

"Yes, why do you ask?"

"You have a sympathetic air, besides, I noticed that you bear less ill-will towards the prisoner than the others; a fact which has not been lost on him."

"I don't understand, Father."

"It is this: To show contrition is easier in a forgiving surrounding; moreover, a person is more hesitant to make a confession in the presence of animosity."

"Making a confession, Father? not this scoundrel."

"Hm, perhaps yes, however, not in the proximity of, of – how should I say it – eyes and ears."

"Oh that? no problem, Father, just give me a hint and I shall step aside."

On the way out, in the company of a guard, he could barely hide his glee. The stage was set, the curtain for the final act had been raised. Before the vesper bell rang tomorrow, Logan, a free man, would be stepping onto Columbia Street. All was arranged, every detail had been incalculated to make his escape possible.

Later in the evening Shehan's mood changed. For unknown reasons he started to fret. An inexplicable foreboding, for days lingering in the back of his mind, came to the foreground. Imageries of an impending evil assailed him, doubts and apprehensions led him a merry dance. Did he get cold feet? Hardly, he assured himself despite a faltering state of mind. But the thought of the coveted Mars property in the Selkirks sustained his resolve. It was part and parcel of the scheme. The defunct mine with all land, machinery, and claims held, will be his. Logan, now the sole owner of the company, had so promised.

Shehan realised of course that he had to face two charges: One, impersonating a priest; two, assisting a felon to escape. No doubt, the book would be thrown at him, but a string of lawyers, the best money can buy, should manage to soften the impact. They might even wangle a suspended sentence from a sympathetic court. With that in mind his confidence returned.

Just the same, he spent a restless night. In the morning his whole body ached. He felt like a man who had lain in the arms of the Duke of Exeter's daughter. Misgivings plagued him, for which he found neither reasons nor understanding. A dread, ominous as much as depressing lay heavy on his mind. Why, he could not say, since all should go well. Changing identities in view of the guard's willingness to relax his vigilance, should take less than a minute. The rest would be easy.

Promising to return the next day, the priest, Logan by now, was scheduled to walk out, never to return. Recognition, considering their clever designs, appeared remote. Even matters like voices, slightly divergent accents, as much as hair colour had been allowed for. Feigning hoarseness was sort of the icing on the cake. A brilliant idea, meant to dissemble the departing priest's voice, plus make him reluctant to speak. After all, following that strenuous session, successful it appeared, surely taxed his vocal cords beyond endurance. Thus, who could blame him for saving his words. Shehan, the new prisoner, intended not to reveal his identity till next afternoon. This should allow his friend an advance start.

It worked like clockwork. The guards evidently suspected nothing, they didn't even raise an eyebrow. True, the jailers outside sensed a change in the prisoner, a fact, so they assumed, attributable to his conversion, as much as his approaching end. Who could blame him for moping hours on end with averted face on his cot. Never loquacious before, he had grown outright taciturn. Besides, the guards' power of observation, not keen to begin with, was further skewed by increasing preoccupation with the impending execution. Whether they liked or hated a condemned man, a hanging always frayed on their nerves.

The day of the execution had arrived, so had the hour of revelation. Rising from his cot, Shehan stepped up to the gate facing the guard, who immediately took umbrage.

"What are you staring at?" he growled.

"I'm not Sid Logan," the prisoner announced.

"Not that again," the guard responded in disgust. Confused, the prisoner repeated:

"You don't appear to understand, I am not Sid Logan, so there will be no hanging tonight."

Receiving no answer, he was about to say more, when the guard cut him short:

"I know, we all know."

Taken aback, the prisoner asked:

"What do you all know?"

"That you are not Logan."

"How do you know that?"

"Because you told us often enough," came a grumpy reply.

"I – I told you, when?"

"Lately, a hundred times at least."

Shehan stood there, stunned, immobile as if bolted to the floor. There was that disquieting premonition again, assailing him with renewed force. Knitting his brow, still not comprehending, alarmed by a gnawing suspicion, he uttered once more:

"Believe me, I am not Sid Logan, my name is ...."

"Brent Shehan," the guard fell in, thoroughly annoyed; then he added:

"I know it, all the guards know it, so does the superintendent and the governor. Now shut up before I summon the prison doctor."

Aghast, Shehan recoiled as if bitten by a krail. At first the guard's words, perturbing as they were, made little sense. But slowly a terrible suspicion seized him, which squeezed the air out of his lungs. Shaking his head vigorously, he staggered towards the cot, where he slumped down heavily, moaning like a wounded beast.

He saw it all. By clever rehearsals Logan had managed to evade future prosecution. He could live freely hereafter anywhere he liked, right under his own name to boot; for he was dead, hung on a raw November night in accordance with the dictate of the law.

"Why, oh why?" Shehan lamented, till the guard told him roughly to be quiet.

"Shut up, Logan, you are getting on my nerves. Play another record, one we haven't heard yet to the point of nausea."

Springing to his feet, Shehan shouted:

"Fetch the superintendent, tell him I demand to be finger printed."

"We have gone through that too, so just take it easy, and for heaven's sake keep your trap shut or I will hang you myself."

Yes, Shehan understood. He was conned, tricked, and irretrievable trapped. What now! Protesting got him nowhere. Ranting and raving would simply result in heavy sedation, and possibly precipitate the execution. Spewing venom at the guard and all his ancestors and heirs? No, there must be a more effective way to extricate himself. A few short hours lay between him and eternity; unless – unless. He perked up, his utter despair yielded to hope, that wondrous deceiver revived his smitten soul. Things should turn out well, he told himself. There might be a last hour reprieve, maybe Logan got caught; maybe the superintendent, or maybe the governor, maybe– maybe ….

Shuffling sounds, followed by voices brought him to his feet. He almost shouted for joy when he saw a group of men and women approaching his cell. He could read it in their faces, they all shone of good tidings.

"Your farewell dinner, Mr Logan," one of the guards said.

Pangnirtung

*E*veryone with feet to walk hastened towards the water. The whole settlement seemed to be astir. Even the huskies skipped excitedly across the brown tundra in the direction of the wharf. Women with laughing faces, carrying their little ones on their backs, shuffled behind the men, in front of their elders, whose tired limbs couldn't keep up. The object of everyone's interest was a ship, barely visible with naked eyes, approaching from Cumberland Sound. It could only be the Nacosbie, laden with the settlement's annual supplies.

Father Perrault stood by to assist with unloading, but first he intended to welcome the new arrivals. He was a sturdy fellow, French Canadian from head to toe, graced with characteristic heartiness and humour. With the inevitable pipe between his teeth, he surveyed the congregation, trying to identify his converts, which could be counted on one hand. However, that did not daunt him, his indomitable spirit was not easily dampened. Fluent in Inuktituk, strong in limbs, fearless like Nanook, he was known throughout the Arctic.

Today's excitement, always considerable at the sight of the Nacosbie, was heightened by the expected arrival of Paul Rusk, the new Hudson Bay factor. He was slated as replacement for Ralph Ponta, who had suddenly disappeared about a month ago.

Meanwhile the ship came to a halt some hundred yards offshore, where dozens of small boats encircled it. Shouts in Inuktituk were answered in French and English. Good-natured banter travelled from mouth to ears and back. Soon the first boats returned fully laden, so that the gunwales almost touched the water.

"Is he on board?" Father Perrault asked.

"Yes, Falla, he is with Amuluk," he was told.

Three hundred pairs of eyes turned in every direction to sight the famous hunter's boat. As he came closer to shore, a hundred voices murmured to themselves. Then a resonant utterance drowned out the droning sounds.

"Siksi," Simon Ivalu announced.

"Siksi, Siksi," others repeated.

The moniker adhered to Rusk from thereon. Siksi–squirrel, he soon was referred to all over the Arctic.

Father Perrault greeted him with sincere enthusiasm, which Rusk found embarrassing. Startled, visible uncomfortable by such effusiveness, he felt an urge to turn away. Noticing the priest's accent, his discomfort changed to outright chagrin. He was not only forward, this priest, but a French Canadian to boot. Rusk couldn't help it, prejudice formed part of his life; it was the strut holding up his self-esteem.

As it turned out both were born and raised in Montreal, a lively city, the only metropolis with a soul north of the Rio Grande. Strange to say, Rusk found no satisfaction on account of that. The opposite was true; it vexed him. He felt no kinship with French Canadians, for they were shockingly different, less than mediocre in his estimation. In any case there existed an unbridgeable chasm between them, a gulch dug by his forebears and steadily widened with hands guided by insecure minds. Below flowed the river of disdain, separating superior Anglo-Saxons and their hangers-on, from inferior Canadiens. Such tenets were fed him with his mother's milk; he believed them as did millions more.

Rusk started work in the morning. When he opened the store he noticed a group of Inuits nearby, who annoyed him at first glance. Their uproarious laughter grated on his nerves, as did the guttural utterances of which he understood not a word.

Seeing Father Perrault among them, talking like a native, irritated him even more.

It was surprisingly mild for the time of year. The sun, still warm, had just pushed over the high promontory jutting out into the bay. Rusk was about to step inside again, when something odd struck him. Unable to make out what it was, he decided to linger and watch. One of the men it appeared, performed sort of a skit to the amusement of the others. His antics, though strangely familiar, made little sense. Rusk had heard about the Inuit's penchant for mimicry at someone else's expense. They possess a canny ability, he was told, to accentuate a person's peculiarities. They are masterful mimics, so it seemed.

"Let them play the fool," he grumbled, then stiffened; for he suddenly realised what attracted his attention. They were making fun of him! One fellow, a mite of a man, was particularly hard at it; he did the utmost to parody his idiosyncrasies. Strutting around as if on wooden legs, trying to imitate his gait, he received encouragement from all sides. When he shook his limbs jerkily and turned his head in the abrupt fashion of a squirrel, they shouted:

"Siksi! Siksi!"

It was a shameful performance to Rusk, rendered despicable by Father Perrault's presence.

Trading turned out to be slow, which surprised Rusk in view of the four weeks' interruption. Many Inuits came, but few bartered, yet talked much. They were surprised, dismayed really by his inability to speak their language.

"He will soon learn," consoled Nuvalik.

"We will teach him," promised Okalik.

It was an empty assurance, uttered naively. None of them were aware of a puzzling truth, which in any case they would not have believed. Paul Rusk, a fourth generation native of Quebec, spoke not a word of French, neither did his ancestors; the thought of it would have thrown them into a snit. He harboured no intention to learn their language, but would force them to speak his. That, however, concerned the Inuits not greatly, for some spoke enough English to make themselves and others understand. Something weightier burdened their minds; namely, Rusk's aura of discontent. It bothered them, for they knew it was the mother of discord. But despite the feeling of a wintry draught up their spines in his presence, they showed a willingness to be companionable.

"Time will tell," Okalik remarked.

They nodded and went their way. In any case more important matters occupied their minds. Winter approached, a biting whiff lay in the air, presaging harsher times. The memory of the great white silence, pushing down from the mountains made them hasten their steps and hustle. Young and old were astir, they had no time to bother about the new man from another world.

"We will look at him later," the shaman promised.

The others agreed, knowing that their physical strength and mental faculties had to be employed to procure provisions and fix the equipment. For soon thick layers of ice would cover the bay, remaining the better part of eight months.

They were a hard pressed lot, exposed to severe storms roaring down the Penny Ice Cap, and punished by never ending dark winters. Yet they seldom worried, rarely complained.

"It can not be helped," the old people said.

"It will soon be better," men and women promised each other. All were optimists from cradle to grave.

After their gears were prepared and the stores had been placed, the Inuits considered Rusk closer. Siksi, the squirrel, they agreed, was not an object of endearment.

"He is lifeless like an inukshuk," Ivalu reminded.

"Only on the inside," Amuluk reasoned.

"True, his outside never rests," Ivalu concurred.

Then Karpik spoke up:

"Is he a man, how can that be? Does he fish, hunt, or keep a dog team like an Inuk?"

"What do you expect from an Eyebrow," Amuluk scoffed.

"Well, at least he is a good trader," reminded someone.

"That is true," agreed Karpik. "He is fair, diligent, and honest," he added.

"A strange individual just the same," Ivalu averred.

Granted, he had his faults, yet the Inuits did not exactly dislike Rusk. But that soon changed when his treatment of

Father Perrault became evident. At first they poked each other in the ribs, pretending to be amused, but really trying to disguise a growing discomfort. After a while, however, the best feigners admitted the truth: Rusk's overbearing treatment of the Father set their teeth on edge. It sent currents of unpleasant sensations up their spines when witnessing the strain in his face the moment he espied the Long Robe. A crackling tension emanated from the trader then that made the Inuits wince. His high and mighty attitude grated on their nerves.

Rusk was oblivious to a disquieting fact, regrettably so. He paid no heed to the severe, never ending winter's adverse influence. Even the most placid natures become irritable, easily offended and vengeful, as days grow shorter and darkness increases. Idleness, the bane of life, does the rest; it awakens one's baser instincts. It was neither a good time nor the right location to be the odd man out; even worse, to lord it over the most independent and self-sufficient people on earth.

Rusk, who until recently moved in conventional circles, who never stepped beyond the shoulders of easy street, had unfortunately made a hasty, wrong turn. True, the pay was substantial, but the exigencies exceeded his capabilities. Living and working among people shaped by raw nature held no attraction for him; quite the contrary: the vast treeless tundra with its unwashed gypsies, revolted him. A force stronger than reason guided, or rather misguided him.

The Inuits did not understand how anyone lacking manly prowess can pretend to be superior. An Inuk who neither fished, hunted, or was unable to build a snow house, would bow his head in shame.

"A strange creature indeed, helpless like a child," more than one said.

"Scared of everything that moves," scoffed Agnakok.

"Like all Big Brows he is useless," offered Okalik.

Ivalu, the wit, added:

"True, he can not even tell the prints of nanook from that of a sea gull."

"He is a weakling, unable to lift a harpoon with both hands, why even mention his name."

Yes, they did mock and laugh and belittle Rusk, the Siksi. Their hilarity had a hollow ring, meant to hide a rising anxiety. Rusk too sensed a ground swell of discontent aiming at him. As he lay awake at night, listening to the moaning wind, fear gripped him, followed by defiance. Confused, harassed by forebodings, his mind turned towards Father Perrault, whom he blamed for his unpleasant situation. The priest, like any Frenchman, could not be trusted, he decided; therefore caution must be exercised when dealing with him, he told himself. It was a superfluous reminder, since such sentiments were involuntarily ingrained in his character.

At the sight of Father Perrault he instinctively drew himself up while scowling disapprovingly. Instantly the Great Barrens took on the shape of the Plains of Abraham. In his ears resounded the bugles of the British, urging their men to attack. By golly, they did; the French were beaten decisively. True, it happened over two hundred years ago, but the memory was kept alive. Rusk, like many others drew sustenance from it.

Father Perrault had sensed his compatriot's predicament at the first handshake. Despite a long sojourn in a harsh, unforgiving land, among people reminiscent of the Neolithic period, he possessed extraordinary insight. Rusk's affliction, as he called it, deserved pity rather than anger. Looking at the trader's face, pinched and furrowed by stifling emotions, roused his compassion. But also his apprehension for valid reasons, in view of Ponta's mysterious disappearance. What happened exactly he could not say; guessing, however, was a different matter.

An inquiry had taken place which led nowhere. Constable Murgh, the investigating officer, went at it with the zeal of an official and the clumsiness engendered by conceit. Finally shaking his head and tugging his moustache, he left empty-handed; but not before talking to Father Perrault.

"Father, you have done a fine job, turning these rapscallions into angels. For lack of wings, they would all fly to heaven," he praised with tongue in cheek.

Barely managing to suppress a smile, Father Perrault held his tongue. He felt disinclined to enlighten the constable about the Inuits' idiosyncrasies. Murgh could not hide his indignation. Travelling from Edmonton, wrapped in layers of authority, sheathed in the majesty of the law, he found that nobody was impressed. It irked him visibly. Awe inspiring down south, up in the Great Barrens he received scant notice. To the Inuits he was just another pesky Eyebrow. His interrogation methods amused, rather than frightened them. The interminable questions, irrelevant to an Inuit, made them drowsy. More than one fell asleep in the overheated barrack. The repeated selfsame queries proved especially onerous to all. Of course they were meant to ensnare an unwary examinee in a contradiction, but the Inuits found them vexing and confusing.

"What a dolt," they said to each other.

"The white man has no memory."

"What do you expect from a Big Brow," they scoffed.

Father Perrault, if asked, could have told the officer a simple fact: The Inuit does not understand suggestive language, deemed clever to a trained policeman. It confuses and rattles him. Had constable Murgh asked:

"Okalik, did you harm Ponta? Okalik, did you kill Ponta?"

The answer would have been a straight yes or no. Seeing, however, that constable Murgh suffered from an inflated ego which made him argumentative, Father Perrault remained silent.

November had arrived. Days grew shorter and colder. Ice started to form on the bay, providing the means for easy travelling. Northern lights lit up the sky, making it possible to find one's way in the increasing darkness. Soon the great white silence would engulf the vast tundra.

Father Perrault stirred hands and feet to prepare for his yearly journey, covering the whole of Baffin Island and Melville Peninsula. His gear, though always well maintained, nevertheless needed to be overhauled. The well-fed huskies, excited since the first snowfall, brimmed with health and expectations.

Before setting out he decided to have a talk with Rusk, who increasingly worried him. Exactly why he could not say, yet a grating premonition made him feel uneasy. Rusk no doubt was the right man for the job, but wrong for the location. Aloofness has no place in the Arctic, where communal life prevails. Being introversive among spontaneous people, was a sure recipe for strife. He blamed the managers of the Hudson Bay Company for sending a man of Rusk's disposition, who neither belonged here, nor wanted to. He noticed that the Inuits felt alienated already, soon they would turn against him. The signs were there, he knew them only too well. A little push, the slightest provocation, real or imagined, could produce the spark that ignites the tinderbox.

"Paul, I shall soon be on my way. As every winter I will travel up and down Baffin Island and across Melville Bay. The ice is still young, but that will change rapidly."

Rusk perked up, he liked what he heard, it made him more amenable than usually.

"How long will you be gone, Father?"

"Two to three months, depending on the weather."

Good news, it flashed through Rusk's mind, it nearly put him in a jovial mood. Generally disinclined to discourse with Father Perrault at length, this welcome information rendered him almost sociable. He started talking as never before, about trade first, then concerning his life in Montreal. Father Perrault, never tongue-tied, grew strangely hesitant. Repeatedly clearing his throat, hemming and hawing, he finally burst out:

"Paul, there is something you should know."

Seeing the other's frosty look, he dared not tell him what lay on his mind; that is to make him privy of the brewing discontent he sensed in the community. Nothing serious yet, he granted, but worthy of attention. He meant to tell him about the Inuits' innate suspicion towards the Big Eyebrows, as they call Europeans, especially in the case of newcomers. Such distrust is best allayed by learning their language and taking part in their lives. Sequestering oneself creates disharmony, which is a poisonous barb that penetrates their leathery skin. But Rusk's ruffled reaction made him swallow his words.

"What is it, Father?" he asked sharply.

"I just wish to draw your attention to the rigours of our winters," he answered evasively.

"Don't worry about me, I know how to take care of myself."

"Maybe so, Paul, but just remember not to venture outside during a blizzard. No one, not even the most intrepid Inuk does it without tying himself to a rope. Believe me, within seconds the whirling, wind-swept snow can turn into a dense wall impenetrable to the keenest eye. Everything gets blurred, one instantly loses any sense of direction."

Rusk, waving the priest's counsel aside, interrupted condescendingly:

"I know all about it."

Father Perrault considered him closer, while nodding knowingly. Rusk's demeanour was an open book to him, he could have recited verbatim what he thought:

"How dare a hewer of wood and carrier of water, a mere habitant lecture anybody, especially me?"

Poor chap, he felt like saying, you carry a cross heavier than our Lord's crux imissa. You are plodding on a path steeper and rockier than the way to Golgatha.

"Well, Paul, I might not see you again for awhile, so take care of yourself," were Father Perrault's parting words.

He would have liked to add: "Mend your ways, give your heart a little massage, it might save you a lot of grieve." But he merely smiled and extended his hand.

A few days later he encountered a group of Inuits on his way to the wharf. They were talking animatedly about Nuvalik's luck, who had harpooned two seals. The excitement over the upcoming feast was obvious.

"Will it be today, Nuvalik?" they asked.

"No, tomorrow, I will call you when all is prepared."

Father Perrault was not deceived. Seeing him coming, they had switched to a more innocuous topic. He came straight to the point:

"You are concocting something," he accused them.

"We, Falla?"

One had to know them to describe the air of affected innocence framing their faces.

"How could anyone fall prey to such an idea?" marvelled Nuvalik.

"Oi, oi," lamented Ivalu, as if in pain.

"The Falla sees ghosts," Karpik offered solicitously.

"Maybe so, maybe so," Father Perrault admitted against his better judgement.

But why fret, he told himself, if they had decided to play a prank on Rusk, no power on earth could dissuade them from it. Then again, is it Rusk whom they had chosen, or himself? Who knows!

A few days later Father Perrault loaded his sled, then harnessed the huskies who bristled with excitement. Turning their muzzles westwards, he cried: "Hurr – hurr," and cracked his whip over the lead dog's head. It was merely a formality, done out of habit, for the dogs needed neither whip nor encouragement. They bolted forward as if stung by a thousand wasps.

Soon the weather changed, the sky took on an ominous hue. Invisible hands seemed to be at work, painting, erasing, creating weird shapes before his eyes. It would have been difficult to say who was more elated: the smiling Father or the bounding huskies. Both were on a mission that stirred their souls, they thanked their maker for being alive.

Pangnirtung gradually disappeared behind the horizon, as much as from Father Perrault's thoughts. The last he saw were dark clouds gathering over the settlement, auguring inclement weather; he was not far off.. Screaming winds, of a force never seen or heard before by Rusk, lashed down from the mountains, reaching a state of fury nothing could appease. Then came the snow which, driven by the wind, formed into streaming sheets of white and grey.

Looking out the window, Rusk rubbed his eyes in amazement, the whole surrounding had acquired an eerie aspect. Nothing could be seen except impenetrable whiteout. Gone were the huts, the church, and the bay, obliterated by whirling snow. Father Perrault's admonishing words, treated with condescension, took on a more heedful aspect. Who indeed would want to step into this raging hell? Not he, in any case.

Why should he? Didn't he sit pretty within sturdy walls under a well anchored roof? The store was stocked with provisions that would outlast any storm. As he still congratulated himself, he heard the door rattle furiously, which made him mutter:

"Gee whiz, that wind does pack a punch."

It was not the wind, however, but someone demanding to be let in. Reluctantly he pushed back the bolt and peered outside where he found himself face to face with a muffled man covered with snow, who moaned:

"You must come, Ruska."

Bewildered, not knowing what to say or do, Rusk asked:

"Who are you?"

"Amuluk, you know me."

"What do you want?"

"Come with me; little Agnorok, my son, is sick. You know him, Ruska, he is terribly sick."

Still dumbfounded, Rusk was stirred to action by the menacing storm. After pulling Amuluk inside with one hand, slamming the door shut with the other, he pushed back the bolt again. It was high time, for snow started to accumulate in the room. The biting cold went right through him, nipping at his very marrow. Still not understanding what Amuluk wanted, he tried to find out:

"Little Agnorok, your son... "

"Is being devoured by fever. His skin is aflame, you must come," Amuluk wailed.

"What for?"

"He needs medicine, good medicine to cool the heat in his body."

"I am not a doctor."

"But you have medicine," countered Amuluk.

"Why don't you go to the Father?"

"The Falla has left, he will not be back soon. Agnorok is burning with fever, your medicine will cool his brow."

Rusk was in a quandary. Not going might jeopardize his career, moreover, harm the sterling reputation of the Hudson Bay Company. Doing Amuluk's bidding, however, might be fraught with danger. But like all Hudson Bay factors, he was duty-bound to tend the sick, administer basic medicine, plus call for help, if necessary. For that reason all factors sent to the Arctic possessed first aid training. Failing to help, foul weather or not, could be construed as negligence, resulting in punitive measures. Remembering Father Perrault's words, Rusk said:

"I will come with you, but first I need a rope."

Looking puzzled for a minute, Amuluk remarked:

"I have one already strung out between my house and the store, it will guide us there and back without any problem. We need a short piece though, to hitch ourselves together."

Rusk understood. Nodding approval, he went behind the counter and got one. At the same time he pocketed some antibiotics. After donning his heaviest clothes, and girding themselves with the rope, they set out.

Amuluk, gripping the line fastened to a bracket near the door, led the way. Rusk followed a few feet behind. As they stepped outside he had to suppress an impulse to jump right back again. The fierce wind almost lifted him off his feet. Had he not been tied to Amuluk, plus been in dread of his scathing mockery, Rusk would have slipped back inside. It was slow going in that Egyptian darkness, made denser by whirling masses of snow. Not a glimmer of light shone through that raging inferno which could have served as a guide.

Had anyone asked Rusk right now for the location of Amuluk's house, his store, or the church, he most likely would have pointed in the wrong direction. Not a single contour, not even a shadow was visible. Indeed, there were moments when even the squat shape of Amuluk disappeared before his eyes. Three feet at most they were separated from each other, yet at times not even the eyes of an eagle could have penetrated that short distance.

The roaring storm took Rusk's breath away. His face, if not averted, instantly bore a layer of snow turning to ice. He could have endured the rigour of the weather, had it not been for a rising premonition of a nameless impending disaster. Shouldn't they have arrived some time ago? Amuluk's hut, not forty steps distance was nowhere in sight. Neither had they passed, nor seen the few buildings in between. Although he did not count the paces, they surely must exceed one hundred. Something odd was going on.

"Amuluk, Amuluk," he bellowed.

There was no response. A strange sensation gripped Rusk when he realised a disquieting fact. Until a moment ago he felt a steady tug on the rope and saw Amuluk's contour now and then. He accelerated his steps while stretching out both hands. He wanted to touch Amuluk, to reassure himself that there existed another beating heart in this howling inferno. But he neither touched, heard, nor saw his guide. When he pulled on the rope he felt no resistance, indicating it was no longer fastened to Amuluk. Dumbfounded, not comprehending anything, he stood there as if petrified. Then the awful truth slowly sunk in. Amuluk had disappeared, somehow the rope about his body untied itself, a fact he must have noticed too late. He was alone in a veritable maw of an enraged behemoth.

Calling for Amuluk till his breath gave out, he tripped over something. In a flash, hope raced through his frozen frame like a darting flame. The rope! he cried in a voice choked with emotion. Groping around he found what he expected. Rising to his feet he gripped the rope firmly with the intention to pull himself along. It was high time to reach a safe and warm place, for his situation, precarious at any time, and worsened by apprehension, had become critical.

When after a few tugs he experienced not a trace of resistance, he frantically started to haul in the line, as one does when a fish is hooked. Meanwhile his surprise changed to amazement, then extreme wonder, and finally while holding one end before his eyes, to paralysing shock. Turning around he repeated the same manoeuvre. Sure enough the other end appeared in his tremulous hands. He understood.

Life in Pangnirtung continued as it did for hundreds of years. After the storm abated, some Inuits showed up at the store, ready to trade. When they found the door locked and saw no trace of Siksi, they shrugged their shoulders and went their ways.

"Siksi is gone," they announced.

"He must be under a snowdrift," suggested some.

"He has gone out in the blizzard," remarked Karpik mockingly.

"Just like a Big Brow," Amuluk ventured to say.

"What do you expect from a white man," chuckled Ivalu.

"They are useless, I tell you," offered Okalik.

After a while the Hudson Bay managers started to ask questions, then notified the police in Frobisher Bay, who sent two constables to investigate. They set out at the first sign of good weather. Meanwhile the Inuits, ever keen-eyed, noticed foxes and bears lingering around a small hillock not far from the settlement. Growing suspicious they took a closer look. Sure enough, they found Rusk partially exposed under a snowdrift. Obeying the Falla's wishes, they piled rocks over him.

Constables Turcotte and Villeneuf arrived a few days later. They were completely at sea after talking to the villagers; yet a report had to be written. The essence of it was this: Paul Rusk, unacquainted with the perilous Arctic, ventured outside in a snarling blizzard. For unknown reasons it was stated twice. True, he held a long rope in his hands, plus had a short one around his body, but that in itself meant little. These fatal occurrences do happen every year, stated the official report in closing.

When Father Perrault returned about a month later, he tried to learn what happened. He did not get very far. Siksi, he was told, vanished in a blizzard, they found him under a pile of snow. Upon reading the police report, a grim smile stole around his lips, which might have expressed pity or guilt.

April arrived, the first snow buntings appeared filling the air with lovely sounds. They were the harbinger of better times. Days grew longer, the sun climbed higher, soon it would not set anymore. Over the still frozen tundra wandered immense herds of caribou, trailed by never missing wolves. Their howls at night made the Inuits smile, and the caribou shiver. Hope lay in the air. Old women cast twinkling glances at their men. Rusk was almost forgotten. The odd Inuit spoke about him now and then.

"Not a bad trader," one said.

"But just another Big Eyebrow," another countered.

"The next one will be better," someone concluded.

The Stranger

They craned their necks till they ached to get a better look at the newcomer.

"My, my, it seems he has a date with the grim reaper," conjectured Rita Hartwig.

"No doubt about it, I can see the shadows of the great beyond on his face," remarked Peter Bruno.

"My soul, he will not grace our fair world much longer," suggested Cathy Honig.

Suppositions to that effect were expressed from all sides by voices mixed with pity and satisfaction. For in an old people's home robustness is not appreciated; it's deemed a source of vexation.

Having just lived through a harrowing experience, they wished not to see it repeated. A man became a resident, who, although near eighty years old, behaved like a prizefighter in his prime.

"Let's have a tussle," he invited the wan, ghostlike figure of Mr Young, who could barely rise from his chair.

"How about some arm wrestling," he challenged the men, and yes, even the women. He paid no heed to fatigue, and even less to decorum. His uproarious behaviour turned the entire institution topsy-turvy. They felt self-conscious, stung to the soul, some even wished to move away; but where to? This was their home, the final stop prior to the last journey.

Fortunately help was on its way in the form of Adam Rickman the new manager, who replaced Marie Warren, a timid and confused administratrix. He was cut from a different cloth than the reserved Mrs Warren. Known as a hands-on person, a doer in other words, he brooked no deviation from the accepted norm; be it in deed or thought. Marching to different drumbeats? Not in his team, he averred.

"I will settle his hash in a jiffy," he promised the string of complainants. He did; not in the twinkling of an eye, mind you, but eventually he succeeded to have the frisky troublemaker transferred.

One look at Jupp Hennig, the new arrival, convinced everyone that a repetition of the previous debacle could be ruled out in view of his broken down condition. A collective sigh wafted through the halls as they viewed this picture of misery. Crippled he seemed, tied to a wheelchair, bowed by abject resignation, a compatible co-dweller, thus unlike that fire-eater.

"He will fit right in," remarked Peter Bruno, which remark he learned to rue.

For now, however, fraternal sentiments, as much as benevolent solicitude were extended him. Soon that changed, for behind the veils of novelty they could see the cloven hoof.

"He is up to no good," Mr Bruno announced.

"Good gracious, here we go again," seconded Mrs Hartwig.

A week after his arrival Hennig reached a horrific conclusion. It was this: Get out of here, or perish before the next solstice passes! Broken limbs were endurable temporarily; confinement, though unpleasant, he could accept for a limited time; but not this bowing and scraping. Come hell or high water, he promised himself to turn his back on this citadel of sweet singers. "Rather scuffle with the notorious grizzlies in the Mackenzie Mountains than be exposed to this stifling atmosphere of saccharinity." So he moaned in the privacy of his room, to little avail, however.

Lamenting hardly eased his plight, blaming others even less, since the source of his misery lay squarely at his own threshold. A fact, though divined, he nevertheless refused to admit. His adversaries were neither the other residents nor the attendants, but old age and a limping sense of reality. Nevertheless, he stamped them all with the mark of the beast, responsible for his grief.

Searching for enemies within the walls of the old people's home rendered him morose, unjust, and no less belligerent. He heaped scorn on his co-dwellers, and groused at the personnel like only an old man can.

"What a fine bunch you are; bleaters, cadging for compassion, humming the Miserere just to be noticed," he scolded.

The timid souls who wished nothing more than live in harmony, hung their heads in dismay. When Mr Bruno, the oldest occupant, suggested:

"My dear Hennig, you might be with us, willing or not, for a long time, so why not accept the fact and be more pleasant?"

Hennig flew at him:

"I should remain imprisoned here for long? man, you must be daft."

Peter Bruno, a man of dignity, considered Hennig closer. An odd expression framed his face, a mixture of reproof and pity. As he turned and walked away he murmured under his breath:

"Brag is a good dog, but holdfast is the better."

Indeed, considering Hennig's age and condition, his was an empty boast, rash, and made in anger. For he, as most others, would likely leave this place in a coffin; so Mr Bruno surmised.

Of course Adam Rickman, an up-and-coming people person, as he called himself, needed no second glance to gauge the newcomer. Alone his outlandish outfit made him bristle. At first sight Hennig's Stetson vexed him no less than his chaps and leather vest.

"They will go first thing," he vowed.

Noticing the old man's haughty bearing raised his eyebrows. Hearing him mention words like independence and individualism, shortened his neck and bowed his head as if ready to charge. Rickman, a burly, squat figure, prided himself to be a product of modern times; in other words a regular fellow. To be proclaimed an average guy made his eyes shine and his head lift up; it was the apex of his aspirations.

"In my team everybody pulls in one direction," was his maxim. Should someone consider slighting the team spirit, that person soon learned to rue his birth. A Torquemada unleashed would have paled beside the glow of Rickman's zeal. Being a fair man in most aspects, except in matters of conformity, the manager counselled to be patient.

"Give him time, he will come around," he comforted grumblers.

That indulgent attitude changed with lightning speed when his ears were set whirring with astounding news: the old man planned to leave! Should he laugh, inveigh, or simply ignore the information? In accordance with his wont, he decided to act. Especially after learning about Hennig's waspish behaviour towards the others. Summoning him to his office, he quickly came to the point:

"Jupp, this can not continue," he snapped.

Hennig, in a foul mood a moment ago, felt amused. So much so that he almost burst out laughing. The man opposite him sure was a sight to behold. Trying to impress, he rather entertained the old-timer hewn from the timbers of Canada's north, whose long sojourn among Native Indians had taught him the ability to separate a tinhorn from genuine men.

Instinctively a broad smirk settled on his ruddy face, as he compared Rickman to a hastily rigged up abbot of unrest. That smirk, plus succeeding comments came back to haunt Hennig. His keen insight recognised Rickman as the man he was; so he thought. But he erred. His perception lacked acuity concerning a crucial attribute: Adam Rickman's dread: abhorrence of independent spirits. Such men and women he considered his mortal foes, begging to be hunted from the face of the earth. A demon in matters of conformity, believing the adage that the masses are always right, he could not abide the slightest opposition to these tenets. Individuals who strayed from the communal path, or even looked another way, ignited his wrath, and a desire to reach for the hammer of witches. To him men should see as others saw, feel collectively, and march in unison.

Rickman frowned, yet was ready to temper indignation with mercy, which turned to vindictive anger after the following exchange. He tried a conciliatory tack.

"Jupp, be reasonable. I realise you had, still have a rough time. But don't take your vexation out on others. Remember, these poor souls have enough grief without your adding to it."

"Oh, don't worry, in two, three weeks I shall be gone," declared Hennig.

Rickman started as if bidden by a viper.

"Gone? Gone? what do you mean?" he cried.

He couldn't believe what he just heard, for in all the years in his incumbency as an old folk's home administrator, he not once remembered an occupant leaving, except in a casket. Suppressing the sharp rebuke which lay on his tongue, he tried to reason with Hennig instead:

"You are seventy-five years old, tied to a wheelchair, impecunious, with no one in the world to take care of you, except us of course. So, in a nutshell, you are completely dependent on us."

"Not for long, not for long," Hennig murmured.

Stung to the quick, Rickman bellowed:

"Till your death!"

A broad smile brightened the old man's countenance. Despite his grief his sporting instinct rose to the surface. Extending his hand he proposed:

"I have some gold nuggets hidden in the mountains, I bet you half, that within a month I'm walking out of here."

Ignoring the proffered hand, snorting derisively, Rickman expelled:

"Not so, old man, you will leave in a coffin loaded on a hearse which will take you to the cemetery."

"All right, you are on," Hennig chuckled.

Afterwards, in a huff, the manager convened his staff to whom he explained the situation. Emphasising one aspect, making light of the other, he summed up:

"Old Hennig suffers from delusions, thus he must be closely supervised; moreover, his movements should be curtailed."

Raising her eyebrows, Fanny Gruber, the head nurse, wanted to know:

"Are you suggesting house arrest?"

Nettled by her question which contained a whiff of sarcasm, he replied caustically.

"Did I say that?"

From there on the ambience within the home changed. A crackling tension, felt by everybody, whisked through the rooms. No one could define it, yet all knew whence it originated.

The manager, growing more restive by the day, seemed to have locked horns with Hennig, who took on an increasing combative stance. Rickman behaved like a martinet towards the old-timer, who oddly took no offence; at least not visibly. He just sat in his chair, unruffled as only a loner can be, saying little, smiling to himself occasionally.

"He is scheming, and no doubt about it," Rickman proclaimed with an air befitting a warden warning his guards about an impending jailbreak.

"Something is up," granted the head nurse.

But in the absence of the manager she sang a different tune.

"The boss is in a dither, he is getting silly," she declared at the table.

Seeing a dozen heads bobbing in consent, she added:

"All on account of an eccentric old man who means no harm. I don't understand it; nobody does, I guess."

Mrs Gruber erred in two aspects. First, she misjudged Hennig's intentions; second, two people did comprehend quite well. One was Adam Rickman who saw his idol, average man, stagger precariously, which the other, Jupp Hennig, pushed wantonly. Indeed, neither the personnel nor the residents had an inkling of the profound struggle in their midst, which both men intended to win.

Hennig's innate optimism started to wane. Unable to walk, feeling stifled by the hemmed in surrounding, importuned by a manager pitted by the notion of team spirit, he lost courage. He pined for his former life among feral beings and solitary men and women, independent till their last breath. Enduring gnawing hunger and numbing cold deemed him a gift of the gods compared to this debilitating comfort, amid clouds of insecurity. He could not have imagined how a man can be so lonely among a crowd, ready to help and ostensibly compassionate. He felt like a beast in a cage whose bars were rattled by a rampaging manager.

"Mr Hennig, you have a visitor," one of the attendants announced.

Taken aback, he asked:

"Who is it?"

"A Charlie Yohin."

"Charlie? send him up," Hennig cried.

What a surprise, what a pleasure talking to his old stomping pal again who lost everything, except his humour, a year ago in a devastating blizzard.

"Charlie, old buddy, what's up?"

"Not much; how goes it with you?

Pointing to his legs, Hennig growled:

"Still can't walk."

Charlie, a Dene Indian, tilting his head inquiringly, asked:

"Are you in the dumps, old man? you surely look it."

Hennig, glad to unburden his heart to a kindred spirit, explained the situation. Not to its full extent, however, for wit and words failed him to describe the hazards from which he felt encircled.

"Something puzzles me," he remarked with raised eyebrows.

"Tell me," encouraged his pal.

"Chuckle all you want, Charlie, scratch your old head, but I swear to you that the entire outfit here is opposed to my convalescence, especially the manager."

"Now, now, Jupp, you are imagining things."

"Am I? listen."

"Go ahead."

"When chiding me for being a stormy petrel, after which I assured him to be gone in a few weeks, he blew a fuse."

"I don't understand."

"I didn't either; then, that is, but I do now. Pounding the table he screamed at the top of his lungs words to the effect that I shall never leave these premises except in a coffin."

"That's a silly thing to say, but it carries no punch," Charlie remarked.

Then his mien acquired that puckish expression known throughout the North. He was getting on in years, that Dene elder, yet now as then could not refrain from letting the imp out of the bottle.

"Let's prove him wrong. Come on, ya old curmudgeon, pack up, we are leaving!"

Startled, raising his head inquiringly, Hennig thought about that for a moment, then remonstrated:

"Fine and good, but what happens after? Remember, my legs are out of action, besides, I have no wish to impose on you."

Charlie, hemming a few times, acknowledged this wasn't one of his brightest ideas. Thinking some more, his face lit up.

"How about wheeling you around the block several times, that would break the spell, as much as ruffle Caesar's feathers."

Magic hands couldn't have done a better job converting Hennig's resigned demeanour to glowing anticipation.

"I'm ready," he chortled.

Scarcely had they reached the bottom of the ramp when Hennig whispered to his pal:

"There is roly-poly."

"Where do you think you are going?" Rickman asked in a menacing tone.

"Out," Hennig replied.

"Out? you mean leaving the premises?"

Charlie said not a word; nonchalantly he proceeded towards the exit in that lumbering stride of his.

Rickman, growing more exited by the second, visibly perturbed upon seeing mocking gazes directed at him, wavered an instant, then lost his nerve. Tumbling more than walking, he rushed to the doorway where he planted himself plumb in the middle.

"You are not leaving!" Did I not tell you the only way is in a..." Biting his lips on time he said no more.

"Get out of our way, shorty," Charlie growled as only a man can who has faced down grizzlies.

"You will not leave these premises," Rickman shrieked, beside himself with rage.

"Hm, hm," Charlie grunted as he lifted the struggling manager off his feet and deposited him gently away from the entrance.

"There now, be a good boy," he counselled amid a chorus of snickers.

When they returned Rickman was nowhere to be seen. However, a small crowd had congregated in the entrance hall. Hennig and his pal were showered with curious stares, some admiring, others reproachful. None displayed approval prior to casting furtive glances all around, since they scarcely cherished the thought of getting into the manager's bad books.

Inwardly, however, they gloated, for with a few exceptions his concept about the glory of the average man found little resonance with them. But having witnessed his mean-spirited persecution of anyone disagreeing with him, they took no chances.

Hennig and his friend, who knew little about characters like Adam Rickman, soon forgot the incident; contrary to Fanny Gruber, the head nurse. Her heart leaped up when Charlie, the Indian, played upsy-daisy with Rickman, despite a certain understanding of dire consequences in store for the old man.

"I'm sure the boss is ogling the whole gamut of dirty tricks right now," she remarked to Miss Curlow, her confidant.

Rickman, set on punishing the old-timer, found his options limited, in any case officially. That, however, did not curb his dominative tendencies, nor the urge to requite an imagined injury. He said little in the ensuing days, although his mind was in a whirr. To tell the truth, he went through a spell of shock. Choked by indignation, humiliated by Hennig's brazen challenge of his authority, he temporarily lost heart, which fact manifested itself in his subdued demeanour.

Curious to say, though few liked Rickman, he was nevertheless pitied, whereas Hennig and his Indian friend were secretly condemned by many for his ignominious slap in the face of authority. By many, but not all: notable Fanny Gruber. Her sentiments diverged from such notions, deemed mawkish to her. She neither trusted nor respected Rickman, whom she not so privately referred to as 'Lord Ruffle'. She knew the type: tyrants to their fingertips, bristling with self-importance fuelled by insecurity. Two things they can not abide: self-sufficiency, be it only in thought, and slight of their beliefs. Being aware of Rickman's fear to lose caste, she anticipated a dark future for Jupp Hennig.

A few days later the old man's cherished western attire went missing. Hennig kicked up a tremendous row, which led nowhere. The manager, fuming over such slackness, let it be known that no stone will be left unturned trying to locate it.

"Have no fear, Jupp, we will find your belongings; if I have to personally turn this place upside down," he assured the hapless old-timer.

"In the meantime you will have to be content with regular clothes from our store, free of charge of course," Hennig was advised.

Did the manager laugh in his sleeve? Hennig could have sworn he did, which supposition the head nurse shared. She more than divined that humiliating a dogmatist with impunity transgressed credulity.

Rickman, visibly vexed on account of his staff's negligence, suddenly regained his wonted bumptiousness. The commandeering voice, borne by recurring confidence, once more resounded through the building. Crisp orders kept the staff on their toes and made the daunted residents huddle. They were back at the old regimentation, seemingly that is; for something peculiar commenced to happen, which neither the attendants nor the old people understood.

Having been blessed with a week's respite from the constant hubbub apparently necessary to manage an old people's home, they felt annoyed by the returning bustle. Some of the seniors, especially the men, balked. Buoyed up by Hennig's recent sally, covertly admired, yet overtly deplored, their attitude towards Rickman underwent a change. The manager's spell cast over them started to crack; soon it broke. The old people's awe gradually turned to disdain, whereas the staff's respect, never pronounced, took a tumble.

Adam Rickman, bent on adherents who toe the mark enthusiastically, quickly sensed the contrary attitude towards him. At first he felt offended; then anger arose and with it the urge to punish; in other words he more than before acted the bully. The staff's diminished deference, never profuse anyway, he could have suffered; but not the lack of homage due him and expected from the occupants.

Like all despots, the need to be appreciated was indispensable to his existence. Browbeating the seniors achieved little; in fact, it rendered them openly defiant plus more amenable to Hennig's influence. A quandary, not unlike the man being charged by an irate bull, faced him. Should he grab his left horn, the right, or both? Independent of his choice he will be tossed. Applying draconian measures would stiffen opposition, whereas tolerating their mutinous behaviour would cause the cessation of his authority. With a heavy heart he decided on a most loathsome step.

He went on a trip across the Strait of Georgia to meet Jens Larsen in Victoria.

"I have an appointment with Mr Larsen," he announced.

"He is expecting you," the secretary advised.

Jens Larsen, the deputy minister of social services, harboured scant sympathy for Rickman, to whom he referred as a brainless windbag who constantly tumbled from Scylla to Charybdis. His unabashed thirst for glory vexed him as much as the roly-poly stature amused him. He always compared Rickman to a hastily assembled manikin.

"Well, Mr Rickman, what brings you here?" Larsen boomed. "Take a seat, take a seat. What do you take? Tea, coffee, or something alcoholic?"

"Nothing, thank you," the manager replied hastily.

He felt ill at ease in the presence of Larsen, who despite his elevated position behaved like a man from the cornfields.

"What brings me here is a delicate matter, embarrassing, yet begging to be aired."

He was miffed, put out by Larsen's decorum, deemed antiquated by a son of the new world, wherein first names are the norm.

"Don't be shy, sir, out with it," encouraged the older man.

"It concerns one of the residents, an old man who, I am sorry to say, is getting quite senile."

Larsen had a way of raising one eyelid, while half closing the other. He tilted his head and blinked.

"Well now, isn't an old people's home meant for such?" he reminded.

Rickman started to fidget; something bothered him about the deputy, who exuded an air of homeliness from every pore. His jovial grandfatherly demeanour, incongruous with senior office holders, touched him unpleasantly. Trying not to lose his composure, he exclaimed:

"Quite true; normally that is, but not in this case."

"Oh?" Larsen interrupted in a tone that startled Rickman, who couldn't believe that anyone managed to put so much scathing rebuke into a simple exclamation.

He continued haltingly:

"He doesn't belong in a place where tranquillity is of the essence. For his own benefit, and the other residents, he would be better off in an intensive care institution."

Larsen nodded, encouraging him to talk. Rickman explained at length while the deputy minister listened; seemingly that is, for in reality he harboured not the least desire to lend him an ear. There was no need for it, since the man sitting opposite him lay like an open book before his eyes. He knew men of his stamp, under whose imprint the whole country groaned.

"Let him talk," he told himself, "it might be his swan song."

Finally he cut Rickman short.

"What are you suggesting?"

"To have Hennig transferred to Riverview."

Did Larsen blink because a speck had entered his eyes? Had it happened involuntarily, or was it a manifestation of anger?

"A mental institution in other words," he declared, emphasising each syllable.

"It would be the most suitable place for the unfortunate man. I understand their programs and treatments are quite effective. Who knows, Hennig might even be cured."

Larsen comprehended nothing of the sort; he knew different. Rising abruptly, he advised:

"I shall give you a written opinion within a week. Good day, Mr Rickman."

Scarcely had Larsen seen Rickman's shadow disappear, when he fell back in his chair. Overcome by a leaden heaviness, he groaned as if caught between two millstones.

"Why do I lose my joy of life at every contact with this man? The fault must be mine, for Rickman isn't such a bad sort," he lamented.

True, he was officious, dogmatic, plus enamoured with the goddess mediocrity. But so were others, who nevertheless did not set his teeth on edge. To tell the truth, Rickman frightened him. Strong he still was physically, resilient mentally, yet the sight or thought of Rickman made his knees wobble.

Some days later a decision arrived.

Dear Mr Rickman;

After careful consideration concerning Jupp Hennig,
I arrived at the conclusion he should remain where he is.
Please keep me informed of any new development.

Signed: Jens Larsen, Deputy Minister

Trying to control his chagrin proved not easy, till Rickman was gripped by a notion which made him rub his hands in glee. Forcing himself not to burst out laughing, he expelled under his breath:

"By golly, I shall yet rid myself of this thorn in my side, and soon to boot. What a gawk that rustic in Victoria is, playing into my hands, while intending to oppose me. What a fool to hand me the stone to kill two birds with, what a duffer!"

He went at it feverishly, time was of the essence, for the old man grew more rebellious by the hour. Spurred by his sudden inspiration, he decided to act. Taking paper and pen in hand, he wrote.

Dear Mr Larsen;

Your missive concerning Jupp Hennig has been received. It shall be followed. However, allow me to express my, as much as the staff's reservation. As mentioned, Hennig suffers from delusions, to which a further evil in the form of suicidal tendencies has been added. We shall do our utmost to prevent a calamity; but I must reiterate that in our opinion an old people's home is not a suitable place for self-destructive individuals.

Yours truly
Adam Rickman

Chortling he remarked: "There now, the cornerstone has been laid."

For the first time in weeks Rickman felt elated, increasingly so as he appraised the state of affairs. Just wait, he would settle Hennig's hash, as much as that bigwig's in Victoria. The wheels were in motion, they only needed to be steered. Should a dire mishap occur, no blame could be attached to him after duly warning his superior. Let him toss it to the wind, as he surely will, his own escutcheon shall be clean.

Rickman's optimism, derived from Hennig's recent habit highly opportune to his intentions, increased by the hour. He could not help chuckling to himself while observing his nemesis lingering at the top of the stairs leading to the entrance hall below. A better spot could hardly be found, even if enjoined to do so.

Rickman had noticed Hennig's latest habit, but paid scant attention to it: till now that is; for the deputy's missive sharpened his perception and gave impetus to a latent design. This was an ideal opportunity to satisfy his fondest desires.

Observing Hennig with more interest now, he couldn't help gloating. There he sat, bowed in his wheelchair like a long-suffering Job, with the mien of a man having dreamt his last dream.

"The old fellow is scheming again," Rickman announced at a staff meeting.

"What is he up to now?" queried the irrepressible head nurse in a deprecating tone.

It earned her a withering look from the manager as if to say: "Your turn will come, just wait."

Then something extraordinary happened; it confounded the entire crew and no less the occupants. Even Evelyn Steir, a regular Griselda, burst out incensed:

"That is unbelievable, outrages, scandalous!"

It was this: Hennig, feeling a stir in his legs again, asked for crutches.

"I can get around much easier with them than in this monstrosity," he averred.

Deeming it a reasonable request, leading to benefits all around, the attendants obliged with alacrity, or rather would have, barring Rickman's objections, which he uttered strenuously. To their dismay he broke out into a regular revilement upon hearing the innocent wish, which they, the staff, were inclined to grant. Remonstrances, neither courteous nor soft reverberated through the building. Renewing his orders to be informed about anything concerning Hennig, he concluded:

"Make sure that gate is securely shut at all times, we certainly don't want an accident to happen. Imagine, tumbling down those stairs; such a fall might be fatal to a helpless man tied to a wheelchair."

When Hennig learned about the manager's strange refusal, he smiled for the first time since his arrival. As before he wheeled himself to that wonted spot, where he sat for hours gazing heaven knows at what.

One morning when he tested the gate as he habitually did, it opened to his touch. Startled, he shrunk back; then after a moment's reflection tried to close it. Being unsuccessful he alerted one of the attendants, when in a twinkle Rickman came charging around a corner. He took it all in with one glance: the partly opened iron gate, as much as Hennig, evidently at sea. As expected Rickman started to rant:

"Confound it! Have I not told you to keep this gate shut at all times? Can I not turn my back for one minute without enduring a thousand fears?"

Amid this torrent of words he grabbed the gate with both hands and closed it. Not, however, before he removed an object from the latch with deft fingers. It was done with lightning speed and clever stealth, imperceptible to anyone not stirred by suspicion, like Hennig, who saw everything, yet understood little.

But soon Rickman's curious sleight-of-hand started to make sense, for strange occurrences started to take place, which defied explanation. Every day amid the silence of dawn, footfalls approached stealthily, ever so furtively, yet audible to Hennig at his lookout. When he turned his head towards these sounds, slowly to be sure on account of his aching muscles, dark shapes, trailed by dim shadows, scurried away as if mortified to be recognised.

"What sort of mummery is this?" he said to himself.

Did someone act out his or her sportive tendencies? wanted to scare him perhaps? or did his imagination run wild? He decided to find out.

Next morning in the shimmer of dawn he sat there pretending to be fast asleep. As usually at this early hour, silence reigned, not a whisper could be heard. Slumped in his chair, Hennig waited. In a short while somebody approached with feline stealth. Though on pins and needles, he neither turned nor moved. The steps in his back, still furtive, yet quickening, steered unmistakably towards him.

"Let them come," Hennig chuckled, he was ready to spoil their fun. Whoever it is will think twice before repeating such shenanigans. Trying to sneak up on a seasoned trapper? Just wait and see what is in store for you, Hennig mused. For he intended to surprise whoever it was with the mighty hoot of the wild mountains, which can shatter nerves and eardrums at close quarters.

Things turned out different, however. What happened took his breath away and stifled the planned whoop in his throat; he was rushed suddenly from behind. Someone grabbed the wheelchair, spun it around, then aimed a kick at the gate which flew wide open. Still not comprehending, Hennig heard the voice of Rickman who hollered at the top of his lungs:

"You see, can you not see what might happen on account of your flagrant negligence?"

Barking at anyone in sight, raising his voice when he saw the head nurse standing midways on the stairs, Rickman seemed beside himself. Mrs Gruber resembled a thunderstruck woman, unable to comprehend, though having witnessed all. While denouncing everybody from the janitor to his assistants, Rickman, with one motion, slammed the gate shut after removing an object wedged in the seating of the latch. Despite his befuddled state, Hennig did not miss the juggler's feat. He gaped, for he understood.

After this episode a curious fact manifested itself: Hennig's churlishness gave way to astonishing blandness. His demeanour, hitherto an embodiment of hostility, changed visibly; he became supportable, at times even affable. Many an inquiring glance borne by suspicion and disbelief, ranged over him, for it seemed to good to be true. The sudden transformation became the talk of the institution. His former resignation, anger and self-pity disappeared miraculously; they were swallowed by forces no one could name.

Indeed, Hennig felt motivated to quit moping and lay the groundwork to perform a feat not seen and heard before. He swore to walk out of this place without the aid of a stick or crutches, plus send Mr Average up-river for life.

Soon rumours started to circulate about odd goings-on in Hennig's room.

"It sounds like somebody throwing heavy objects onto the floor," Rita Hartwig declared.

"And at the walls," Peter Bruno avowed.

No one griped to the manager, but some grumbled in the presence of the attendants, who mentioned the complaints to Mrs Gruber. When she questioned Hennig, he quipped:

"Let them twaddle, they have nothing else to do."

Privately she agreed, but intrigued by his recent change in personality, she couldn't resist remarking:

"You are up to something, tell me about it."

Observing her with one eye half closed, puckering his brow, he revealed:

"I am exercising."

"Well, there is nothing wrong with that, I reckon," she admitted.

Fanny Gruber, being the only person whom he trusted, came close to be taken in his confidence. He thought better of it, but promised to keep noises in check.

He exercised alright, with the ardour of a zealot, and determination bordering on temple madness. Spurred by images that made him giddy, he grit his teeth while sweating it out. He frequented that preferred spot less and less. In fact, when he saw the gate in a captious position, he wheeled past it. This occurred more often than not. Should he stop for a while, Rickman seldom failed to show up to ingratiate himself with offers difficult to refuse.

"Don't be shy, Jupp, to ask for assistance," he encouraged.

"Assistance? from whom?" Hennig inquired coyly.

"From me of course. By the way, how are your legs?"

"Wobbly like reeds in the wind."

As he walked away Rickman reminded:

"Don't put on airs and graces, my personal services await your command."

"No doubt," Rickman muttered to himself. "No doubt at all."

He harboured scant uncertainty about Rickman's intentions, of which he breathed not a word to anyone. Designs were hatched with utmost deliberation and fiendish cleverness; every eventuality received consideration. Branding him, Hennig, delusional, and suicidal for good measure, deserved mention. Decrying the entire staff as negligent, opened the door for misadventures. Shifting blame on the resented deputy in Victoria surely inspired him with glee. The scheme could have been predicated as genial, had it not been for one hitch, a shortcoming really.

Rickman, hidebound by notions of sameness in demeanour, appearance, and speech, deemed it impossible that anyone outside this pattern would catch on to his plan, let alone thwart it.

Hennig harboured no illusions about Rickman's intentions to see him one way or another landing at the bottom of those stairs with broken bones, or dead preferably. He understood the mechanism of self-closing gates quite well, but not the mind of a man riven with hate, bent on sending an old, helpless fellow to his doom. Thinking about it saddened and angered him. Like this evening for instance, as he watched the darkness descending over the mountains. Lights flickered, gradually bathing the fringes of the bay in a warm glow. The sight, hitherto soothing and reassuring, made him shudder this evening, for he expected an unwelcome visitor.

"He will strike tonight," he told himself.

It was a propitious time, since pretty well everybody will attend the annual party given in the big hall. One eye directed at the lights flitting like will-o-the-wisps over the water, the other fixed anxiously at the door, Hennig waited. His nerves were on edge; his senses on high alert.

The knock came shortly after eight o'clock.

"Who is it?" Hennig asked, trying to sound unconcerned.

"Your friend."

"Come in, come in."

Scarcely had the last syllable rolled over Hennig's tongue, when Rickman stood in the room.

"Excuse the disturbance, Jupp. I know you are averse to parties and crowds, but the gang wants to say hello. Have no fear, I shall bring you right back again."

Although having anticipated the move, he nevertheless felt apprehensions surging through his spine.

"Let's be on our way, people are waiting," Rickman urged while taking hold of the chair.

Then everything happened so fast that Hennig almost missed the chance to act as planned.

Rickman said not a word as he practically raced towards the spot which Hennig knew so well. As expected the latch of the gate was disengaged. A well aimed kick opened it wide; a mighty push sent the wheelchair tumbling down the stairs.

"There you go," Rickman hissed; then chuckled while feasting his eyes at the crashing conveyance.

Rubbing his hands he readied himself for the next move. Pretending to arrive fortuitously at the spot, noticing Hennig's mishap, he would race to his assistance, while calling for help. It was a careful thought out scheme, which failed for lack of an essential part: Hennig's that is. As it turned out he neither required anyone's pity nor assistance.

Driven by blind zeal, his attention distracted by a ticklish bend in the corridor, Rickman ignored the significance of an amazing event which he saw, but deemed an illusion, till the awful realisation hit him: Hennig was not in or around the chair; he stood sneering at the top of the stairs, leaning against the rail. Looking wild-eyed from the shattered wheelchair below to the grinning man on top, Rickman muttered:

"No, no, it can not be!"

Then he moaned:

"I have been tricked, ignominiously duped."

Shaking himself like a wet dog till his wispy hair flew from temple to temple, he hurled himself at Hennig:

"Dog, miserable hound, you are following that chair," he shrieked.

"Mr Rickman, what are you doing?" someone cried.

"Have you gone berserk?" Mrs Gruber shouted.

The enraged attacker saw and heard nothing while his hands closed around the old-timer's neck. An indescribable confusion ensued.

Rickman, beside himself, unable to control his rage, had to be forcefully separated from Hennig, who doubled up in pain and gasped for air. Bellowing with anger, Rickman suddenly darted towards his office.

Meanwhile a crowd had gathered. Excited voices, some timid, others demanding, filled the air.

"What's going on?"

"Where is Mr Rickman?"

"Yes, where is he? Someone go and fetch him!" a man ordered.

"Look at that wheelchair, it's a heap of scrap."

So it went till Mrs Reifel cried out:

"Look! look!"

All eyes followed her outstretched hand. Did they witness a mirage, or was it really Hennig standing there?

"He is walking," announced Rita Hartwig.

The time had arrived for Jupp Hennig to fulfil his promise. Amid 'aahs' and 'oohs' he proceeded towards the stairs. Eyeing bystanders triumphantly, he set his foot on the first step, then froze in terror. Looking down, his weather-beaten face turned pallid; the door leading outside seemed miles away, and unreachable besides.

Instinctively he shrunk back when the entire stairway appeared to move up and down; then to his dismay one step after the other disappeared before his eyes. Attacked by dizziness he gripped the rails with both hands till the knuckles blanched. Slowly, groaning abjectly, he sank to the floor.

"Fetch a chair!" someone ordered. It was provided in a hurry, onto which helping hands placed the choked-up old-timer. If anyone saw the tears welling up in his eyes, they did not mention it.

Then a shot rang out, causing heads to turn towards the manager's office. Mrs Gruber, the head nurse, said aloud what others felt.

"It's the best way out, the strife has ended."

Instilling Fear

*S*arah Lukas was not a vixen yet, but certainly on the way of becoming one. She increasingly wrangled with life, questioned her marriage, and planted seeds of discontent wherever she went. Weariness was etched all over her face, it made her eyelids droop and her face sag.

Viktor, her husband of seventeen years, cast quite a different figure. Friendly disposed, tall, and prone to laughter, he could be called prepossessing. Sarah took umbrage at his cheerful nature and good looks. His supple built she perceived as a personal affront. It contrasted sharply with her own appearance, which resembled that of a dying duck in a thunderstorm; in other words, she was chapfallen.

Lukas would soon be on his way to the Caribbean, starting construction projects in several islands. By tomorrow afternoon everything, gear, materials, personal belongings should be ready to go. Once underway he intended to follow.

First, however, he wanted to say farewell to his friend Kevin Lars. They met at the Upper Duck lounge on the Ontario side of the Ottawa River. Soon the conversation drifted to Lukas' forthcoming sojourn.

"Remember one thing, Viktor, you must show them who is boss," Lars advised.

"Show whom?"

"The natives; otherwise they will be all over you, plus rob you blind besides. Believe me, I am talking from experience."

"You were stationed in Barbados, I understand."

"Yes, for over two years," Lars commented.

"Your work is all done, I presume?"

"Yes, and I thank heaven for it." Lukas chuckled.

"Come now, Kevin, from what I hear it's a most charming place, inhabited by friendly and peaceful people."

"Don't be daft, Viktor, listen to me. Those black scallywags only understand one thing."

"What would that be?" Lukas asked.

"Force, old buddy, resolve and force. Show them you mean business; dare them to transgress, or you will rue it."

"I don't understand," admitted Lukas.

"It seems you don't, so let me explain."

Casting appraising glances over his friend's slender frame he remarked jokingly:

"Are we agreed that your physique does not easily frighten?"

"I have no intention to do so," Lukas replied affably.

"True, that's why you need a dog in those places."

"I can't stand them," Lukas snorted.

"A pistol then," his friend suggested.

"That's too drastic for me; besides, I don't know how to shoot."

"Who is saying anything about shooting? Just be seen with it, aim it the odd time, unloaded if you prefer, at nothing or no one in particular; they will get the message."

When Lukas poohed that idea, Lars gazed at him significantly, like an object of pity.

"Well now, I feel duty-bound to warn you. In any case, here is the police chief's card."

Reaching in his pocket, he handed it to him with the words:

"He will fix you up. Don't forget to give the old gander my regards."

That conversation took place two months ago. Lukas barely remembered a word of it. Indeed, how could a man occupy himself with such bugaboos in a land of smiles, good will, and courtesy? In those days, Barbados, as other islands, was not yet overrun by tourists, by bumptious, guzzling men, and lonely women foraging for a night or two of romance.

True, they did come in the winter months, but not yet in droves; besides, being leery of natives, and repelled by conditions outside the sanitized hotel grounds, they rarely ventured beyond its confines.

After Lukas had found appropriate quarters, an office conveniently located, plus a fine residence overlooking the city, he sent for his wife. Their son, being of school age, stayed behind with Viktor's parents.

Sarah hesitated to oblige for two reasons. First, she hoped to renew a love affair with Lars, with whom she was intimate many years ago; second, leaving little Ferdinand in care of her in-laws filled her with resentment. To be sure, both were decent, loving grandparents, but they had two strokes against them; speaking a foreign language was one; using it exclusively with the boy constituted the other.

To her growing chagrin Viktor did the same, despite their unending bickering, which culminated in pitched battles of wit and will, wherein Sarah stood no chance of holding her own. But she dug in anyway, like any mother would when fighting for the soul of her child.

Little Freddie, as she defiantly called him against her husband's wish, needed protection from this alien influence. What irked her most, alarmed her really, was the eerie transformation when he spoke that abhorred language. His features softened, his eyes shone and his voice attained an engaging lilt. Worst of all, she felt rebuffed, shut out from her cherished boy's life.

She took umbrage, seriously so. A desire to hit back, to humiliate Viktor overwhelmed her. How should it be done? Belittling his foreign birth came to her mind, an idea which she repudiated almost immediately. To begin with, he took pride in his heritage; moreover, his speech, though marked by a slight accent, was faultless. Yet humbled he must be, if only to raise her self-esteem.

Imagination, a boon to healthy minds, bane to anguished ones, played havoc with Sarah Lukas. It drove a good woman off the rails. Hunted by wild conjectures and erroneous ideas, she eventually reached a stage of divine wrath, when any deed, no matter how shabby or self-destructive, looks attractive.

She finally discovered a path of retaliation, as only a woman could. She started a love affair with Viktor's friend Kevin Lars, thereby giving her counter-attack more thrust. Lars, an incorrigible lady's man balked at first, but deeming it quite save, could not resist the temptation, if only to stick another feather in his cap.

It seemed strange that a man intimate with more than just a few women, should know so little about them. Secretiveness, so important to him in this case, meant nothing to Sarah. She told her friend May Simms who, quite intrigued, wanted to know:

"When did this start?"

"Two weeks ago."

"I hope Viktor will not find out."

"He will."

"Not from me, he won't. I doubt Kevin would tell him."

"I will," Sarah announced.

"Are you mad?" her friend remonstrated.

"Not quite. Yet considering the circumstances known to you, he must be made privy of it. May, I have to fight back or else suffer a nervous breakdown."

"I don't follow your reasoning."

"Quite simple. How can I make him suffer if he is unaware of being punished?"

Incredulous, May Simms uttered:

"You are doing it out of spite?"

"Exactly. I feel cast aside, thrown overboard like flotsam with no intention to be retrieved again. So when Viktor finds out, he will wake up."

Her friend did not share that optimism, but she kept quiet.

Sarah told her husband the same day; it was a mistake. The hoped for awakening, a rude one, happened alright, but not as anticipated. Did her husband of seven years rant and rave as expected of a man? Did he threaten to kill the louse who marred his honour, plus give the wife a proper hiding? No! he behaved far worse; he remained calm and smiled.

"Why are you telling me this? Wouldn't it be more fun if done behind my back?" saying so he winked at her.

One could have knocked her over with a feather. Not understanding she just stood there stunned and speechless. Finally she managed to stutter:

"But – but, don't you mind?"

"I do, but for you, not me," he countered.

"Aren't you – aren't you feeling dishonoured?"

That elicited a Homeric laughter which drove her out of the house.

This happened about ten years ago when both were still fairly young. After a while all was forgotten, they patched things up and life went on. Lukas worked hard and smart, thus over the years he became a successful contractor. Rumours about him and his wife took some time to abate, whispers that never ruffled his water lingered on. He and Sarah, while no longer billing and cooing, nevertheless got along tolerably. Their relationship, a marriage of convenience, was loosely held together by the existence of Ferdinand, a boy of fifteen by now.

When Sarah arrived in Barbados her first complaint was the weather.

"Too hot and muggy," she announced, however, not in that usual petulant voice, but to his surprise in a conversational tone accompanied by a smile.

On the whole she appeared to be unwontedly conciliatory, amiable really, like a woman desirous to please her man.

Bewildered, trusting neither eyes nor ears, Lukas nevertheless felt intrigued. When she started to cast suggestive glances at him he knew what to do. Within a week they became amorous like in younger years.

Lukas understandably was in high feather; business went well, his wife pleased him exceptionally; added to it an unconstrained atmosphere, one could understand why he felt like walking on air.

But within a month all that changed. It started innocently enough, but nevertheless the wheels of misfortune began to turn. The house on the hill, affording a resplendent view, little by little became a place of weird occurrences of which Lukas remained unaware for some weeks. No doubt he noticed Sarah's frequent musings, when she seemed to be oblivious to her surrounding, but he hardly heeded them.

Once, however, when she stood deeply engrossed staring forlorn into space, he could not refrain from asking:

"What's the matter, Sarah, are you homesick?"

A thunderclap could not have startled her more than this teasing remark. She positively jumped like someone caught in a compromising act.

"No. Why do you asked?" she inquired sharply.

"For no particular reason. Anyway, I was just kidding," he replied, taken aback by her vehement response.

"I am not homesick," she repeated, ready to belabour the point.

No, Sarah was not homesick, he granted, something more earnest bothered her. Indeed, why should she, or anyone else pine for a lacklustre place inhabited by lifeless people, where the clouds hang low and the cold nips at one's limbs for over six months? He felt right at home among these cheerful men and women, who want so little, yet give so much. The unconstrained ambience of yesteryear suited him well.

Somewhat cowed by her curt reply, Lukas nevertheless was determined to keep his eyes open, for he harboured no wish to see his wife relapse into the previous moroseness. He spent more time at home, even during working hours when his presence at the office or job site was not essential.

As time past he couldn't shake of a feeling of discomfort. There were too many peculiar circumstances to be shrugged off. Take the gates for instance. Sarah kept them locked at all times; moreover, she seldom ventured beyond the walls of the house. How she could endure the midday heat confined inside puzzled him. Especially since the property resembled a park-like setting where palms, fruit trees, and fragrant jasmine shrubs abounded. Added to it a constant breeze, where could one find a cooler, more comfortable place for miles around?

"Viktor, they were here again," she called out before he set foot inside the yard.

As always it annoyed him to be rushed, it made him ornery, thus he pretended not to have heard. His wife, once in swing was not readily discouraged. She repeated her words, more insistent and louder.

"Did you hear what I said?"

"Yes, Sarah, who are they?"

"The men I told you about yesterday."

"Ah, Sarah, they are just curious, don't mind them, they mean no harm."

"That's what you say. I tell you they are up to no good, something must be done."

"Did they say anything?"

"Yes, but I told them to go away."

Lukas, undecided how to treat these exercises in petulance, as he called them, said no more. She will settle down, he comforted himself, gradually accept the behaviour of the locals, whose concept of privacy differs from ours. He saw no grounds to be at sixes and sevens with the entire neighbourhood over insignificant occurrences.

On the whole he felt uneasy about Sarah, who acted increasingly like a dragoness on the lookout for enemies to be fought by him. She was developing into a stormy petrel; in his opinion because of boredom plus too many rum punches. He decided to talk to her in a placatory way, for peace must reign; he abhorred the thought of being once more washed about by waves of rancour.

A good opportunity presented itself the same evening while sitting outside on the balcony. Tentatively, anxious not to rock the boat, he spoke to her in soothing tones. As if by chance the subject concerning the mores of the islands came up. Casually he explained:

"You must understand, Sarah, these people do not perceive privacy like we do. What we deem obtrusiveness, they consider to be friendliness."

Sarah, mollified by the soft evening air, redolent with the scent of jasmine and the stirring cries of whistling frogs, appeared to be amenable to his entreaties. Nevertheless, she voiced her concern again:

"It may be as you say, Viktor, but something is weird here. I can't banish the thought that an effort is made to be troublesome."

Raising his glass, winking at her in his most seductive manner, Viktor joked:

"Maybe your womanly instinct is leading you a pretty dance."

Ready to bridle, but noticing his well-meaning smile, she suppressed her annoyance.

"They are climbing up and walking along the wall now," she announced accusingly.

"A bunch of youngsters I suppose, feeling their oats."

"Not at all. They are quite grown up, anyway the ones that were here today."

"Just tell them to get off, and stay off."

"I did."

"So, what happened?"

"They just laughed and kept on gambolling around."

"I will talk to them," he promised eagerly.

Fearing his amorous expectations foiled, he added:

"Don't worry, you will be left in peace, I guarantee it."

It turned out to be an empty promise; things got worse. One afternoon when Lukas arrived at the house, his wife seemed ready to burst at the seams. He had never seen her in such a state, she evidently was at the end of her tether. On the verge of tears she declared:

"Viktor, I can't stay here any longer."

"What happened?"

"They are now making pictures of me, the house, and the grounds."

"Are you sure?" he asked in disbelief.

"Absolutely," she snapped; then added:

"That's not all."

"There is more?" he asked alarmed by now.

"One of them, not quite so raven black as the others, called me an unprintable name. Something must be done, Viktor, or I am returning to Ottawa."

Kevin Lars' words rang loud and clear in his ears.

"From day one you must instil fear in them, otherwise they will be all over you."

Next morning Lukas presented his card to the desk sergeant at the police station.

"I wish to see the chief," he requested.

Within the twinkle of an eye Mr Sinclair, the police chief, appeared. He was a jovial man, a native Barbadian sporting a British accent. Black, large, not lacking in gainliness, he appeared to be pleased to meet Lukas, of whose presence he was aware.

"Does your visit serve a purpose, or is it just a social one?" the chief inquired.

"First let me convey Kevin Lars' compliments."

At the mention of that name the chief started.

"Do you know him?"

"Quite well, we consider ourselves friends."

Mr Sinclair's reaction upon hearing that was not as expected. He seemed to be uncomfortable, visibly vexed. Eyeing his visitor inquiringly as if anticipating further elucidation, he lowered his head in disappointment when none were offered.

"I come to broach a ticklish matter, Mr Sinclair," Lukas declared.

"Well, let's hear it," the chief encouraged.

Lukas explained the situation, emphasising his wife's fears, which understandably heightened his own concerns. The chief, listening intently, soon broke out in a wry smile, evidently uncertain of Lukas' intentions.

"Did anyone enter the house or the property unauthorised, in other words, intrude?"

"Not exactly, but they are getting there."

"Wouldn't a dog help?" the chief mused.

"That is not a solution for two reasons. First, both of us dislike them; moreover, since we are absent quite a bit and have no minders, it would create an insurmountable problem. A pistol will be the answer."

"You wouldn't want to shoot anybody, I hope."

"Of course not, it would merely serve as a deterrent," Lukas assured the unenthusiastic chief. Fearing a refusal, he quickly added:

"It should make existence, ours as much as the neighbours, more agreeable. Alone the knowledge of a gun in the house…"

Raising a hand Mr Sinclair interrupted:

"If we issue a weapon it will be unloaded, it may not be fired."

Surprised, Lukas looked up, uncertain what that meant. Reflecting for a moment, he understood.

"Only you and I would know that," he countered.

A broad smile crossed the chief's face.

"That's one way of looking at it," he admitted.

Then he rose, opened the door of his office and called out:

"Sergeant, give me form A16, application for a gun license."

Handing it to Lukas, he advised:

"Fill it out and we shall see. Understand now, should a license be issued, it will be conditional."

"Tell me the provisions, chief," Lukas requested.

"The pistol may not be discharged unless authorised by us. To enforce it, plus guaranty its return, a bond is required, plus a personal undertaking."

"I understand," Lukas remarked.

"One more thing: character references are required."

Four days later Lukas held the pistol in his hands. Showing it to his wife he declared in his most menacing voice:

"That will settle their hash."

"It is high time," Sarah proclaimed.

Indeed, it was, for circumstances had reached untenable proportions. Sarah maintained that some criminal elements were intent on mischief, she felt like a prisoner in her temporary home. Her endurance was stretched to the limit, she avowed. Another day or two without some drastic measures, would have found her packing, she professed.

Viktor, at sea on account of the apparent hostility surrounding them, hardly knew what to say or think. In his experience the islanders, with few exceptions, generally behaved commendable; so why the rancour in one of the friendliest island in the Caribbean? Did Sarah's overwrought demeanour contribute to it? his own behaviour? or existed an

inherent feud between the locals and this property? Daggers
were drawn on both sides, no doubt about it.

No matter, things should improve now. A pistol in the
house, loaded or not, would surely induce Sarah to settle down,
and make the locals more careful.

His reveries were interrupted by Sarah's request:

"Shoot the darn thing a few times, that will make their
bones shiver."

Capping her ears in anticipation of a report, she spurred him
with flashing eyes:

"Fire away, shoot in the air if you must, but shoot."

Lukas, neither enamoured by his wife's frenetic behaviour,
as he termed it, nor the fact that he could not, rather should not
pull the trigger, felt a column of anger rise within him. Sarah,
pouting, pulling a face that would have many a man shrink into
himself, taunted unabashed:

"What's the matter, are you afraid to frighten those black
devils?"

No, he explained, he was not afraid, just loath to terrorise
the neighbourhood on account of a few troublemakers, who
may be outsiders to begin with.

Lukas nevertheless made a point to be seen with the pistol, a
habit seemingly bearing fruit. For a whole week peace reigned.
Sarah uttered not a word of complaint, her spirit revived. Lukas
too relaxed when his unfailing inquiries about her well-being
received a positive response.

"The situation is improving, Viktor, the gun has done the
trick."

Just the same he ceaselessly looked for another place to
live. Who could have described his astonishment when she
repeatedly declined to look at available properties, suitable in
his estimation. Their lives improved considerable since the
procurement of the weapon. But the day arrived when
Aristotle's rules for a tragedy held true.

It was now late October, the trade winds gathered force, the
air became drier, rain had almost ceased. The season of delight
approached step by step.

Sarah and Viktor were sitting in the garden, content with the
world, themselves, and each other. They said little, for fear

perhaps to disturb a perfect peace in a true land of Beulah. Yet Sarah's eyes, unnoticed by her absorbed husband, found no rest. They shifted constantly, as if expecting momentarily something explosive to happen; it did.

"There they are again!" she suddenly shouted.

Viktor, looking up, perceived three or four dark figures on top of the wall. Jumping up he murmured:

"All right, you asked for it."

He raced into the house towards the gun, laying as always in a sideboard securely locked.

"They are mocking us," he heard his wife moaning as if mortified. It was the impetus needed to strengthen his resolve and put sparks under his feet. Unlocking the little door which he almost tore off his hinges, he took hold of the gun and stormed outside. Meanwhile Sarah had risen from her chair, she pointed at the wall and screamed:

"Look at him, look at that big ape, he is daring you, Viktor."

Was someone really challenging him? Viktor felt in no position to judge. His limbs were astir and his brain on fire. He was deeply upset, ready to physically attack all three of them. Added to it Sarah's urging, he hurried forward in a fury. As he approached all but one jumped off with a hoot. An older fellow, more defiant, remained as if unconcerned.

"Shoot, Viktor, shoot," Sarah now behind him entreated.

Hearing the shrill command, the man on the wall scrambled down.

"Why didn't you shoot?" Sarah remonstrated strangely agitated. "Why didn't you shoot?" she repeated.

Seeing his wife beside herself, insisting to be answered, he explained:

"What's the use, Sarah, it would only give the show away."

"What do you mean?"

"The gun is not loaded."

"You fool, of course it is loaded," she sneered.

Turning the pistol towards her, intending to put an end to this argument, he declared:

"See, it is empty, hear the click, no bullets are in there."

"No, no, no!" she screamed, while pressing both hands over her face.

Lukas, to convince her, pulled the trigger. The ensuing explosion shook him to the core. Seeing his wife sink to the ground, evincing neither a sound nor moving a limb, froze the blood in his veins. Standing there like the proverbial pillar of salt, gazing at the lifeless figure on the ground, his mind hovered between a thin line of hallucination and reality. Not comprehending, the smell of horror in his nostrils, he remained immobile as if nailed to the ground. Though unable to collect his wits, an inexplicable impulse bid him to stir, to overcome his shock and act.

His wife was dead, his subconscious told him, attempts at revival would be futile. Moving his eyes from the wife he had just killed to the gun in his hands, he made an awful discovery: the pistol was not the one issued to him. A voice from somewhere whispered: "It must disappear."

Like a catatonic who obeys forces only he understands, Lukas shuffled towards a deep well near the house. He barely heard the splash, but nevertheless felt secure in the knowledge it would not ever disclose his secret.

Gradually regaining command of his senses again, he realised what must happen next. The gun, lawfully issued to him had to be found, it was the ticket to his continued freedom. Rummaging about the house, trying to subdue a rising despair, he finally found the weapon. Having learned a lesson, he opened the chamber and turned the drum; the pistol was empty.

"Just in the nick of time," Lukas sighed when he saw the police outside the gate. Statements were taken from him by three different officers, who suspected him openly. No homicide caused by firearms had occurred in Barbados since the tenure of any officer present. But since evidence against Lukas was not solid, they let him be for now, after confiscating the pistol and securing the corpse for an autopsy.

The ensuing ballistic tests, while not exonerating Lukas, did ameliorate his plight. No bullet was fired from his gun in many weeks, besides, its calibre did not match the extracted bullet's. Though not all was clear sailing, Lukas, by no means a fool, stuck to the truth wherever possible. He unreservedly owned up to everything except the fatal shot and the disposal of the gun. He felt secure as long as he remained steadfast and collected.

One snag, however, did exist. Being within touching distance from each other, how could he have failed to notice his wife's assailant who by virtue of the powder marks on her clothes, had to be rubbing shoulders with her.

"You claim not to have seen her attacker," a persistent juror inquired.

"You were standing beside her, were you not?" the coroner pointed out in the hope to catch Lukas napping, for they did not entirely believe him, it all sounded far-fetched.

Intruders armed with lethal weapons in Barbados, prepared to use it on a defenceless woman? tell that to the marines, their miens appeared to be saying. Lukas replied:

"I was not standing nearby when it happened. As I said before, seeing that one defiant fellow remained on the wall, I rushed inside to find a stick, cudgel, or any weapon to scare him with."

"But you had a gun."

"It was not loaded, a fact well known to me." And to you too, he almost added.

"So you loaded it inside the house."

Lukas, looking baffled, trying to conceal a smile, repeated what he had said before:

"I had no bullets."

"While inside the house searching for a stick, or whatever, you heard a report?"

"Yes. I rushed outside, where I almost stumbled over my prone wife."

Lukas' testimony remained unshakeable. Although not convincing, it was repeated verbatim every time. The jury had no choice but rendering the verdict: Homicide by persons unknown.

A week later Lukas received a visitor.

"Just a social call," chief Sinclair announced.

After a convivial half hour or so, the chief, not in uniform, sort of jauntily turned up his head:

"Remember when you applied for a gun license my pouting reaction upon learning about your friendship with Kevin Lars?"

"I do, it surprised me."

"I had reasons to be out of sorts."

"Do you mind telling me?"

"A pistol was issued to Lars about two years ago, along with a box of ammunition."

"That does not surprise me, for I am aware of Kevin's predilection for fire arms."

"He never returned the gun, nor the unused bullets."

"Kevin didn't? I shall remind him at our next meeting to do so," Lukas promised.

"That will not be necessary," the chief countered.

Lukas, taken aback, eyed his guest inquiringly.

"Chief, you are trying to tell me something," he declared.

"It is this: The bullet retrieved from your wife's body was fired from Lars' gun."

Whether Mr Sinclair noticed Lukas' sudden pallor is not known. One thing Lukas realised: the chief's visit could be termed anything but casual, it reeked of an ulterior motive. He was trying to tell him something, which he just did.

Sarah's words, innocuous at that time, took on a sinister meaning. "Shoot, Viktor, shoot," he recalled her shrieking; and, "You fool, of course it is loaded." Kevin and Sarah were at it again, he knew.

"By the way, Mr Lukas, do you know where Lars' gun is?"

A different colour rushed into Lukas' face, scarlet red this time. Mr Sinclair, the portly Bajan with an old world demeanour, broke out in chuckles, totally unseemly for an upholder of the law.

Lukas, at sea for a moment, chimed in. As the chief raised his glass and winked, Lukas understood the purpose of his visit.